A New Home
for Lily

THE ADVENTURES OF LILY LAPP

❧ *Book Two* ❧

A New Home *for* Lily

Mary Ann Kinsinger and Suzanne Woods Fisher

Revell

a division of Baker Publishing Group
Grand Rapids, Michigan

© 2013 by Suzanne Woods Fisher and Mary Ann Kinsinger

Published by Revell
a division of Baker Publishing Group
P.O. Box 6287, Grand Rapids, MI 49516-6287
www.revellbooks.com

Printed in the United States of America

Library of Congress Cataloging-in-Publication Data
Kinsinger, Mary Ann.
    A new home for Lily / Mary Ann Kinsinger and Suzanne Woods Fisher.
       p.   cm. — (The adventures of Lily Lapp ; bk. 2)
    Summary: From age seven, Lily finds it difficult to adjust to life in Pennsylvania, following a different set of rules, and going to school with judgmental Effie and annoying Aaron, but her second year brings some wonderful surprises.
    ISBN 978-0-8007-2133-6 (pbk.)
    1. Amish—Juvenile fiction. [1 Amish—Fiction. 2. Moving, Household—Fiction. 3. Family life—Pennsylvania—Fiction. 4. Schools—Fiction. 5. Friendship—Fiction. 6. Pennsylvania—Fiction.] I. Fisher, Suzanne Woods. II. Title.
PZ7.K62933New 2013
[fic]—dc23   2012040319

Scripture quotations, whether quoted or paraphrased, are from the King James Version of the Bible.

The internet addresses, email addresses, and phone numbers in this book are accurate at the time of publication. They are provided as a resource. Baker Publishing Group does not endorse them or vouch for their content or permanence.

Published in association with Joyce Hart of Hartline Literary Agency, LLC.

13 14 15 16 17 18 19   7 6 5 4 3 2 1

Mary Ann

I would like to dedicate this book to my five little brothers
who were always there for me.

Suzanne

This book is dedicated to my beautiful and talented nieces:
Hilary, Heather, Stacey, Whitney, Katie,
Kelly, Becca, Sara, Taylor, and Paige.
I love you, each and every one.

Contents

The Big Day Arrives

*T*here was only one thing Lily Lapp liked about her new house in Pennsylvania. One thing.

She had a very long list of things she didn't like: The color of the house was an ugly olive green. The kitchen countertop was a shiny bright orange, so bright it hurt her eyes. There weren't enough bedrooms for Mama and Papa, seven-year-old Lily, and her little brothers, Joseph and Dannie. In fact, Lily's bedroom wasn't a real bedroom at all. Her bed was tucked into the corner of an upstairs hallway. She had a hallway bedroom. A wave of self-pity swept over her whenever she climbed the steps to her hallway bedroom.

But here's what Lily liked about the new house: the light switches worked! On, off, on, off. Lily and Joseph tried them in every room. Amazing! Papa said they could use the electricity only for a few weeks. As soon as he installed a new water pump for the well and found a refrigerator that could be run with a little gas engine, the electricity would be turned off.

Lily was sorry to learn that they couldn't use those electric lights for much longer. They were so much brighter than the dim oil lamplight she was used to. Electric lights filled every corner of the room with bright cheerful light.

This very day, Lily's family had moved to Pennsylvania from their farm in New York—a cold, gray, snowy day that made the long drive even longer. Lily wanted to tell the hired driver to hurry, hurry, hurry! Her papa had gone ahead with the moving van and was already at the house. Sally, her one and only doll, was in a box in the moving van, and Lily wanted to unpack her and play with her.

But when they arrived in Pennsylvania, Lily was disappointed to find strangers in the yard, helping Papa move furniture and boxes into the house from the moving van. As Lily and Joseph followed Mama into the house, they found other strangers inside, opening boxes and unpacking dishes and putting them into cupboards. They didn't seem at all concerned if that was where Mama wanted them. A girl stood posted by the front door to open and close it as the men carried in furniture and more boxes. Every time the door opened, snow swirled inside and a cold draft whooshed in. Lily shivered. The men tracked snow in on their boots and it melted in dirty puddles on the floor. Even the snow, Lily thought, was crying.

This move to Pennsylvania didn't suit Lily at all. Sadly, common sense had not prevailed, and here they were. She wished they could just pack everything right back up and return to New York. She had hoped, at the very least, that Grandma and Grandpa Miller and Aunt Susie would be here to greet them since they'd moved to Pennsylvania ahead of

Lily's family. But they had gone off to visit Great-Grandma. Another disappointment.

The couch had been brought in and pushed against the kitchen wall. Mama set two-year-old Dannie on it and asked Lily and Joseph to read to him while she helped with the unpacking. Now that Joseph was six and learning to read, he sounded out words to Dannie in the picture book. Lily listened absently to the women's conversations in the kitchen. She heard one woman say to Mama, "Rachel, you will probably want to send the children to school tomorrow. Our boys walk right by your house every day on their way to school. I'll tell them to stop in tomorrow morning to walk with your children."

School? *School?!* In the busyness of moving, Lily had forgotten all about school. She hadn't even found a bathroom yet in this new house! She hadn't found Sally in the boxes. How could Mama possibly think that she and Joseph were ready to start school? Too worried to stir, she could barely hold back until the strangers left so she could tell Mama that starting school tomorrow was a terrible idea.

As the sun began to set, people drifted off to their own homes. Now Lily could talk freely. As the last stranger shut the door, she turned to Mama. "Do we have to go to school tomorrow?" she asked. "I think it's a good idea that we wait until next week." Or next month.

"I think it's a good idea to go to school tomorrow," Mama said, sounding certain. "The longer you wait the more you will dread it. Once you're there, you'll enjoy it."

Lily wasn't at all certain. She could tell from the look on Mama's face that her mind was made up. Suddenly, she was looking into a terrible future. She sat there without a sigh left in her.

That night, as Lily slipped into her nightgown and hopped into her bed in the hallway, she thought and thought. Soon, an excellent idea took shape. She would stay awake all night long. That way, she reasoned, she would have a terrible headache in the morning and Mama would have to let her stay home from school. She snuggled deep under the covers and kept her eyes wide open, pleased with herself for thinking up a way to avoid school. It was always a good idea to have a backup plan.

Her eyelids drooped, and it was morning.

"Time to wake up, Lily," Mama's voice called from the bottom of the stairs before she flipped on the light switch. Lily blinked her eyes a few times. She thought the electric lights were wonderful at night, but in the morning they were much too bright. They hurt her eyes.

She hopped out of bed and put on her dress, then went downstairs to help Mama with breakfast. When she stepped into the kitchen, she noticed two lunch pails on the bright orange countertop. Mama was wrapping sandwiches and placing them inside.

School! Lily had forgotten. She didn't stay awake all night like she had planned. A feeling of dread covered her like a blanket. She did not want to go to this new school.

Mama chatted cheerfully as she finished packing lunches. "This will be exciting for you and Joseph," she said. "You'll get to make new friends. And it will be nice to learn with other children and a real teacher instead of at home."

Lily had liked having school at home when they lived in New York. It was easy and fun and there were days when Mama was so busy that they skipped schoolwork. Now and then, Lily had missed seeing her friends, but she thought staying home was worth that small sacrifice. She was about to say as much, but from the look on Mama's face, Lily's fate was sealed.

After breakfast was over, Mama sent Lily and Joseph to change into school clothes. She reminded them to brush their teeth and wash their face and hands until they were shiny. They would not have to help with the dishes this morning.

Lily cheered up a little. At least there was one good thing about having to go to school. She could skip dishwashing. She hated, hated, hated to wash dishes. Drying wasn't so bad, but washing dirty dishes in gray, soapy, slimy water was disgusting.

A knock on the door interrupted Mama as she inspected Lily's and Joseph's faces. She opened the door to find three boys on the porch. The biggest boy said, "Our mom told us to stop by so we can show your children the way to school."

Mama smiled and invited them inside. "Come in and warm up a little while I help Lily and Joseph into their wraps. It's cold outside this morning."

The boys did look cold. Their noses were red and their ears even redder as they peeped out from under their straw hats. Lily wondered why they would wear straw hats on such a cold day. These Amish in Pennsylvania seemed odd. Joseph looked much more cozy with a warm stocking cap on his head.

"This is Lily and Joseph," Mama said. "What are your names?"

"I'm Marvin Yoder," the biggest boy said. "And these are my brothers, Ezra and Aaron." Ezra nodded and smiled but Aaron looked Lily over and didn't like what he saw. He glared at her with angry blue eyes. So she glared back.

Mama helped Lily slip into her winter coat and close the

snaps. She stood quietly as Mama draped her shawl over her shoulders and pinned it firmly under her chin. After the ribbons of her heavy black bonnet were tied, she and Joseph were ready to go.

The bright sun made the snow glisten and sparkle, so shiny and bright that Lily had to squint to see where to walk. Marvin and Ezra walked alongside Joseph and Lily, but Aaron ran up ahead. Marvin asked questions about the school in New York. Lily told him she had attended school for only one year but had two teachers. Teacher Ellen had been a very nice teacher, but after she was hurt in an accident, she couldn't teach any longer. Teacher Katie had finished out the school term, but Lily had been scared of her.

"You won't be scared of Teacher Rhoda," Marvin said. "We all like her."

"Did you have a farm in New York?" Ezra asked.

Joseph chimed in. "We sure did." Only six, he had already decided he was going to be a farmer when he grew up. "A big farm with a lot of animals."

Up ahead, Aaron stopped and spun around. "How many cows did you have?"

"Only one cow," Joseph said. "And lots of chickens and our big horse, Jim, and a little horse too. We called him Chubby."

Aaron sneered. "That's not much of a farm. One measly cow? Sounds like Pennsylvania had better start sending their milk to New York to keep the people there from dying of thirst."

"New York does not need Pennsylvania milk!" Lily said, indignant. "Grandpa Miller and a lot of other people had big farms with lots and lots of cows. Hundreds and millions of cows!"

Aaron was not impressed. "New York needs Pennsylvania

milk. See? New York girls can't even walk very fast. You need milk!" With that he took off and ran ahead to school.

What a rude boy! Lily planned to stay clear of him.

"Don't pay Aaron any mind," Marvin said, reading her mind. As they continued on their way, Lily couldn't deny that Aaron was right about one small thing: she was walking much too slow. But she couldn't help it. Her feet felt heavy in her heavy winter boots and sank in the soft snow. She tried to walk a little faster, but then she would get out of breath and couldn't talk.

They arrived at the one-room schoolhouse just as Teacher Rhoda, tall and slender, stepped outside to ring the bell. Lily teetered on the threshold, reluctant to go in, until the children pushed around her and she ended up inside. Her fingers were cold and stiff from the mile-long walk to school. She couldn't open the large safety pin that Mama had used to pin her shawl. Teacher Rhoda saw she was struggling and stopped to help her.

That was a good sign. School might not be too terribly awful if the teacher was kind. Lily hung her shawl on the wall peg, feeling eyes on her from all over the room. Everyone was watching. Lily's cheeks flamed with embarrassment as Teacher Rhoda showed Joseph and her to their desks. She longed to be somewhere else. Anywhere. Like, at home. Better still, at home in New York.

Joseph sat with the first grade at the very front of a long row and Lily sat in the same row with the second grade. A girl named Beth sat right in front of her. She turned around to give Lily a bright smile. Another good sign! She had met Beth on the house-hunting trip and was relieved to have one friend in this school.

But here was a bad sign, a terrible sign: seated right across the aisle was Aaron Yoder. He looked different with his straw hat off. His hair was curly. So curly that it shot out in every direction.

Mama taught Lily to never stare at anyone, but she had never seen such curly hair. She peeped over to look at the wild hair again just as Aaron glanced her way. He stuck his tongue out at her. Lily narrowed her eyes. She fought an urge to stick her tongue out right back at him, but she didn't want to have to confess to Mama what she had done on the very first day of school. Instead, she just sighed.

Teacher Rhoda stood behind the teacher's desk. "Good morning, boys and girls," she said in a cheerful voice.

"Good morning, Teacher Rhoda," the children responded.

"We have two new pupils in school today," Teacher Rhoda said. "I want everyone to welcome them to Green Valley School."

Lily squared her shoulders and folded her hands in her lap, expecting everyone to turn and stare at her again. Instead, they opened their desks and retrieved little homemade packages. One by one, they walked over to drop them on her and Joseph's desks. There were cards that said, "Welcome to Green Valley School!" Some had tucked bookmarks or stickers inside. Lily loved stickers. A few had written a cheerful little note. Even that curly-haired Aaron gave her a yellow balloon. It looked used, though.

Lily stole glances around the schoolhouse at the children and wondered which ones might be her friends. She was disappointed that there weren't many girls. Two girls who looked to be Lily's age caught her eye. One girl wore glasses and had her nose in a book. The other girl was scribbling away in a workbook. She had dark brown hair and a handful of freckles scattered over her nose and cheeks. Her big green eyes snapped and sparkled. That girl looked like she would know how to have fun. Lily hoped that green-eyed girl might be one of her friends.

Teacher Rhoda handed several new books to Lily to put into her desk. She browsed through them, pleased. She enjoyed working in schoolbooks and was eager for an assignment from the teacher. Teacher Rhoda called the first graders up to the front of class to read aloud. The school day had begun.

During recess, all of the boys ran outside to play. They didn't pay any mind to the cold and wind. The little girls gathered by a table at the back of the room. The girl with glasses told Lily that her name was Malinda. She had a worried look on her face that made Lily start worrying too, so she turned to the girl with green eyes and asked what her name was.

The girl drew her shoulders back and lifted her chin. "My name is Effie Kauffman. And I am so glad my parents gave me a nice humble name instead of a fancy one like yours."

Shocked, Lily didn't know how to respond to Effie Kauffman. She had always liked her name. Now that she thought about it, she couldn't think of one other little Amish girl named Lily. Maybe it was a fancy name. Maybe it wasn't humble at all. But she couldn't change it now. Oh, what a terrible discovery!

Beth yanked on Lily's sleeve. "Don't pay any attention to Effie," she whispered. "Her father is a minister and she thinks she's the boss of everybody."

Beth got a box filled with jacks and a little red ball while Lily's thoughts drifted back to a girl in New York named Mandy Mast who liked to boss everybody around. Beth dumped the jacks on the table and the girls started to play. Much too soon, Teacher Rhoda rang the bell and the children hurried back to their desks.

The rest of the day inched along slowly. As Lily worked in her new schoolbooks, she couldn't stop thinking of Effie's accusation. It bounced around in her mind like an echo: *Fancy like yours. Fancy like yours.* She sighed.

When school dismissed for the day, Teacher Rhoda helped Lily pin her shawl. It was time for the long, cold walk back home. Marvin and Ezra waited until she was ready and then walked beside Joseph and her. Aaron ran ahead with his friends. Lily was glad he didn't stay to walk with his brothers. They were much nicer than he was.

A wave of exhaustion rolled over Lily as she trudged through the thick snow. She hoped Mama would have a nice snack waiting when they got home. She sighed all the way home.

When they reached Lily's ugly olive green house, Marvin and Ezra didn't stop to come inside. They waved goodbye and said they would see them tomorrow. Then they crossed the road and disappeared on a little path that led into the woods.

As Lily entered the warm, cozy kitchen, she found Mama working at the sink. Dannie stood on a chair next to her, watching everything Mama was doing, the way Lily used to when she was little. He nibbled on a slice of raw potato that was sprinkled with salt. Mama offered a potato slice to Lily and Joseph. "So how was your first day of school?"

Joseph launched in eagerly about his first day of real school. He told Mama about his desk and his books and the boys that he could play with at recess. So many boys! An abundance. He told her about the story Teacher Rhoda had read to them after noon recess and about his shiny new pencil. Sometimes Lily thought that Joseph babbled like a brook.

Lily felt pale and droopy and all she could think of was what Effie had said about her name. When Joseph ran out of things to report, Mama turned to Lily. "How did you like your first day of school?" she asked, because Lily wasn't saying.

Out blurted, "Why in the world did you and Papa give me such a fancy name?"

Mama's brown eyes widened with surprise. She set the potato she had been peeling aside and carefully washed her hands and wiped them on her apron. "Let's go talk about it."

Lily followed Mama into the living room and sat next to her on the sofa. Joseph and Dannie followed them in and sat on the floor, all eyes and ears. There was absolutely no privacy with those two brothers.

"When God gave us a little baby girl, Papa and I were very

happy," Mama said. "We wanted to give her a special name. Papa's great-grandmother was named Lily and she was a very kind woman. We hoped that our little girl would grow up to be kind and sweet just like she was. And we both liked the name Lily. We knew it wasn't a name that many other Amish girls had, but we wanted you to have it. Papa's great-grandmother was very pleased when she heard what name we had chosen for you."

Relief flooded through Lily. She should have known that Papa and Mama always did the right thing.

"Is there a reason you are asking about your name today, Lily?" Mama said.

Lily smoothed out her dress. "A girl named Effie Kauffman said it wasn't a humble name."

Mama smiled. "I don't think I would worry too much about what this Effie Kauffman thinks. I think Lily fits you just fine."

After eating the soup Mama had made for supper, Lily helped wash and dry dishes, and then it was time for bed. Tonight, for the first time that Lily could remember, she didn't mind when Papa announced, in his deep, soft voice, that it was eight o'clock. "Bedtime for little lambs." He had a fine voice, Papa did.

As she snuggled under the covers, she reviewed her day. All in all, it wasn't as bad a day as she had feared it to be. Teacher Rhoda was nice, much nicer than Teacher Katie. And then there was Beth. But two things she knew for certain: she would never be friends with sassy-mouthed Aaron Yoder or with snooty-faced Effie Kauffman.

She sighed.

The Red Door

$\mathcal{L}$ ily's bedroom was cozy and comfortable, but it wasn't really a bedroom. It was the corner of a hall. Next to her bed was her dresser. On top of the dresser was her pretty little white lamp with pink flowers. A door beside the dresser opened into a bedroom and that's where Joseph and Dannie slept.

And in the boys' room was a painted red door.

Mama told Lily and her brothers that they needed to wait for permission to open that red door. Lily couldn't stop thinking about it. What was behind the door? Where did it lead? Maybe it just opened to the outside, like the hayloft in the barn. Then she worried that Joseph and Dannie might get too curious and open the door. They would fall to the ground like a couple of stones. Boys could be like that. Too curious.

Lily whispered her worry to Mama. "No," Mama said.

"The red door doesn't lead to the outside. Please remember not to let your imagination run away with you."

Finally, on Saturday morning, Mama said to Lily, "Today, you can take your brothers and go exploring behind that red door." Carefully, holding her breath, Lily opened the red door. It led to a set of stairs.

Lily held Dannie's hand as they climbed the stairs. When they reached the top, they had to stop while their eyes adjusted to the dark. It was just a cold attic. Lily was disappointed, but on top of the disappointment rushed in curiosity.

On one side of the room were boxes, piled high. Those boxes had been brought with them on the big truck from New York, waiting to be unpacked until Mama had room for the things. Lily hoped the box that held Sally in it was here. She still hadn't found Sally.

On the other side of the room were piles and piles of things that the former owners had left behind. There were stacks of puzzles and games and boxes filled with books and newspapers. In front of a little window, Lily spotted several pink and yellow Easter baskets. Propped up against the wall were two guitars.

Lily's fingers wiggled at her side. She wanted to strum the strings on the guitars. What did they sound like? What did a guitar feel like? But she didn't touch the guitars. She knew that they didn't belong to them. Papa and Mama wouldn't be happy if they heard Lily had poked into other people's things. Still, she could look. She and Joseph and Dannie walked all around the boxes and tried to see everything they could without touching anything. Too soon, they heard Papa's voice at the top of the attic stairs. "Lunch is ready," he said. He took a few steps into the attic and looked around, hands on his hips. "Looks like we will have a lot of sorting to do. They sure left a lot of things here."

Lily clambered around the boxes to reach Papa's side. "Do you think we can keep everything?" She hoped Papa would say that they could play with all those wonderful toys and games and read those books and maybe—just maybe—strum the guitars.

"It's all ours now," Papa said. After catching the excited look on Lily and Joseph's faces, he quickly added, "But I don't want you to be playing with anything until Mama and I have sorted everything and decided what to keep and what to sell."

Lily knew what *that* meant. More waiting.

One Saturday later, Papa told the family to get their coats on. "We're going up in the attic," he said, grinning. It was much colder up there than in the rest of the house.

Papa carried one of the kitchen chairs up for Mama to sit on while they sorted through boxes. Mama said he was spoiling her, but she seemed pleased. "I'll bring things over to show you, Rachel," he said. "Lily and Joseph can help me and you can decide what to keep or not." Dannie's job was to sit beside Mama and play with toys and books.

Papa started with the boxes that were the closest to them. Box after box held nothing but clothes, clothes, clothes. They weren't even clothes that they would wear. Boring! But Mama seemed delighted. "We'll remove all the buttons and cut everything up," she said. "Some of the clothes can be used for quilt patches. Others will make good dust cloths for our Saturday cleaning. The rest we can tear into strips to make woven rugs."

Now the clothes seemed a little more interesting to Lily. Wouldn't it be wonderful to have a purple woven rug? Mama sat on the chair and sorted all the clothes. Lily put the sorted piles into boxes, pulling all of the purple clothes into one pile, and Papa wrote on the boxes in his neat handwriting: *MAMA'S WINTER PROJECTS*. Underneath that label, he wrote *QUILTS* or *RUGS* or *RAGS*.

On one side of Mama's chair was a growing pile of things to be thrown away. There were books that they didn't want to keep and boxes of old newspapers. When Papa put the two guitars on the throwaway pile, Lily asked Papa if she could strum them. Just once. Papa shook his head. "I don't think that's a very good idea," he said. "Doing it a little bit will only make you want to do it some more. Since we can't keep them anyway, it's best not to play with them at all. It will only tempt you for fancy things that we Amish don't want to have. We believe in singing our praises to God."

Lily looked at the guitars in the pile. Soon, other things were piled on top and they were out of sight. How sad.

But Lily didn't have much time to feel sorry about the guitars. Papa brought another box over to Mama and opened it. Lily could feel her heart skip a beat when she saw what was inside. Dolls! Real dolls, with pretty faces and cute hands and feet. Some of them looked like they were sleeping until Mama picked them up and their eyes popped open. Some had long, soft hair, while others had only hair painted on their heads.

Papa chuckled at Lily's delight. "Looks like we found a treasure chest for our little girl."

Mama examined each doll. "You can choose one doll to keep, Lily. Then I'll make Amish clothes for it. If you want one with hair, I'll take a pair of tweezers and pluck all the hair out so that it can wear a nice covering."

Lily looked at all the dolls. Every single one. She tried to make up her mind over which one she wanted the most, but it was so hard to choose. They all looked so pretty. She held them in her arms to see which felt the best. She didn't like the dolls with hard plastic bodies. She finally settled on a doll with a nice soft body that she could hug and cuddle in her arms. Its hair was painted on. Lily was afraid if she chose one with real hair, her doll would be left with a head full of little holes once Mama plucked its hair. That wouldn't do at all.

She held up her choice. "I'll take this one."

"Let's take it downstairs," Mama said. "You can play with it once I have time to make it some Amish clothes to wear."

Lily knew what that meant. *More waiting.*

Three weeks had passed since Lily's family had moved to Pennsylvania from New York. Papa had found the equipment he needed so that he could turn off the electricity in the house. Lily was sorry that they would no longer be able to use those bright lights. She would miss hearing the pleasant hum of the refrigerator in the kitchen. But watching Papa work and being his helper took her mind off all they would miss without electricity.

First, Papa took a little gas engine and attached it to a funny-looking gray box that had slits in it. An ice compressor, he explained to Lily. Last week, Papa had measured the space inside the freezer compartment in the top of the refrigerator. He knew an Amish man who could create a stainless steel pan to fit inside. Papa slipped it right in and smiled: a perfect fit. He moved the refrigerator forward and tipped it up while Mama slipped a rug under it. Then Papa took a firm hold on the rug and pulled the refrigerator out on the porch as Lily watched, wide-eyed.

She followed behind him. "Why can't you leave the refrigerator in the kitchen?"

"This community doesn't allow refrigerators in kitchens," Papa said.

"Why not?"

Papa shrugged. "No one knows. It's just always been that way. It probably started way back when the first refrigerator was invented." He fit the refrigerator snugly against the house wall. "Our house is too small to have it anywhere else, unless we put it upstairs in your bedroom." He stopped for a moment, stroking his beard, as if he were giving the matter some serious thought.

How awful! There was barely enough room for Lily's bed and dresser in that hallway. Joseph and Dannie galloped through like wild colts to get to their bedroom.

Then Papa's eyes twinkled and she knew he was teasing her. "But I don't think there's quite enough space up there."

Lily didn't think so, either. The porch seemed like a much better place for a refrigerator than her hallway bedroom. Though, it might have been nice to be able to get some snacks during the night without going downstairs. Then she remembered her little brothers and their bottomless appetites. They would be in and out of the refrigerator in Lily's hallway bedroom all night long. She could just see them eating leftovers from dinner in their bunk beds, getting crumbs everywhere. Soon mice would move in. Maybe a rat. She had overheard Aaron Yoder talk about killing a rat that was cat-sized.

No. The porch would just have to make do for the refrigerator.

On Saturday afternoon, an English stranger arrived at the house. He had a funny tool satchel and a big roll of copper pipe. He took the copper pipe and made a stack of coils that fit neatly inside the pan in the top of the refrigerator. The rest of the pipe was strung neatly beside the house and down to the ice compressor. Once everything was fastened, he told Papa, "It's ready to try out."

Papa brought the garden hose up to the porch from the basement. He told Lily to turn on the faucet in the basement and wait there until he told her to turn it off.

Lily ran to the basement and turned on the water. When she heard Papa call out to her, she quickly shut it off and ran back to see what they were doing next.

The pan was almost filled to the top with water. The copper coils were completely immersed.

Papa started the gas engine. Soon, the copper pipe beside the house was covered with thick white frost. He peeped into the refrigerator. "It's working. I'll stop the engine as soon as the pan is full of ice," Papa said. "Mama will have a place to keep food nice and cold."

"Let me see," Lily said.

Papa hoisted her up so she could look inside the pan. There were glossy layers of fresh ice all around the copper coils.

"Don't ever touch that pipe," the man said, peering over his glasses at Lily. "You would stick to it. It would be quite painful to try to get free."

Lily was stunned. A warning to her, of all people? The strange thing was that she was planning to lick that pipe as soon as the man left. The frost looked just like ice cream. Sometimes, she thought being grown-up meant you could read minds.

Sugar Weather

It was the time between winter and spring. Cold at night, warm during the day. The snow that fell was soft and turned into slush piles on the way home. It was fun to walk and splash through the piles on the way home from school. Lily liked this time of year. Beth called it sugar weather.

Lily wasn't sure what sugar weather was. All she knew was that the children rushed home from school each afternoon so they could go sugaring. Lily loved sugar. One evening at the supper table, she asked Papa what sugar weather was. "Why don't we go sugaring?" she said. "Everyone else is doing it."

Papa chuckled. "We would need to have big maple trees to go sugaring. We don't have any."

Lily was disappointed. She had no idea that sugaring had something to do with trees. There were so many trees on their property. Why couldn't they have had a sugar maple tree? Sometimes, life just didn't seem fair.

Several days later, Teacher Rhoda came to school with several pie pans filled with something mysterious. At noon, she set the pie pans on her desk. She took a sharp knife from her dinner bucket and began to cut whatever was in those pans into pieces.

"We made some spotza this week," she said. "I brought some along for all of you."

Children scrambled to line up. When it was Lily's turn, she whispered to Teacher Rhoda, "What is spotza?"

Teacher Rhoda seemed surprised that Lily didn't know what it was. "Why, it's sugar maple candy. From our maple trees."

A tree that made candy? Lily was amazed. How could Papa have not bought a house that had a candy tree? Everyone else seemed to have a candy tree.

Lily went back to her seat and examined the candy. It was pretty. The soft amber color was almost see-through. For a fleeting moment, she thought about saving it to share with Dannie. Maybe next time. This looked too delicious. She took a lick and . . . practically gagged. It didn't taste very sweet. It tasted like it should have stayed on the tree.

Lily couldn't understand why spotza was such a big treat. The room was quiet as each student licked away at their pieces. All but Aaron Yoder. He popped the whole piece into his mouth and started chewing it. The next minute he was making funny noises. His teeth were stuck together and he couldn't chew. Lily burst out laughing. She wished he would eat spotza every day so his mouth would be glued shut. Spotza was good for something, after all.

Just then, Aaron started to cough and spit. He held up a bloody tooth for everyone to see, smiling like he had just won a prize.

How disgusting! As soon as the class was dismissed for recess, she ran outside and buried the rest of her spotza deep in the snow. The last thing she wanted was to be toothless.

A month had passed since Lily had moved to Pennsylvania. One day, during recess, she was playing pick-up sticks with the other girls as Effie leaned toward her. "Lily, when are you going to start wearing a real covering?" she whispered in that too-loud-to-be-considered-whispering voice.

It was Lily's turn to try to get another stick from the pile without moving any of the others, but she paused to look at Effie. And frowned. "I am wearing a real covering," she said.

"No, you're not," Effie said. "It isn't made out of the proper fabric and the strings are too narrow. It isn't even made the same way. It makes you look funny."

Like usual, Lily didn't know how to answer Effie's proclamations. She knew that her head covering looked different from the ones the other girls in school had. Making a Pennsylvania-style covering for Lily would have to wait until Mama had time. Mama was sewing new clothes so that they would match everyone else in this new church. Lily knew it wouldn't be long before she had a new covering, and she wasn't sure how she felt about it. She liked the one she had on. She'd worn that style since the day she was born. It reminded her of her happy life at Singing Tree Farm in New York.

"Well, don't just sit there," Effie said. "We want to play too."

Beth smiled at Lily. "I think your covering is nice. It doesn't make you look funny at all."

Beth's encouragement made Lily feel a little better. She decided she would not let Effie spoil another day for her.

Effie was always saying things to make others feel like they'd bitten into a sour lemon. From now on, Lily wouldn't pay any mind to things Effie said. She concentrated on carefully lifting a pick-up stick from the pile. Another stick moved ever so slightly and her turn was over.

That afternoon, Lily and Joseph walked home from school. All the other children had run ahead of them, but Lily didn't mind. She enjoyed the walk home from school much more if they slowed down to see things.

This afternoon was much too nice to hurry. The snow banks beside the road were growing smaller. They didn't look very pretty with all the clinging dirt. The melting snow ran into the ditch along the road. Little Coltsfoot flowers were blooming. So brave. The first flowers to blossom after winter. They weren't very pretty, but they still made Lily feel happy when she saw them. A sure sign that spring would be here soon.

Lily stooped to pick a few and drop them into the water in the ditch. She watched them bob along the ripples in the water and wondered where their journey would take them. They might drift into a creek that could take them to a river. Maybe those little flowers would end up bobbing in the ocean. She wished there was a way that she could follow them and see where they went. If she were a flower on a creek, she might try to float all the way back to her little farm in New York and go visit Chubby the miniature horse and Stormy the dog. Chubby had been sold at auction and Stormy had been given to a family at the church. She missed them and she was sure they missed her.

Lily and Joseph stood and watched until the flowers disappeared from sight, then they started for home.

It was getting late. They walked a little faster now. Lily was hungry and couldn't wait to see what Mama was making for supper tonight. When they reached home, Mama was working in the kitchen. Three glasses of milk and three cookies were waiting for them.

Dannie stood next to his chair. "Hurry and change," he said. "I'm hungry." He was starting to get bossy. It was a worry to Lily.

Lily and Joseph changed into their everyday clothes and then sat at the table to enjoy their snack. Ever the copycat, Dannie sat on his chair and dunked his cookie into his glass of milk just like Lily and Joseph were doing.

"So how was school today?" Mama asked.

Lily listened patiently as Joseph told Mama about his day. When he was done, she said, "I like school but I don't like recess."

"What's wrong with recess?" Mama asked. "I thought you liked to play with Beth and your other friends."

"I like playing with Beth," Lily said. "But not all the children are as nice as she is." *Effie*, she meant.

"Always remember, Lily, it is much more important to treat others kindly than to think that they have to be nice to you," Mama said. "I hope you are nice to all the children and not just Beth."

"I do try to be nice to everyone," Lily said. *Malinda*, she meant. It was hard work to say only nice things to Effie when she didn't care what kinds of things she said to Lily.

Besides, Lily doubted that Effie's mother would give the same advice as Mama gave. Effie's mother was a big-boned, full-voiced lady who acted like her little girl could do no wrong. Lily had already learned that Effie Kauffman could do no right.

Two days later, Lily and Joseph walked in the door from school and Mama said to hurry and change their clothes. "Then come down and eat your snack. I want Lily to try on her new covering that I made today."

Lily ran upstairs and slipped into her light blue everyday dress. She felt excited. Finally, she would look like the other girls. Effie could no longer make fun of Lily. At least, not about her unusual covering.

Mama had spread peanut butter on apple slices. The apples were waiting for them to eat as Lily ran into the kitchen. She wished that Mama had given them a glass of chocolate milk instead of the apple. She could drink faster than she could chew apples and today was not a day to waste time on a snack.

Lily offered the rest of her apple slices to Joseph and he was happy to take them. Joseph was always hungry. Lily washed her hands and hurried to the living room to try on her new covering.

There it was, resting on top of the sewing machine cabinet. It was a beautiful shiny black satin instead of the thin black organza she had always worn.

She removed the covering she was wearing. Mama carefully placed the new one on her head and tied the wide satin ribbons under her chin. Lily went to find a mirror to admire the fluffy bow that these wide ribbons made. The bow looked nice, but something was wrong with this covering. Terribly wrong.

It was noisy! Every time Lily talked or moved her head she could hear her covering. Coverings weren't supposed to make sounds.

Mama smiled at her. "Well, how do you like it?"

Lily hesitated to tell her that it was broken. After all, Mama had spent time making it. "It is pretty," she said. "But it rattles."

A puzzled look came into Mama's eyes. "It rattles?"

"Every time I move, even a little, it makes a rattle."

Mama removed the covering and held it to her own ears. She grinned. "It's the thick fabric. I think you'll get used to it. Before long you won't even think about it. You can wear it to school tomorrow."

Lily wondered how she was supposed to concentrate on her lessons if she had to wear a covering that rattled all day long. She removed the new covering, glad to get away from the noise it made, and replaced it with her old, comfortable, quiet covering. She wished Mama had waited a little longer before making her a new one. Like everything else in this new town, it was strange and uncomfortable.

The Mirror at Midnight

$\mathcal{L}$ily glanced at the clock on the schoolhouse wall. Only ten more minutes until recess. Teacher Rhoda was busy with the first graders, who were trying to learn a new letter and its sound. Lily liked watching the first grade class. They were cute and little and their schoolwork was easy. Much easier than the math problems she was working on. Rain beat against the windows. The gentle patter of raindrops made Lily feel sleepy. She yawned as she turned her attention back to the last few subtraction problems. Only three more.

"Put your books away for recess," Teacher Rhoda said.

The room was filled with the sound of books closing, papers shuffling, and the opening and closing of desk lids. Lily tucked her arithmetic workbook and pencil into her desk. She wished she had hurried to finish those stupid math problems. She would have to finish them after recess.

She closed her desk lid and waited as Teacher Rhoda

dismissed one row of students at a time. She wondered what they would be playing today. They couldn't play outside in the rain. It had been raining for weeks now and she was tired of indoor games.

The children gathered at the back of the schoolhouse, but nobody had any ideas of what to do. Someone suggested they could play Still Waters, but that suggestion was met with groans. Lily was relieved. She didn't like when it was her turn to be *it* and she had to wander around the schoolhouse blindfolded, hunting for children. They could walk and run away from her until Teacher Rhoda called out "Still Waters" and everyone froze in place. They had to hold still until Lily had found them. It always took her a long time to find everyone. Last time, Aaron Yoder had stuck out his foot and tripped her.

Jay Troyer, one of the first grade boys, opened up his umbrella and walked around the schoolhouse with it.

Effie planted her hands on her hips. "Close that umbrella right now!"

Jay kept right on walking. "Why?"

Effie didn't like for her orders to be ignored. "Don't you know bad things happen to people who open umbrellas indoors?"

Jay's mouth opened in a silent O. He quickly closed the umbrella, horrified. Lily hadn't known that, either. She tried to think back and remember if anything bad had ever happened to her after she had opened Papa's big, black umbrella in the house. Once, she had stubbed her toe as she put the umbrella away. But she often stubbed her toes, even when there was no umbrella in sight.

A few children started to talk about other things that were bad to do. Marvin Yoder—who was nice, unlike his younger

36

brother Aaron, who was not—said that when a lamp chimney broke or cracked while the lamp was lit, it meant that someone in the family had died.

Effie said that if your left ear itched it meant that someone was saying something bad about you.

One of the eighth grade girls added that if a girl walked up the stairs and accidentally stepped on the skirt of her dress, it meant she would not be getting married that year. Right then and there, Lily decided to step on her skirt every year. She didn't want to get married. She never wanted to leave Papa and Mama.

Beth rubbed her hands together. "If you look into a mirror when a clock strikes midnight, you will see what you will look like in your coffin."

Lily shivered. How awful! She wondered if it was really

true. It must be true. Beth never lied. Effie did, but Beth never did.

Lily was glad when Teacher Rhoda rang the bell and it was time to return to their desks. This recess had been spooky.

When Lily got home from school, she changed into her everyday clothes and looked at her reflection in the mirror. It was the same as it always was. Big brown eyes, a few freckles splashed across her nose and cheeks, and mousy brown hair. She couldn't help but wonder what she would see if she looked into the mirror at midnight. Fear trickled down her spine.

Later that night, after bedtime, Lily snuggled under the covers and soon drifted off to sleep. Suddenly, she jerked awake. She could hear the chimes of the clock downstairs. Lily's heart beat faster as she sat up and counted every strike. One . . . two . . . three . . . then, seven . . . eight . . . nine. Everything went quiet. Lily fell back on her pillow with a sigh of relief. It was only nine o'clock.

She hopped out of bed and turned her mirror to face the wall. Too risky. She did not want to see what she would look like in a coffin if she happened to wake up at midnight.

Each evening after that, Lily made sure the mirror was turned toward the wall. It became part of her going-to-bed routine.

Until one evening, when she forgot. The chimes of the clock woke her. Outside the moon was shining brightly and its soft light filtered into her window. Lily sat up in bed and counted as the clock struck ten . . . eleven . . . twelve!

She couldn't help herself. She looked! She looked in the mirror. Lily expected to see an old, old woman, as old as Great-Grandma, staring back at her. But all she could see was her own reflection. She breathed a sigh of relief and snuggled back under her covers.

Then came a dreadful thought. What if that meant she was going to die soon? How *awful*! How sad.

Lily was wide awake. She might die in her sleep! She lit her oil lamp and opened her dresser drawer to find a piece of paper and a pencil. Since she was going to die, she might as well write out a Last Will & Testament. She would give Joseph all of her books and games. Dannie could have her doll Sally. And Papa and Mama could have the rest of her things.

She folded her will and set it on top of the dresser. Then she blew out the lamp and climbed back into bed. She tried to imagine how much Papa and Mama, Joseph and Dannie would cry when she died. Buckets and buckets of tears. Just thinking about it made her cry. She sniffed and pulled the covers up over her head. She would never sleep tonight. Never.

"Lily! Time to get up!" Mama called from the bottom of the stairs.

Lily blinked twice, then opened her eyes wide. She hopped out of bed and grabbed the will she had written last night. She had better get this over with. Poor Mama. She tucked it into her pocket. In the kitchen, she handed it to Mama.

Mama opened it and read it quietly. She looked at Lily. "What is this all about?"

"I'm going to die soon," Lily said. She was trying to be brave, but it was sad. So sad.

"What makes you think that?"

Lily told her all about what Beth had said about the mirror at midnight. She told her that she had woken up and seen herself, at age eight, so she knew she wouldn't live to be as old as Great-Grandma. So sad, so sad.

Lily glanced up to see if Mama might need a handkerchief

to wipe away her tears. But no! Mama's eyes were smiling. In fact, it looked as if she were trying not to laugh. "Oh, Lily. That's only a very silly superstition. The mirror only shows a reflection of who looks into it. It doesn't have any special powers. It's just a mirror. You don't have to worry about seeing an old wrinkled woman in it until you are old and wrinkled."

Mama bit on her lip as if she was trying very hard to hold back a smile. She turned back to the frying pan where several pieces of bacon sizzled and popped. Instantly, Lily felt light and happy. And very hungry. She wasn't going to die soon after all. She would get to keep all her toys and books and never have to worry about looking in that mirror again.

She wondered if all those other things she had heard from her new friends were only silly superstitions. Probably so. But she thought she would still step on her skirt while going up the stairs at least once every year. Just in case.

Papa had found a job with a construction crew only a few days after moving to Pennsylvania. Unlike in New York, he didn't work on Saturdays. That made Lily happy. That was the second good thing about moving to Pennsylvania. The first good thing was making friends with Beth. Those were the only two things on her list.

On Saturdays, Lily and Joseph were Papa's little helpers as he worked on the house. Lily loved to watch and help Papa with all the interesting things that he did.

Earlier that week, Lily and Joseph had come home from school and had seen that someone had delivered a big, empty propane tank. It was set under the big spruce tree beside the house. Lily and Joseph liked to climb on top of the tank to slide over the side. It was only a short ride, but it was fun.

On this particular Saturday, Papa was putting gauges on top of the tank. He told them that he didn't want them to climb on it any longer. He didn't want them to touch the gauges. "The best way to make sure that doesn't happen is to stay off the tank."

Papa dug a ditch across the yard to the little gas engine. He placed another compressor behind the engine. Once it was hooked up, he started the engine and pumped air into the propane tank until he was satisfied there was enough pressure.

Lily grew bored watching Papa work on the propane tank. It wasn't as interesting as fixing the refrigerator. You could see ice, but you couldn't see air.

When the tank was full of compressed air, Papa took the lid off the water well. He started to pull at the pipes and wires that were attached to the electric pump that pumped water to the house. It was hard work. Soon, Papa gave up trying to do this project by himself. He went inside and sat at his desk to write a note. He handed it to Lily. "Run to Grandpa Miller's and give this to him."

Lily hurried down the road to Grandpa Miller's house and handed him the note at the door. He read it and said, "If you can wait a little, I'll walk back with you."

Lily would never mind waiting for Grandpa. It would be special to have time alone with her grandfather. Soon, Grandpa finished his task, plucked his hat and coat from the wall peg, and the two were on their way.

Grandpa walked with a purpose. He did everything with a purpose. Lily did the best she could to keep up, but her short legs had to take two steps for every one of his long, graceful strides. She chattered happily as they strolled down the road. Grandpa pointed out some birds that Lily had never noticed. He knew about all kinds of things—birds and wildlife and trees and clouds. Sometimes, Lily thought that Grandpa knew everything, even more than Papa. The walk didn't take nearly long enough. It was the first time she had ever wished Grandpa lived farther away, so they could walk longer together.

When they reached the yard, Grandpa helped Papa pull the electric water pump out of the well. Together, they made quick work of it. They fastened the air hoses to the new pump and slid it down into the well.

Once they were satisfied that everything was secure, it was time to try it out. They went into the house and opened the kitchen faucet. Water sputtered out but it was dirty and muddy and brown. And then it stopped coming altogether.

Papa didn't seem to be concerned but Lily thought it was a terrible thing to have to drink such filthy water. Soon, the water started sputtering out of the faucet again. Papa stood there watching as the water flowed. He said that changing the pumps had stirred up some dirt. They needed to be patient until it had time to settle and become clear again.

Lily watched the water run. Every once in a while it would stop and make a long gasping noise before it started to flow again. "Why does it do that?"

"That's the way air pumps work," Papa said. "Every time the pump has to bring another load of water, it pauses until it fills up."

Grandpa brushed his hands together like he was dusting off flour, a sign that he was satisfied. "It looks like everything is working so I guess I may as well start for home."

Papa thanked him for coming over to help. He turned

back to the sink to watch the water. It was starting to run clear.

Lily could get used to having a refrigerator on the porch instead of the kitchen. She could get used to having flickering oil lamps again instead of electric lights. But she wasn't sure she could ever get used to a gasping faucet.

Lily's New Doll

Another week went by and Mama was still too busy to make clothes for Lily's new doll. Mama explained to Lily that she had many clothes to sew for the family so that they would be dressed the same as everyone else in the church. There was a way of dressing in the Pennsylvania church that was different than Lily's New York church: the fabrics were different, the pleats in Mama's dress and cape were different, Mama's apron had to be one inch shorter than it had been, no snaps allowed on Papa's coat—only hooks and eyes. Lily asked Mama what difference it made and she had no answer for her.

"It's tradition," she said.

"But why?" Lily said.

Mama sighed. "We don't question why. Each church has their own way of doing things."

And didn't that just say it all?

Papa had found the box with Sally, Lily's doll, and even though Lily was happy to see Sally, she was anxious to play with the new doll. She had already given it a name: Irene. It seemed like a perfectly lovely name for such a pretty doll. She was trying so hard to be patient. She only asked Mama about it twice a day. Surely, Mama could see Lily's patience.

One afternoon, Lily came home from school and was handed a bag by Mama. "Lily, I just don't think I'm going to be able to make doll clothes for a very long time," she said. In the bag were the doll and some fabric. "Take this bag to Grandma Miller and ask her to make the clothes for it."

Lily didn't even wait for an after-school snack. She ran all the way to Grandma Miller's house. Grandma had plenty of time to sew doll clothes. It wouldn't be long until Irene was ready to be played with.

Grandma opened the door to Lily, surprised to see her. Lily blurted out the story about the doll in the attic. Grandma looked at the doll and fabric and listened as Lily explained that this would be her very own doll as soon as it was wearing Amish clothes.

Grandma smiled. "I'll try to have it ready by Saturday."

Lily skipped all the way home. Only three more days and she could finally play with Irene. At last! It almost seemed too good to be true.

On Saturday, Lily worked extra fast to help Mama with all the day's chores. They finished cleaning the house in record time. "Can I go see if Grandma has finished the doll?"

"You worked very hard today, Lily," Mama said. "Today is a special day. You waited patiently for your doll to be ready, and I know how much you wanted to play with her. I think it would be nice if you stopped by Mr. Wilson's Corner Store and treat yourself to some candy." She handed Lily a quarter.

Oh, what a wonderful day! The best day ever. A doll *and* candy! Lily already knew what she would buy. A Snickers candy bar. It cost a quarter. As she walked into the store, she spotted a box of Tootsie Rolls on the counter. Each Tootsie Roll cost five cents. Instead of the Snickers bar, Lily decided to buy five Tootsie Rolls so everyone in the family could have a piece of candy.

Slowly, ever so slowly, Mr. Wilson counted five Tootsie Rolls and put them in a little brown paper bag. *Hurry, hurry, hurry!* she wanted to say to Mr. Wilson, but of course she didn't say it out loud. That would be rude. But she was *that* eager to see her new doll. When Mr. Wilson handed her the bag, she thanked him, walked carefully out the door, and then ran up the road to Grandma's house. She could barely control her excitement.

In the house, the doll was sitting by Grandma's sewing machine. Irene looked beautiful. She was dressed in a pretty royal blue dress and a crisply starched white apron. Her black covering was tied neatly under her dimpled chin. The blue dress made her eyes look even more blue. As blue as a summer sky. And her pink cheeks looked like roses. Lily held Irene in her arms and hugged her against her chest. Sally was no longer Lily's favorite doll. Irene was much more like a baby and so much prettier than her old limp rag doll.

Lily thanked Grandma Miller for sewing such nice clothes for Irene. She was eager to get home and play with her new doll. At the door, Grandma handed her an envelope. "Please give this to your Mama when you get home."

Lily tucked the doll beneath her shawl to keep Irene from getting cold. Spring was nearly here, but the air was still cold.

When she reached home, she showed Irene to Mama. Even Joseph and Dannie were interested in seeing her. Lily started up the stairs to get her bag filled with doll toys and her doll blanket when she remembered the Tootsie Rolls in her pocket. And then she remembered the envelope Grandma had given to her.

Mama opened the envelope and read the letter. She looked surprised, then sad. She folded the letter and slipped it into her pocket. "I think it might be a good idea to wait to play with your new doll until Papa comes home."

What? *More* waiting?

Lily thought it was a terrible shame not to be able to play with her lovely doll. She sat on the corner of the sofa and watched out the window for Papa to come home. She wanted him to hurry, but then, a part of her didn't want him to hurry, either. She had a funny feeling about what might be in Grandma's letter. It didn't seem like good news.

When Lily spotted Papa coming up the driveway, Mama told her to stay in the house with Joseph and Dannie while she spoke to Papa privately.

Afterward, Papa came into the kitchen to wash his hands and face. He crossed the room to where Lily was reading a story to Joseph and Dannie. He picked up her new doll and looked at it carefully. Then he sat down on the sofa. He held Irene in his lap. "Grandma Miller said that she doesn't think it's wise for a little girl to play with a doll that has a real face, hands, and feet."

Lily felt tears prick her eyes. She was afraid of something like this. She knew her doll was too good to be true. "But Papa, other girls in my school have dolls who look just like Irene. Beth does, and Effie does too."

Papa nodded. "We realize that other little girls in this community might have dolls like Irene. Still, we don't want to offend your grandma. She thinks those kinds of dolls make girls vain. Besides, Lily, you already have a doll that you love very much."

Sally, he meant. But Sally was so . . . threadbare and worn-out.

"Mama and I talked it over and we decided to sell this doll. We will let you keep the money. Then someday we will take you to a thrift store and you can buy a whole pile of books with it."

One tear leaked down Lily's cheek.

Papa wiped her tear away. "You will be able to read those books a long time after you have outgrown dolls. I think that's the best thing to do."

Lily didn't think it sounded like a good idea at all. She had waited patiently for Irene and she was never patient! She wanted to play with that doll more than she had ever wanted anything before.

Tears were coming faster than she could blink them back. She knew she was much too big to cry about a doll, but it simply didn't seem fair. It didn't matter if she bought a hundred zillion books with the doll money. She would rather have Irene. She would rather be back in New York. If they had just stayed there, she would never have seen Irene and discovered what she was missing. None of this would have happened. Everything about Cloverdale, Pennsylvania, was awful. Everything.

Cherry Pie Barn

The snow was melting away. Winter was fading and spring would be here soon. Today, Mama's youngest brother, Uncle Jacob, was moving to Pennsylvania with his family. He had already bought a little house close to Grandpa and Grandma Miller so that he could work at Grandpa's sawmill. Lily didn't remember Uncle Jacob from New York. He had married and moved to his wife's community when Lily had been a baby. She was eager to meet Uncle Jacob. She had never seen Mama so excited.

On Saturday, Mama and Lily had joined some of the other women in the community in a work frolic to clean Uncle Jacob's house. Joseph and Dannie had to stay at home with Papa.

Uncle Jacob's house didn't look very dirty to Lily. Still, every inch had to be scrubbed spotless. Effie's mother, Ida Kauffman, stood by the front door and gave people jobs to do as they arrived. She directed some women to wash the walls and ceilings. Others cleaned the insides of closets. It reminded Lily of school recess, with Effie bossing everybody around.

Lily helped Mama wash the kitchen cupboards. Grandma and Aunt Susie washed windows. Aunt Susie was Grandma's youngest daughter. She was all grown-up but seemed like a little girl. She was born with something called Down's syndrome, and Lily loved her.

Soon, the house began to sparkle. It was cleaned from top to bottom and ready for the move-in. Lily hoped the men wouldn't track in muddy puddles like they had done on her family's moving day.

Several days later, Lily and Joseph came home from school and couldn't find Mama or Dannie. The house was strangely quiet. On the kitchen table, Lily found a note from Mama: "We went to Uncle Jacob and Aunt Lizzie's to help unload their belongings. There is chocolate milk in the refrigerator. Help yourselves and then come join us at Uncle Jacob's house."

Lily found the chocolate milk and poured it into two glasses. Joseph gulped it down and started to head out the door as Lily grabbed him by the collar and made him wait. She wiped his face with a clean washrag, just like Mama did. It would never do to arrive with a chocolate milk moustache. Uncle Jacob would think Joseph was a messy boy. He *was* messy, but Uncle Jacob didn't need to find that out today. Satisfied that they looked presentable, they ran down the street to Uncle Jacob's.

They found lots of people carrying furniture and boxes into the house. Joseph saw Papa and ran off to join him. Lily ducked into the front door, darting between men who carried heavy boxes. She looked around to see if she could find Mama. Boxes were stacked on the floor. Furniture was pushed against the wall. There were dirty puddles on the floor, tracked inside from the rain. Lily sighed. All of her housecleaning was for naught.

Lily slipped into the kitchen. There was Mama, unpacking dishes and placing them into cupboards. Next to her was another woman. She held a baby on one hip and tried to work with her free hand. She looked exhausted. Lily felt sorry for her.

"Lily," Mama said, "meet your aunt Lizzie."

When Aunt Lizzie saw her, she brightened. "Hello, Lily, would you mind taking care of baby Anna for me?"

Lily was thrilled! Holding a baby was much more fun than unpacking dishes. Aunt Lizzie must think Lily seemed very grown-up if she let her take care of her baby. Lily carried Anna into the living room and sat on the couch. What did babies like to do? Dannie liked to play patty-cake when he was a baby. Lily held Anna's hands and started to chant, "Patty-cake, patty-cake, baker's man." Anna smiled a big toothless grin.

A little boy clambered onto the couch. "I'm Noah," he said. Lily thought he looked to be about Dannie's size and age. Noah watched Lily play with Anna. He squeezed in front of the baby. "I want to play patty-cake too." He held his hands out to Lily.

Lily shook her head. "I can't right now," she said. "I have to take care of baby Anna."

Noah slid off the couch and ran to the kitchen. Soon, he was back with Aunt Lizzie, pulling on her skirt. "I want her to play with me too."

Aunt Lizzie gave Noah a weary smile. "Your cousin Lily has her hands full right now. Maybe she could tell you a story."

She turned to Lily. "It would be a big help if you could keep an eye on Noah for me too."

Lily tried to think about the kind of story a boy like Noah might enjoy. She wished she had a picture book to read to him. Noah stood beside her, staring at her with his big blue eyes, eager for her to start the story.

Whenever Mama would wash and braid Lily's hair, she told a story about a horse that sneezed each time it smelled a flower. That would be a good story to keep a busy little boy's attention, Lily decided.

As soon as Lily finished the story, Noah hopped off the couch and started crawling around the room pretending to be that horse. He sniffed at the boxes and sneezed loudly. He didn't pay any attention to where he crawled. His pants became soaked from crawling through puddles on the floor. A man nearly tripped over him when he came into the living room with more boxes. Lily yanked Noah out of the way just as baby Anna rolled over and nearly fell off the couch. This went on for the rest of the afternoon.

Lily had never been so happy to hear Papa say it was time to head home and do the chores. It was hard work trying to take care of two little children. Now Lily understood why Aunt Lizzie looked so tired. Lily was worn-out.

But Mama wasn't at all tired. She chatted happily all the way home. She had invited Uncle Jacob and Aunt Lizzie for Sunday dinner. Lily hoped that didn't mean she would be expected to take care of Noah and Anna. She thought that Joseph and Dannie had too much energy, but she had never seen a little boy with as much energy as that Noah. He couldn't hold still for more than a minute. And he talked and talked and talked! It made her head hurt just thinking about it. Poor Aunt Lizzie.

Lily and Joseph followed Papa out to the barn to help with chores. Dannie liked to help with chores too, but the barn was too cold tonight. Papa told him to stay in the house with Mama. When Lily saw the disappointment on Dannie's face, she felt sorry for him. But Papa was right. Jim and Jenny snorted out big white clouds of air each time they breathed.

Papa got the milking stool off the peg on the wall and sat down beside Jenny. He washed her udder with warm soapy water before he started to milk her. Lily scooped several handfuls of oats into Jim's grain trough as Joseph scooped grain and corn sweetened with molasses into Jenny's trough.

"When you're done there, Lily," Papa said, "come and hold Jenny's tail so she won't swat me in the face." Jenny looked back at Papa, batting her big black eyelashes at him as if to say, "Who, me?"

Lily hurried over to hold Jenny's tail. A big gust of wind whistled through the cracks between the boards in the barn walls. Snow blew through the cracks and Lily shivered. Papa noticed how cold she was. "I'll do something about those cracks before another winter comes."

Lily wished he would do something about the cracks right away, but Papa said there wouldn't be many more cold days. He stood and stretched, then put the milking stool back on the peg and picked up the pail of warm, steaming milk to take back to the house. Lily and Joseph followed behind. As another blast of cold wind hit Lily in the face, she wondered about Papa's prediction that spring was here. The calendar might say March, but today it felt like January.

Early Saturday morning, Papa hitched Jim to the wagon and hurried off to town. He returned with a stack of thin boards. He said they were batten strips, and he piled the boards on the ground beside the barn. Lily thought that was a funny name for such thin, narrow boards. Mostly, she hoped Mama wouldn't need her in the house so she could help Papa outside. Being indoors was fine, but being outdoors with Papa was better.

"Go ahead, Lily," Mama said, smiling at the way Lily was staring out the window at Papa. "I don't think much dusting is going to get done with you wondering what Papa is up to." She laughed. "Just be sure to stay out of Papa's way as you watch him work."

Lily dropped the dust cloth and hurried outside. She hoped she could do more than watch Papa. She wanted to help him.

Outside, Papa was nailing a batten strip over a crack between the boards on the barn wall. He nailed in several nails, then stepped up on the stepladder to climb to the top, nailed in more nails, then climbed down to the bottom. There, he pounded more nails in the strip to make sure it was tightly fastened to the barn. Then he climbed halfway up and started the process again. Nail the middle strip, climb up the ladder, hit some nails, climb back down again, hit more nails. Over and over.

As Lily watched him, she was pretty sure she could nail those boards on the bottom so Papa would only have to take care of the nails in the middle and the top. She ran to find another hammer and came back to help.

Papa was already up the ladder, working on the top of the next strip. Lily picked up a strip and leaned it against the wall. She found a nail and held it firmly with her left hand on the bottom of the strip. She took a hammer and gently tapped the nail, taking care so she wouldn't hit her thumb with the hammer. The nail made only a tiny little pinprick hole. It tumbled to the ground when Lily let go. She picked it up and pounded harder. This time, the nail stayed in the board. But the next whack with the hammer sent it tumbling to the ground.

Papa grinned when he saw what she was doing. He climbed down the ladder, tools clanking in his carpenter's apron. "It's a little harder than it looks," he said. "But keep trying on this board. I'll keep working on the other ones."

Lily tried harder, but she couldn't pound a nail all the way into the board. Sometimes, it went in a little deeper, but with the next blow, the nail would bend and twist. It would have to be pulled out. Fortunately, the nails always seemed to come out of the board much easier than they had gone in.

This was hard work! She took hold of the nail and hit it as hard as she could with the hammer. The hammer slipped and whacked her thumb. *Ouch!* Lily dropped the nail and hammer and held her thumb in her other hand. Tears stung her eyes.

Papa came down the ladder to take a look at her thumb. "You had better run inside and let Mama put something on it to help it feel better," he said.

Lily went to the house, tears slipping down her cheeks. She had not been able to help Papa at all. Not one nail.

Mama crushed an aspirin into a small bowl with warm water. She told Lily to hold her thumb in it until it started feeling better.

Lily sat at the kitchen table with her thumb in the water. This was boring, even worse than helping Mama clean the house. She could hear the steady *bang, bang, bang* from Papa's hammer as he kept working on the barn.

After a while, the throbbing in her thumb started to subside. Lily went back outside to see what the barn looked like. Papa had already finished one side of the barn. Lily thought it looked funny. The barn had been red. The unpainted batten strips that Papa had placed over the cracks reminded Lily of a big cherry pie with a lattice top.

Papa noticed Lily at the foot of his ladder and asked her how her thumb was feeling. "It's a little better," she said. She looked up at the wall. "I think we should call our farm 'Cherry Pie Barn.'"

A laugh burst out of Papa. "The barn does look like a cherry pie right now. I don't think Mama will want to call our farm 'Cherry Pie Barn,' but maybe it will work until we find a better name."

Lily felt pleased. Maybe she wasn't old enough to pound nails, but she did help in one small way. She had found a name for their farm. At least for a while.

CHAPTER 7

An Angry Billy Goat

One spring Saturday afternoon in early April, Lily and Joseph were outside helping Papa clean the yard. There was so much to do. Leaves, sticks, and rocks littered the yard. Junk too. Lots and lots of junk. It looked like a tornado had come and gone. Papa said the people who had lived here before them must have been too worn-out to work outside. Lily said maybe they just liked to collect trash, but Papa said it was best to think well of others.

Even though Lily still didn't like the olive green house, and she didn't like her hallway bedroom, she wasn't bothered by such a messy yard. It was fun to help Papa work outside. Lily and Joseph's job was to pile sticks in the wheelbarrow. When it was full, Papa would dump them in a pile behind the barn. When he had time, he would burn the sticks.

Papa whistled as he worked. He was always whistling. He dug bunches of tiger lilies to replant in a neat row beside the fence. He paused to wipe the sweat from his forehead as a big noisy truck rattled to a stop in front of the house.

Lily and Joseph stared at the truck. Rusty red gates on the back were held together with baler twine. A big puff of wind might blow them right off. Several goats stuck their heads up over the gates.

A man jumped out of the truck and walked over to Papa. He wore baggy overalls and a dirty white shirt. He kept spitting brown stuff on the ground near his feet.

"You wouldn't be interested in buying these goats, would you?" the man asked Papa.

"How much do you want for them?" Papa asked.

"Give me twenty dollars and you can have all four of them. There are three nannies and one billy. Two of the nannies will be having kids any day now."

Papa walked over to the truck to examine the goats more closely. Lily and Joseph followed close behind, but Lily walked carefully around the man's spit spots. Disgusting.

But the nannies looked nice. They were a soft brown with a white patch on their foreheads and white legs. The billy was bigger. He was black, with eerie yellow eyes and long curved horns.

Papa took off his hat and ran a hand through his thick hair. "We hadn't given any thought to buying goats."

"I'll let you have them for ten dollars," the man said. "I have to get rid of them. They're nice and tame, but I can't keep them. My wife doesn't like them. She said either the goats go or she goes." He spit another long brown wad into the grass beside the road.

Lily was shocked. How could a wife say such a thing? She hoped Papa would buy the goats. It would be terrible if the man had to go home with the goats and his wife would go away. But maybe, Lily wondered, if the man stopped spitting, his wife wouldn't be so mad at him.

Papa looked at each goat for a long time, thinking and thinking. Then he jammed his hat back on his head. "You back the truck up to the barn while I go get the money."

The man jumped into his truck. The whole truck shuddered and lurched forward when he started it. Lily and Joseph ran into the house with Papa to hear him explain to Mama that he had just bought four goats. Mama looked stunned. Papa hurried off to pay the man.

"Goats?" Mama said as the door slammed shut behind Papa. "You bought goats?"

After the truck rumbled away, they all joined Papa outside to look at the goats.

Papa had tied the goats outside of Jenny's pen. He gave them several handfuls of hay to eat. Lily liked to listen to their sharp little teeth crunch the hay with quick, fast bites. It sounded so different from the slow, contented way Jenny munched her hay.

"I think I'll have to spend the rest of the afternoon making a pen for these goats," Papa said. "And it looks as if I'll need to milk one of the nannies tonight."

"Can I milk the goat?" Lily asked. "She's just about my size."

Papa hesitated. "I guess you could give it a try."

Lily was excited. Chore time would be even more fun if she could milk a nanny goat while Papa milked Jenny. Joseph could hold Jenny's tail for Papa. No one would have to hold the goat's tail because it was too little to swat anyone in the face.

By chore time, Papa had finished the goat pen in the barn. He put the three nanny goats in the pen but tied the billy goat near the back of the barn. Lily felt a little sorry for the billy goat, but Papa said that he didn't want that goat anywhere near the nannies. Lily thought that might be a good idea. If they were going to get kids soon, she didn't want the billy to hurt them with his big horns. But she thought she might gather fresh fistfuls of grass every day to feed to the billy. He might not feel so lonesome if he were given fresh grass to eat.

Papa handed Lily the milking stool. "Here, Lily. You can try milking the goat first. I can milk Jenny after you're done." He tied the nanny so she wouldn't walk away while Lily was milking her.

Lily sat down beside the nanny. She placed a little bowl on the floor under the goat and tried to milk her. Instead of nice long streams of milk like Papa got, she was able to get only a few drops into the bowl. *Plink, plink, plink.* Papa tried to help Lily, but as hard as she tried, she couldn't get the milk to stream. Her hands just weren't strong enough.

"We'll wait until you're a little older," Papa said. "I'm sure you'll learn how to be a good milker when you get bigger."

Lily was crushed. Papa finished milking the goat and handed her the bowl of milk to take to the kitchen. Mama strained the milk into a quart jar and put it into the refrigerator to get cold.

The next morning, Mama poured milk into a glass by each person's plate for breakfast. "Can I have goat milk this morning?" Lily asked. She'd been wondering what it would taste like.

Mama looked up, surprised. "You can if you want to."

Lily ran out on the porch and got the goat milk from the refrigerator to fill her cup. Papa and the boys decided they wanted to try the goat milk too. Lily took a sip and made a face. It didn't taste like milk was supposed to taste. It tasted like . . . Lily tried to think what it tasted like. What was it? Hmmm . . . then she knew. It tasted the way that big billy goat smelled.

Papa didn't like the milk either. "Tastes like goat to me," Papa said as he pushed his cup of milk aside. Joseph and Dannie liked it. They drank it all and asked for more. Little boys were funny that way. It didn't seem to matter what they ate. They just wanted to eat.

The next afternoon, Lily and Joseph ran all the way home from school. Lily wanted to get home fast so that she would have more time to feed fresh, sweet grass to the billy goat.

They gulped down the snack Mama had waiting for them at the kitchen table. Then they jumped out of their seats to hurry back outside.

"Not so fast," Mama called after them. "It's still too cold to be outside without a coat." She handed them their thin spring coats.

Lily slipped into her coat and ran out to the pasture. She grabbed fistfuls of grass in her hands and ran to where the billy goat was tied. She dropped the grass in front of the billy goat and watched as he munched it down appreciatively.

She ran back to get more. This was fun. She pulled even more grass and made a big pile before gathering it up to take to the billy. She dumped her armload in front of the billy. He kept on munching, happy to have such a tasty snack. As Lily spun around to get more grass, she saw some dropped grass on the floor just out of the billy goat's reach. She bent down to pick it up. As she tried to rise, something caught her coat. As she had bent over, the billy had stepped forward a little to eat more grass. His long horns got caught in the back of

Lily's coat. She tried to slip her coat off the horns, but the billy knew something was wrong. He started to bleat and shook his head to get away. He was so strong that Lily lost her balance. She dangled from his horns. Her feet and hands weren't quite touching the floor.

The billy grew angry. His bleating grew louder and louder. Lily started to cry. Joseph stood there, frozen, watching Lily hang in the air by the billy goat's horns. "Go get Mama!" she said.

Joseph turned and ran to the house. Lily had never felt so helpless. The billy jerked her back and forth, back and forth. His bleats were getting wilder and more desperate, as if he were crying too.

Mama came flying. She took one look at Lily and opened

her coat to lift her away from the billy. He shook his head and gave a few more short angry bleats. He backed as far away from Lily as he could. As if he was frightened of her, of all people!

Mama sat down on the ground and started to laugh. She laughed and laughed, so hard that tears ran down her cheeks. Lily had never seen Mama laugh like that. Joseph and Dannie started to laugh too. Lily didn't think it was at all funny. Not at all, but at least the scared, shaky feeling was going away.

Mama wiped the tears from her face and rose to her feet. "Let's all go back to the house and do something less exciting until Papa comes home. I'm sure he'll want to hear about your adventure too." Mama started giggling all over again. Lily wondered if Mama would be able to stop laughing before Papa came home. She wondered if he would laugh as hard as Mama. Probably more.

Lily tried to think how she might have looked hanging from the billy's horns. A little smile tugged at her lips. Maybe it was funny. Just a little bit.

CHAPTER 8

The Sawdust Mountain

Suddenly winter was over and spring had come. It wasn't like New York, though, where the air was scented with lilacs. Sometimes, Lily missed New York so much that she walked around with a lump in her throat. It was especially hard after she got a letter from her cousin Hannah. Yesterday's letter reported that Hannah had seen Chubby, Lily's miniature horse, taking some children for a pony cart ride. Lily sighed all afternoon.

Robins were back in the trees, filling the air with sweet birdsong. Lily wondered where they had flown during the winter. She liked to watch them hop around the patches of snow hunting for worms to eat.

Grandma Miller had a favorite saying: "Your year will end up just like the first robin you see in the spring. If it is flying, you will get a lot done. If it is hopping about looking for food, you will be comfortably busy and have steady work. But if it is holding still, you will be lazy."

Papa would quietly add that Grandma's saying was only a fun way to tease each other. "Robins have nothing to do with how lazy a person is, Lily," he said. "Even Grandma doesn't really believe it."

Still, Lily wished that the first robin she had seen had not been sitting on a tree branch, singing, instead of flying across the sky. She wondered if she might have a lazy year.

And if Grandma's saying was true, Lily was sure everyone in her family must have seen robins in full flight. Ever since the snow started to melt, life had become very busy. Grandpa Miller was building a long building behind his little barn that would become a sawmill. He was also adding a room to the house for Grandma's mother. Great-Grandma had a stroke last year and had to stay in bed. Grandma needed a place for Great-Grandma to live. Until then, Great-Grandma was staying with Grandma's sister, but she was much older than Grandma and couldn't take care of her as well.

Secretly, Lily didn't mind that Great-Grandma hadn't been able to stay at Grandma Miller's. Great-Grandma was very old and very scary looking. Bony hands like claws, not a tooth in her mouth, whiskers on her chin. She reminded Lily of a wrinkled apple doll.

Lily wondered what it would be like at Grandpa Miller's after his sawmill was built. In New York, Grandpa had a harness shop. In Pennsylvania, there were too many harness shops, so Grandpa decided he would cut lumber out of logs that loggers brought to him.

Lily was worried that Grandpa would not want little children to spend time with him while he worked in the sawmill. Even she knew it would be much more dangerous than the harness shop had been.

Grandpa asked Papa and a few other neighbors to help

him build his sawmill and the new room for the house. Work frolics were fun, but this frolic would be on a Wednesday, and Lily and Joseph had to go to school. Lily felt a little miffed. She wished that the grown-ups would ask her opinion about the best days for things like frolics. She definitely would not have scheduled it on a school day. If she didn't know better, she'd think the grown-ups didn't want the children at the sawmill frolic.

On a Sunday afternoon in early May, Papa and Mama thought it would be nice to go visit Grandpa and Grandma Miller. It was such a beautiful day that they decided to walk. Papa said he had a hunch Dannie would tire of walking, so he pulled him on the little wagon.

Lily loved to visit at Grandpa and Grandma Miller's house. She had the visit all planned out. Aunt Susie would be eager to play dolls or color in coloring books. Joseph and Dannie could play with the wooden blocks and toy animals. They weren't very good colorers. Dannie only scribbled and Joseph colored outside the lines.

Here's what Lily liked best: Grandma would give a bowl of apples to Mama to peel and slice while she popped popcorn. And then everyone would sit around the table and talk while they snacked.

The part Lily liked least was visiting Great-Grandma. After Grandpa had finished building the little room, he and Grandma had gone to New York to bring Great-Grandma to Pennsylvania. Great-Grandma's room was very nice. It had cheerful light-honey-colored walls and fluffy white curtains at the windows. At one end, Grandma had a big desk and several shelves filled with craft and scrapbook things.

Grandma thought that Great-Grandma wouldn't be so lonely if she were working in the room beside her.

Whenever they visited, Mama always went in to talk to Great-Grandma. She brought Lily in with her. Lily tried to stay far away from Great-Grandma's bed, but she would still stick her bony arm out to shake Lily's hand. Her fingers were twisted and gnarled and her skin looked like crepe paper. Lily was always glad when this part was over and she could go play with Aunt Susie.

On this particular Sunday afternoon, as they reached Grandpa Miller's house, Lily could see a big pile of sawdust outside the sawmill. There were stacks and stacks of logs waiting to be cut and even more stacks of neatly cut lumber waiting to be picked up.

The mountain of sawdust looked like it might be fun to dig and play in. Joseph and Dannie had the same idea and asked Papa if they could play in the sawdust. "We'll have to ask Grandpa first," Papa said.

Grandpa and Grandma welcomed them at the door and ushered everyone into the house. Aunt Susie hurried off to get her dolls to bring to Lily. Joseph waited as long as he could, at least ten seconds, before it burst out of him. "Grandpa, can we go outside to play on the sawdust pile?"

Grandpa chuckled at Joseph's and Dannie's eager faces. "As long as your mother isn't worried about getting your clothes dirty."

Before Mama could finish saying that she didn't mind, Joseph and Dannie galloped outside to play. Lily looked at the doll in her arms. As much as she liked playing dolls, she really wanted to go out and play on that sawdust pile too. She cast a sideways glance at Aunt Susie. "Do you think we should go outside to watch the boys?"

Aunt Susie was always happy to do whatever Lily wanted to do. They put their dolls away and went outside. Aunt Susie found some little shovels and they started to dig.

It was a little different than Lily had expected. It wasn't like digging in sand. She grew bored with digging and decided to climb to the very top of the sawdust pile. It was almost as high as the roof of the sawmill. Lily could see for miles and miles. The sawdust shifted a little under her feet. She thought it would be fun to run down, so she started down the hill, picking up speed. By the time she reached the bottom, she was sure she had never run that fast before. So much fun! Almost like flying!

Lily scrambled back up the sawdust hill. "Let's all run down together," she called to Joseph and Dannie. They were busy digging a big hole in the side of the sawdust pile.

Joseph popped his head up. "No, I want to dig."

"Me too," Dannie piped up. "Gotta dig."

Aunt Susie didn't want to run down the pile, either. She went to help the boys dig the big hole. Lily climbed all the way to the top again. She paused for a moment, then jumped. She practically flew down the sawdust hill! She couldn't remember ever having so much fun. She didn't even mind if little bits of sawdust got all over her, from inside her prayer covering to her socks. She was dusty with chaff and didn't mind a bit when it scratched her. She climbed up several more times and ran down as fast as she could.

Lily was getting tired, but she thought she would jump down one more time. She climbed up the side of the pile and stopped halfway up to admire the deep hole that Joseph and Dannie were digging. It was the biggest hole those little boys had ever made. It was so deep that they were both in the hole to dig it deeper. Aunt Susie had stopped digging to watch them.

Lily made it to the top of the sawdust hill. She took a deep breath and started to run down the hill one last time. As she ran past the hole, the sides caved in, covering most of Joseph and all of Dannie. Aunt Susie sent up a scream that tore the sky in two. Lily worked to free Joseph and Dannie from the cave-in before they suffocated.

Grandpa and Papa came running out of the house. They quickly uncovered Dannie and Joseph and pulled them out. Dannie was bawling. Joseph was spitting sawdust out of his mouth. Aunt Susie was crying her eyes out.

Papa held Dannie in his arms and patted his back to soothe him. "I think it would be a good idea if everyone stays in the house or finds something else to play. Playing here is too dangerous."

Everyone went back inside. Lily felt like crying. She had spoiled everything. She knew Grandpa would never allow them to play on that sawdust pile ever again. Not ever.

CHAPTER

9

Pumpkin Pie in the Woods

Lily's mouth watered when she saw Effie Kauffman's store-bought cookies. One side was white and the other side was dark brown. White frosting oozed out of the middle. Both sides had a pretty design. They were the most beautiful, delicious-looking cookies Lily had ever seen.

Beth had offered a piece of chocolate cake with thick, fluffy chocolate frosting in exchange for Effie's store-bought cookies. Lily peeped into her lunch box. She hoped she might find one of Mama's big chocolate chip cookies that she could trade with Effie for one of her pretty cookies, but there were no cookies today. Only a sandwich baggie filled with sliced apples. Lily sighed.

Tonight, she would ask Mama to make cookies so she would have something to trade tomorrow.

As soon as Lily arrived home from school that afternoon, she made a beeline to the kitchen to find Mama. Her heart dropped when she saw a row of pumpkin pies cooling on the countertop. Mama was trying to use up her canned pumpkin before summer. On any other day, Lily would have been happy to see such a sight. But she knew that Mama would not want to bake cookies after she had already made pies and cleaned up the kitchen.

Instead, Mama had another suggestion. "You can take a pie to school tomorrow to share with your friends."

What a horrible idea! "I don't want to take a whole pumpkin pie to school," Lily said. "I only need one cookie to give to Effie so she'll give me one of her store-bought cookies."

Mama didn't look very pleased. "It's good to want to share your things, but you should share without expecting or asking for anything in return."

Lily went upstairs to change into her everyday clothes. She sat on her bed instead of going downstairs right away. Mama didn't understand. All the other children in school exchanged things whenever they saw something they wanted in someone else's lunch. No one had ever asked to trade for something in Lily's lunch. Right now, nothing seemed as important as being able to eat a pretty store-bought cookie. She flopped back on the bed. She would have to wait until the next time Mama baked cookies. She hoped Effie would keep bringing store-bought cookies to trade before school ended for the year.

The next morning, there was a grocery bag waiting on the kitchen counter beside Lily's and Joseph's lunch boxes.

Mama came into the kitchen as Lily peeped into the bag and saw a pie. "I got a pie ready for you to take to school," Mama said. "I cut it into eight pieces for you and Joseph to share with your friends."

Lily was mortified. No one ever carried a whole pie to school. She could just imagine what Aaron Yoder would say.

She was sure that she could never face anyone again if she had to carry an entire pie to school. "I don't want to take it to school."

"It's not that heavy," Mama said. "Joseph will take turns carrying it with you if you get tired."

Lily didn't know how to explain to Mama that she didn't want to take a pie to school without hurting Mama's feelings.

Joseph was happy to take a pie to school. Pumpkin pie was his favorite. He couldn't wait to give a piece to his friends, Jay and Elam. As they walked down the road, each holding on to a handle of the grocery bag, Lily frowned. "Joseph, don't you realize how embarrassing it is to take a big pumpkin pie to school? We have to do something about this. Quick."

That way of thinking was new to Joseph. He didn't embarrass easily. He was quiet for a while, then said, "We could

73

eat the pie before we get to school this morning and hide the pie pan under a tree in the woods. Then we could pick it up on our way home."

Lily thought that was the smartest thing she had ever heard Joseph say. Ever.

Together they hurried into the woods and sat down by a tree. They set their lunch pails down, took the pie out of the bag, and started to eat a piece. They took another piece and ate it, a little more slowly. Lily was no longer hungry, yet there were still more pieces left. Joseph took his third piece. Lily wished that pies weren't so big. She took another piece and took a bite. She couldn't do it. She couldn't eat one more bite of pumpkin pie. It wasn't worth it. Putting it back into the pan she said, "Let's leave the rest of the pie here. We can eat it on the way home from school."

They picked up their lunch pails and ran the rest of the way to school, arriving just as the second bell rang. They slid into their seats, breathing heavily. Lily felt a prickle of guilt as she thought of the pie that was hidden in the woods. Mama would not be pleased with what they had done, if she ever found out. Lily hoped, hoped, hoped Mama would never find out.

At noon, Effie took store-bought cookies out of her lunch. Lily thought they looked good, but she wasn't very hungry for desserts. She wasn't hungry for her sandwich either. Or her apples. She wondered how she could possibly eat more pie on the way home. Maybe, by then, she would be hungry again.

As soon as Teacher Rhoda dismissed school for the day, Lily and Joseph started up the road. Joseph was eager to eat the rest of the pie. His appetite was a constant source of amazement to Lily. When they got to the woods, they hurried to the tree where they had hidden the pie plate. They looked all around, but there was no grocery bag or pumpkin pie in sight.

"We must have left it under some other tree," Joseph said. They walked around to other trees, but there was no pie. Lily started to feel worried. They couldn't go home and tell Mama what they had done. And the missing pie plate created a bigger problem. Mama took good care of her things. How could they tell her that they had lost her pie pan?

They looked and looked but still couldn't find the pie. They had to go home without it.

Lily put her lunch box quietly on the kitchen table. Mama was in the other room, sewing in her chair by the window. Lily tried to tiptoe to the stairs before Mama heard her, but Joseph was clomping around, making boy noises, as he pulled his shoes off. "Did the children enjoy the pie?" Mama called out.

"It was good," Lily mumbled. She turned to quickly run upstairs to change her clothes before Mama could ask more questions.

Not fast enough.

"What did you say?" Mama said. She was in the kitchen now.

"The pie was good," Lily said.

Mama pinned her with a look. "Did you forget to bring the pie pan home?"

Before Lily could think of how to answer, Joseph piped up. "No, we didn't forget. We couldn't find it because we couldn't remember which tree we had put it under."

Oh, Joseph! Lily thought. *What have you done?*

"Why would you have put a pie pan under a tree?" Mama asked.

Lily gave up. It was no use trying to hide it. Out of Joseph poured the whole story.

Mama listened to everything. She laid the shirt she had been mending for Papa on the kitchen counter. You never saw

75

Mama lose her temper, but she didn't look happy. "We have to go find that pie pan," she said in a low and steady voice. "I'll go hitch Jim to the buggy. Joseph, you come and help me while Lily gets Dannie up from his nap. You can show me where you think you hid it."

Mama and Joseph headed out to the barn while Lily woke Dannie. The ride to the woods was quiet and Lily wondered what Mama was thinking. When they were nearly at the school, Mama got out of the buggy and led Jim to the edge of the woods to tie him to a tree.

In the woods, they spread out to look for the pie pan. It wasn't very long before Dannie let out a happy yelp. He had spotted the grocery bag under a nearby tree. Mama picked up the bag and looked inside. An army of ants covered the pie. "You ate this much all by yourselves?"

Lily nodded. They had eaten a lot of pie. There were only two and a half pieces left. She still wasn't hungry. She didn't think she would ever be hungry again.

They returned home just as Papa was coming home from work. He looked surprised to see them come up the driveway. Mama got out of the buggy and handed the reins to Papa. "The children can tell you all about their day while you do the chores," she said. "I need to go get supper started."

Naturally, Joseph reported everything they had done. He didn't leave anything out. Lily thought it looked as if Papa wanted to laugh when he heard how much pie they had eaten. He looked even more amused when he heard that it was Dannie who finally found the pie pan.

That evening, Papa, Mama, and Dannie each had a piece of pumpkin pie for dessert. Lily and Joseph weren't served any. Papa said they had probably had enough pie for one day.

Lily couldn't have agreed more. Joseph was disappointed.

10

Aaron Yoder
and the Lunch Box

*I*t was a rainy day in May. Teacher Rhoda stood at the front of the class. "Third grade geography class," she said.

Lily glanced across the aisle. As usual, Aaron Yoder was making a lot of noise. He hunted for his geography book buried in his desk while trying to hide some kind of cardboard project. He was up to something. Aaron was always up to something.

The other third graders had found their books and filed to the bench at the front of the room. They waited patiently for Aaron to join them.

Lily was glad that Aaron wasn't in her grade. He was the most annoying, exasperating boy in school. It was bad enough that he sat directly across the aisle from her. It would have been too much if he were in her grade too. A person could only bear so much.

Lily turned her thoughts back to her own book, blocking out the lively discussion that was coming from the geography class. It didn't seem very long until the third graders were back in their seats and working on an assignment. All except Aaron. He had come back to his desk, stuffed his book back inside, and gone right to work on his secret cardboard project. Lily thought it might teach him a lesson if Teacher Rhoda made him stay after school to finish his geography assignment.

Lily tucked her books in her desk. She was finished with all her lessons and had some free time to read a storybook. She settled down comfortably to start reading when something whizzed past her. It bumped into the wall next to her and landed on the floor. She leaned over to see Aaron's contraption. He had made wheels and fastened them to a small cardboard box. It looked like a cardboard wagon.

"Give it back to me," Aaron hissed at Lily.

Lily shook her head. It was just out of her reach against the wall and she was not going to break a rule by leaving her desk without permission. Aaron scowled at her. He waited until Teacher Rhoda turned her back, then he slipped quietly out of his desk and picked up his little wheeled box.

Back in his seat, Aaron turned the wheels again until the long, narrow strip of paper inside the box was wrapped tightly around the axle. He set it down on the floor again and pointed it in a different direction. It went whizzing up the aisle to Teacher Rhoda's desk at the front of the room.

Lily held her breath. As much as she thought it would serve Aaron right to get into trouble, she still hoped Teacher Rhoda had not seen what he was doing.

She saw.

Teacher Rhoda glanced at the clock. "Put your books away. It's time for school to dismiss. Whoever sent this little box flying up the aisle can come pick it up."

No shame. Aaron had no shame. He jumped out of his desk to retrieve the box. Beth's job was to walk around the desks with the trash can so everyone could throw their trash and paper scraps into it before going home. After Beth returned to her desk, the pupils sang a little parting song and it was time to be dismissed. But instead of dismissing them all like she usually did, Teacher Rhoda asked Aaron to stay. "Everyone else may go."

Lily hurried to get her bonnet and lunch box and join Joseph outside the schoolhouse. She felt a tiny twinge of pity for Aaron. It would not be fun to have to stay after school. She wondered what Teacher Rhoda was going to do to Aaron. Maybe, she would dump the trash can on his head like Teacher Katie did once to Levi, Lily's cousin. But that didn't seem like something Teacher Rhoda would do.

79

The other children ran home while Lily and Joseph walked slowly like they always did. They were about halfway home when they heard loud footsteps grow closer and closer. Lily turned around to see Aaron splash in every puddle he passed. He even ran loud. Everything about Aaron was loud.

As he passed them, he reached out and knocked Lily's lunch box from her hand so that it crashed on the road. Her thermos spilled out. So did her empty little dish and spoon. She gathered them up and tucked them carefully back inside. That tiny twinge of pity she had felt for Aaron Yoder quickly evaporated, like a wisp of steam from a teacup. Now she wished Teacher Rhoda *had* dumped a trash can on his head. He deserved that and more. She closed the lid and picked her lunch box up. The lid popped open and everything spilled out again.

The latch was broken.

Now Lily was angry. She gathered everything back up and closed the lid. She had to put her finger against the lid to keep it from popping back open as she carried it the rest of the way home.

As soon as she got home, she showed it to Mama. After examining the latch, Mama said, "I don't think this can be fixed, but there are only a few more weeks of school left this year. You can use it like it is and then we'll buy you a new one before school starts next fall."

That made Lily feel a little bit better, but she wasn't looking forward to having to hold the lid shut every day on the way to and from school.

The next morning, Mama got a big rubber band out of her desk drawer and stretched it around the lunch box to keep the lid shut. Lily didn't think it looked very nice, but it was better than having to hold it.

At noontime, the students hurried to get their lunch boxes off the shelf at the back of the schoolhouse. In his loud voice, Aaron said, "Look at Lily's lunch box. She has to use a rubber band to hold it shut because her parents are too poor to buy a new one."

Lily wanted to smack Aaron. *Hard.* It was the first time she had ever wanted to hit someone at school. She had often wanted to say bad things to Effie and Mandy Mast—a girl from New York—when they were rude, but this was worse. Aaron was making a jab at Papa and Mama.

Lily hurried back to her desk with her lunch. She stripped the rubber band off and placed it on her desk beside her lunch box. Suddenly, Aaron snatched it off her desk and snapped it at one of his friends on the other side of the schoolhouse. Teacher Rhoda saw what was happening and made Aaron return the rubber band to Lily.

Lily finished eating her lunch and slipped the rubber band around her lunch box again. It wasn't fair. It was Aaron's fault in the first place that she had a lunch box with a broken latch and had to use a rubber band to keep the lid from falling open.

She knew Papa and Mama said it was important to forgive people who weren't nice, but she didn't think they had ever met anyone as not nice as Aaron Yoder. He was *mean.*

CHAPTER

11

Tractor Troubles

Day after day, warm breezes swept in across the hills. Lily didn't know how it could be so windy in Pennsylvania with so many big hills and trees. Any direction she looked, all she saw were hills and trees.

Papa was working hard to get everything cleaned up in the yard before it was time to plant Mama's garden. Right beside the house was an old gray building where Papa kept the little open buggy. Several wooden workbenches stood along the side walls where Papa hung his tools. In the workbenches were things that the former owners had left behind. Nothing much of interest, Lily had concluded, after poking through everything.

But there was one thing of interest in this old building. A rickety staircase led up to a loft. Cobwebs covered bunches of dusty dried herbs hanging from the rafters. There were

82

old broken chairs, a spinning wheel, and other old and for-gotten things. Papa said it would take a lot of work to get everything fixed and cleaned up. For now, he was too busy to worry about the loft. The junk in the loft would have to wait awhile.

That was good news to Lily's ears. She felt sure that there were treasures to be found in the cobwebby loft, maybe as good as the junk in the attic. She just had to talk Joseph and Dannie into coming up to help her poke around. That wouldn't be hard.

Each day, Papa came home tired from his construction job only to work another few hours until the sun set. He would eat a quick supper and hurry outside. A big garden plot had to be cleared for Mama so she could plant the vegetable gar-den. As soon as it was cleared, Papa and Mama decided to raise a lot of extra sweet corn and strawberries to sell. Papa would need to plow five additional acres.

Papa hitched Jim to the buggy and went to see if he could find someone to come do the plowing. When he came home he was grinning ear to ear. He had asked an Amish neighbor if he might be able to plow the fields, but the neighbor was too busy trying to get his own fields plowed and planted. He gave Papa a phone number for an English man who had a little tractor and did spring work for people. Papa said the English man would come tomorrow to plow and harrow the garden and field.

Joseph and Dannie were excited that a real tractor would be coming. Lily didn't think it sounded at all exciting. Trac-tors were big and noisy and you couldn't pet them like you could pet a horse.

The next afternoon, a truck arrived, pulling a trailer with the tractor, plow, and harrow on it. Lily and Joseph watched while the man unloaded all of the equipment. Dannie was taking a nap and Lily was sorry he had to miss out on the unloading. But she knew from experience that waking Dannie up from a nap meant a crabby boy for the rest of the day.

Mama went outside to show the man what fields they wanted plowed and made ready for planting. Afterward, she walked back to the house and the man climbed up on his tractor. The tractor roared to life! He drove it back and forth across the field, slow and steady. Black smoke poured from the stack whenever he went uphill. Lily and Joseph watched by the kitchen window. Joseph was so mesmerized by the tractor that he was silent for a long, long time. That was very unusual for Joseph.

Back and forth, back and forth. The man and his tractor worked all afternoon, leaving beautiful furrows of black, moist earth behind. Then the tractor noise stopped and it seemed so strangely quiet. A knock came on the door and Mama went to answer it. "It's getting late," the man said, "so I wondered if it would be alright if I parked the tractor up there on top of the hill until tomorrow. I'll come back in the morning to do the harrowing."

Mama told him that would be fine. The man drove off in his truck and left the tractor parked at the top of the hill.

As soon as the man disappeared down the road, Joseph turned to Lily with excitement in his brown eyes. "Let's go look at the tractor!"

He didn't even wait for her to respond. He ran out the door and started up the hill. Lily jumped up and ran after him. When they reached the tractor, they walked around it, taking in every part of it. They had never been so close to a tractor before. It had the name FORD on the side. The man had unhitched the plow and backed up to the harrow, but he hadn't fastened it yet. Joseph climbed up on the tractor. He sat on the seat like he owned it.

"I don't think you should be sitting on the tractor," Lily said.

"You worry too much," Joseph said. "I'm not hurting anything. And it's fun to pretend to be driving it." He grasped the steering wheel and made engine sounds, as if he were driving.

It did look like fun. "Let me have a turn," Lily said as she climbed up. Joseph sat on the fender to give Lily room to sit on the seat. This *was* fun! She held the steering wheel with both hands and pretended to drive over a big field. She made sure not to touch any levers. She did not want the tractor to start up its noisy engine.

Then it was Joseph's turn again. His pretend tractor noises grew louder and louder. When it was Lily's turn, she leaned forward as if she were going very fast. She accidentally-on-purpose pressed her foot against a pedal. The tractor rolled slowly forward a little bit. Lily and Joseph grew still.

"What did you do?" Joseph asked.

Lily showed him how she had pushed the pedal in with her foot. The tractor rolled forward some more.

Joseph scrambled off the fender. "Let me do it too!" Lily let him sit on the seat. Joseph pushed his foot on the pedal and the tractor inched slowly forward some more. It was much more fun to be on a tractor that moved.

They took turns making the tractor roll until they reached the bottom of the hill. The road was right in front of them. There was no way they could get it back to the top of the hill where it had been. They looked at each other in dismay. What should they do?

"Let's hide!" Lily said. Together they scrambled off the tractor and ran to the old building. They hurried up the rickety old stairs and crouched behind some dusty, cobweb-covered furniture. There was a sudden silence except for the wasps in the eaves. The loft didn't seem as exciting as usual today. Lily felt as grimy as all the dusty things around her. She wished she had never even seen that tractor.

What would Papa say when he got home from work and saw what they had done? Lily wasn't sure she wanted to find out. She knew he would not be happy.

Joseph read her mind. "Maybe Papa will think that the tractor rolled down the hill by itself."

Maybe. They brightened at that thought.

It wasn't long before Papa came home. On any other day, Lily and Joseph would run out to meet him. Not today. They peeped out the window and watched as he got out of the truck and waved goodbye to the driver. Dannie met him on the porch. Then the door closed behind them.

Lily knew what would happen next, just as if she were in the kitchen. Mama would be happy to see Papa was home. They would talk about their day while Dannie would look through Papa's lunch box for a leftover piece of sandwich or cookie. Then Papa would get the milk pail and it would be time to do the chores.

Lily wished she could be in the house. It was always a happy time when Papa came home from work, but today she and Joseph were hiding out in this dusty old loft. She looked over at him. He looked pitiful. His eyes welled up with tears.

Papa and Dannie came out of the house. Dannie held on to the side of the handle of the milk pail. He thought he was helping, but Lily knew Papa was just pretending that he was a big helper.

It must be nice to be as little as Dannie. It would be a relief not to have to worry about getting in trouble.

86

Papa stopped outside the old building. "Lily! Joseph!" he called. "Chore time."

Lily and Joseph wiggled out of their hiding place. They had to go when Papa called them. Joseph had cobwebs stuck in his hair and Lily felt dirty and grimy all over.

They walked over to the barn to help Papa. He had brought Jenny in from the pasture and tied her in the stall. As he started to milk her, Lily held her tail. Everything was quiet. Too quiet. On any other evening, they would be interrupting each other to tell Papa about their day. They would talk and laugh and sometimes Papa would sing. But not today. Even Dannie seemed to sense something was wrong. He sat quietly on a hay bale, stroking a kitten. He didn't say a word.

After Papa finished milking Jenny, he hung the milking stool on the wall peg. He turned Jenny out into the pasture and gave the cats a bowlful of fresh warm milk. He set the big pail of steaming milk on the ground. "Well, Lily and Joseph," he said. "You've been rather quiet tonight. Is there something you want to tell me?"

As usual, Joseph blurted everything out. He told Papa all about how they had wanted to see the tractor after the man went home. He explained how they climbed on it to pretend to drive it. Then he admitted that they had discovered how to make it roll downhill. "We didn't mean to!" Lily chimed in at last. "It just happened." Again and again.

Papa listened to them with a sober expression on his face. "I hope you realize that you should never have touched that tractor. Making it roll down the hill was very dangerous. It could have rolled out on the road. You could both have been hurt. I'm glad nothing happened, but I do expect both of you to tell that man all about it when he comes tomorrow. You need to tell him you're sorry for touching his tractor and that you won't touch it again."

Lily and Joseph nodded, relieved. She hoped the man wouldn't be too mad at them. She decided she was not going to try to drive a tractor again.

But she definitely wanted to get back up in that cobwebby loft and see what treasures she might discover.

Jenny the Cow and Mayapples

 ach morning and evening, Papa would milk Jenny, the
cow. It was Lily and Joseph's job to bring Jenny in from
the pasture and lead her to the barn before Papa got home
from work. It was an easy job for them. Jenny knew that
dinner would be waiting for her in the barn so she would
wait by the fence and moo for Lily and Joseph to hurry. Papa
always said that Jenny could tell time better than a clock.
Those moos would start bellowing right at the time when
Papa was due home. Every time.

But not today. Jenny didn't moo for Lily and Joseph to
come get her. She wasn't standing by the fence like she usually
was. Lily thought Jenny might have found some good green
grass to graze behind the barn. She and Joseph ran through
the tall grass to find the cow. As they came around the corner
of the barn, Lily stopped abruptly. Jenny was lying on her
side. Her mouth was open, her tongue was hanging out of

her mouth, and her ribcage was jerking in a funny way. It seemed as if she was struggling to breathe.

Joseph started to cry. Lily felt tears prick her eyes, but she knew she had to be calm for Joseph and for Jenny. "Let's go tell Mama that something is wrong with Jenny," she said. They ran to the house and bolted up the porch stairs.

Mama was ironing her Sunday dress. The room smelled of steamed cotton and starch. Dannie was playing with his farm toys on the kitchen floor.

"JENNY IS DYING!" Joseph said. He started to cry again, which set Dannie to wailing.

Calmly, Mama set the iron on its stand. "Tell me what she is doing."

"She is lying behind the barn with her mouth open and her sides moving in a funny way," Lily said.

Mama bit her lower lip. That meant she was worried.

"Let's go have a look at her and see if we can get her up," Mama said.

She picked up Dannie and took Joseph by the hand. The four of them walked out to the area behind the barn. Jenny looked even worse than she had moments ago. Her legs stuck straight out instead of being tucked underneath her like they usually were when she lay down to rest and chew her cud. Her eyes, normally so calm and gentle, looked wild and frightened. Her long rough tongue hung out of her mouth. Joseph and Dannie started sobbing all over again. Lily tried to be brave and not cry like her little brothers. She started to go to Jenny to pat her, to help her to feel better and know she wasn't alone, but Mama held her back from touching her.

Mama was worried. "I'll have to run to the neighbor to call the vet right away. I don't know what is wrong with Jenny but I think she needs help. Lily, I want you to keep Dannie in the sandbox and mind the boys until I get back."

Lily took Joseph and Dannie over to the sandbox while Mama ran through the field to the neighbor's house to use their phone. She was only gone a few minutes. When she came back, they went out to check on Jenny again. She still looked like she was suffering. Worse.

When the vet arrived, he gave Jenny a big shot to help her. He crouched down to listen to her heartbeat with his big stethoscope. Suddenly, Jenny's sides stopped moving.

He rose to his feet. "I'm so sorry I wasn't able to save her," he said to Mama.

Jenny was dead.

Lily felt a big lump start to rise in her throat. She would never be able to feed Jenny again or hold her tail while Papa milked her. Jenny wouldn't bat her big eyelashes at Papa anymore. It didn't seem possible that Lily would never see Jenny graze happily in the tall, sweet grass in the pasture. Or lie in the shade of a tree to chew her cud. There would be no more of Jenny's fresh sweet milk or homemade butter and cheeses. Tears started leaking down Lily's face. Soon, she was sobbing as loud as Joseph and Dannie.

"What happened to her?" Mama asked the vet, raising her voice to be heard over the children's wails.

"Do you have any mayapples in your pasture?" the vet said. "Some people call them umbrella plants. They produce a little poisonous apple under their leaf. Every spring, I hear about a cow or two that eats a mayapple. Unfortunately, there isn't anything I can do."

After the vet left, Mama led everyone back to the house. Lily tried to stay busy by helping Mama. She tried not to think about Jenny. She would let Joseph tell Papa the bad news about Jenny when he came home. She couldn't say it out loud. She was hardly past bawling over that silly, wonderful cow.

Papa was quiet for a long time when Joseph told him the news. Grandpa Miller had bought Jenny for Mama's birthday. Lily fought back an urge to point out that their farm in New York didn't have mayapples, and if they had just stayed there, Jenny would still be alive. But Papa looked so sad that she didn't want to say anything that would make everyone feel worse, if that were possible. Finally, Papa went over to the neighbor's house to call someone who would take Jenny's body away.

That night, no one said anything at dinner. There was nothing to say.

On Saturday morning, Papa hitched Jim to the buggy. He said he was going to see if any of the neighboring farmers had a Jersey cow to sell. Joseph and Dannie went with Papa, but Lily was needed at home. Saturday was the day for cleaning house. Lily liked helping Mama work, but on days like today she wished she had been born a boy. Or at least, she wished she were still Dannie's age so that she could go with Papa too. That would be much more fun than dusting furniture and washing windows and wiping up muddy footprints made by two little brothers.

When Papa and the boys came home, they had some happy news to share. Mama set a plate of cookies on the table. Everyone sat around the table to hear Papa's story.

Papa's eyes were twinkling. "Well, I found a cow. A gentle little Jersey. I paid cash for her and the farmer said that he will bring her over to us on Monday."

Lily missed Jenny, but she was happy to hear that they

would be getting another cow soon. They would not have to go without milk, butter, and cheese. She hoped the new cow would have pretty eyes with long, dark eyelashes like Jenny.

Papa pushed his chair back from the table. "I'm going out to the pasture to dig up all those mayapple plants. We don't want to risk losing another cow."

"Can I help too?" Lily said. She had been inside most of the day.

Mama smiled. "We're almost done with our Saturday cleaning. I think I can finish it up by myself so you can run along with Papa and the boys."

In the barn, Papa got the wheelbarrow and two garden hoes. Dannie sat in the wheelbarrow for a ride while Papa pushed it, and Lily and Joseph each carried a hoe.

When they reached the pasture, they checked under all the trees. Papa said mayapples liked to grow in the shade. He pointed out a mayapple plant so the children knew what it looked like. Whenever they found the plant, Papa would take a hoe and chop the plant down. Then he would dig his shovel deep into the dirt until he had removed every bit of the root so that it could never grow again.

Lily tried digging with the other hoe, but the ground was hard. Papa always had to finish digging the roots out. Papa didn't seem to mind that she couldn't do it as well as he could and said, "Every little bit that you chop and dig is a bit I don't have to do."

When the last mayapple plant had been dug up and piled into the wheelbarrow, they carefully dumped them all into a big garbage bag. Now the pasture would be a nice safe place filled with only good grasses for the new cow to eat when she came on Monday. Lily was getting excited to meet her.

❧⚭❧

Late Monday afternoon, the farmer came with the new cow and led her to the pasture. He left before Mama had time to come outside to thank him.

Lily and Joseph ran to the pasture to meet the new cow, but something seemed odd. This cow was too thin. Lily could count all her ribs. Her udder almost touched the ground.

Mama came up behind them and she didn't look happy. She was frowning. "At least the poor thing can eat plenty of grass until Papa decides what to do next."

When Papa arrived home from work, he went right to the pasture to see the new cow. He stood there awhile, just looking at her, frowning. "Run into the house, Lily, and bring me a cake pan and the milk pail."

Lily hurried to get the things Papa wanted but she had no idea why he would need a cake pan. Papa slid the cake pan under the cow's udder and started to milk her. Now Lily could see why Papa wanted a cake pan. The cow's udder was too low to the ground for a milk pail. It didn't take long until the cake pan was full. Papa slid it out and dumped it into the milk pail next to his milking stool. It took a long time to milk this cow because he had to keep sliding the cake pan under the udder and emptying it.

When he was finished, Papa said, "We can't keep this cow. I'll have to go call a cattle dealer and see if he can get us a good cow."

After supper, Papa went to the English neighbor's to make a phone call. When he returned, he told Mama that the cattle dealer would come and pick up the cow tomorrow, take it to a livestock sale, and bring back a nice cow for them.

As Lily lay in bed that night, she thought about what a mean trick that farmer had played on her papa. Lily wanted to march down the road and shake her fist at that awful man. She couldn't believe it! He belonged to Lily's own church.

Papa often told her that whenever she had bad thoughts about a person, she should try to substitute them with good thoughts. Lily couldn't find anything good to think about that bad, bad man. She yawned and rolled over. Maybe tomorrow.

The next morning, the cattle dealer arrived at the house early and loaded the cow in his trailer. A few hours later, he returned. Mama hurried outside to talk to him. She didn't want him to leave this cow without a chance to see it first.

Lily liked the cow the very instant she saw it. The cow was fawn-colored brown with big, gentle brown eyes. Thick, long black eyelashes too. Not too skinny and the udder was just the right size. Lily was glad when Mama paid the cattle dealer for the cow and asked him to unload it. This cow was going to stay.

Now the family had a nice cow again. Lily and Joseph and Dannie tried out a few names: Joseph wanted to name her Eagle and Lily liked Cupcake and Dannie chose Kitty, which made no sense. No sense at all. Mama said that they would wait to pick a name until Papa came home from work.

Papa was happy with the new cow. "I'll let you pick out a name for her, Rachel."

Mama had already thought about a name for this cow. "How about Pansy?"

"Pansy it is," Papa said, pleased.

Lily rolled the name over and over in her mind. *Pansy*. She liked it. Pansies were Mama's favorite flower. It was nice to think that this sweet new cow with big brown eyes would be named after such a pretty flower. She would never forget Jenny, but there was room in her heart for Pansy.

95

Summer Lists

*I*t was a beautiful morning in late May. The rain that had swept through last night had left the air sweet and clean. Birdsong filled the trees. Squirrels chattered at each other. Dandelions made pretty yellow splashes of color in the fields beside the road, the grass looked so bright and fresh, and the sun made everything soft and warm.

On any other school day, Lily would have wanted to run and skip and sing with the birds. Today, she felt too sad. Her right hand felt empty on the walk to school with Joseph. It wasn't holding her lunch box with the big rubber band around it. They didn't need to take lunch to school today. Teacher Rhoda was going to dismiss the class before noon because today was the last day of school.

All in all, Lily had liked school. She wouldn't miss Effie Kauffman and she wouldn't miss Aaron Yoder. But she would miss seeing Beth each day. She would miss working in her books and learning new things. She would miss her teacher. Teacher Rhoda was kind, friendly, and patient. Lily thought she was almost as nice as Teacher Ellen, in New York, had been. Not quite, but almost.

Joseph stopped to collect glittering little stones beside the road to put in his pockets. He didn't seem to mind that today was the last day of school. In fact, he seemed happy about it. He had a long list of things he was going to do this summer, and he hadn't stopped talking about it since they left the house. "First, I'm going to climb every tree in our woods."

"There are hundreds of trees in our woods," Lily said. "It would take years and years to climb all of them."

Joseph didn't pay her any mind. "And I hope Papa buys a puppy for me. Soon. Then I could train it all summer and teach it to do tricks." He hopped on one leg for a few steps until he toppled over. "I hope Papa and Mama will send us to Wilson's Store every day for ice cream or popsicles." Now he was jumping with both feet, like a rope was tied around his ankles. "Every." Hop. "Single." Hop. Hop. "Day." Hop. Hop. Hop.

Lily brightened. She doubted they would be allowed to have ice cream every day, but maybe once in a while. For a treat. So that was one thing she could look forward to this summer. Her list had begun:

1. Eat ice cream and popsicles at Wilson's Store.

Joseph prattled on. "I'm going to take wagon rides on the hill behind the house. And help Dannie play in the sandbox. And fish in the spring beside the house."

"There aren't any fish in that spring," Lily pointed out. Joseph was always getting carried away with his crazy plans, but this one was impossible. Just impossible.

"I can pretend there are fish there."

As they came around the bend to the schoolhouse, Joseph saw some of his friends playing softball. He ran ahead to join them, but Lily wasn't in a hurry. She walked slowly the rest of the way. When she reached the schoolhouse, she removed her heavy black bonnet and hung it on one of the hooks in the wall. The shelf above it, the one that held everybody's lunches, was empty. Lily sighed. This was a very sad day.

Teacher Rhoda rang the bell and the pupils hurried to their seats. Usually, she began the day with assignments. Not today, though. They sang a few songs. Teacher Rhoda had a few fun quizzes for them. And then it was time to get their report cards for the last time.

One by one, Teacher Rhoda called each student up to her desk to get a report card. She started with the eldest and made her way down to the youngest. Lily was glad she was no longer the youngest one in school. She didn't have to wait until last any longer.

Teacher Rhoda spoke quietly to each child, then handed him or her a report card and a little brown paper bag. What could be in that bag? The big girls and big boys peeked in the bag but closed it up again. Lily wished one of them would take it out so she could see it too. This was taking a very long time. Aaron Yoder was getting a long, serious talking-to by Teacher Rhoda. Lily tried to listen, but Aaron noticed and scowled at her. Probably, Lily decided, he was being told to behave next year. Or else. She wasn't sure what "or else" could be, but if she were Aaron's teacher, she would definitely think up an "or else" to make him mind.

Finally, Teacher Rhoda called Lily's name. She hurried to the teacher's desk. She hoped the talk with Aaron hadn't put Teacher Rhoda in a bad mood. He was always putting

Lily in a bad mood. But no—Teacher Rhoda smiled at her. "It was nice to have you join us at our school this year." She handed Lily a report card and a little brown bag.

Lily went back to her desk and sat down. She opened the bag and peeped inside. There was a big chocolate chip cookie and a beautiful brand-new flowery handkerchief. She folded the top back down. On Sunday, she would have a pretty new handkerchief to slip in her pocket to go to church. She glanced over at Effie. Maybe, just maybe, Effie had some extra store-bought cookies that Lily could trade for this cookie. She just had to try one of those store-bought cookies! They looked so good.

Lily noticed that Effie was looking at what was written on the back of her report card. Lily slid her own card out of its brown envelope and turned it. In neat handwriting, Teacher Rhoda had written: "Lily Lapp has been promoted to grade three." Lily wasn't sure what that meant, but getting promoted must be a good thing.

After each student had been handed a report card, Teacher Rhoda rang the bell for the last time and dismissed them. "School is done for the term. I'll see you all again this fall."

Lily was pleased to hear that Teacher Rhoda would teach next term. That was something else for her things-to-look-forward-to list:

2. Teacher Rhoda will be back in the fall.

Then came a scramble as all of the children ran to get their hats and bonnets. The air was filled with happy goodbyes as they ran out of the schoolhouse and started for home. Lily hurried after Effie and held up her brown bag. "Would you want to trade for a store-bought cookie?"

Effie smiled and pulled a baggie filled with store-bought cookies out of her pocket. "I happened to have these in my

desk. You can have them all." She handed the baggie to Lily. Then she took Lily's paper bag and ran off. Lily was so pleased! She could always have a homemade chocolate chip cookie, but she had never tried store-bought black-and-white cookies. And to have a baggie full of them! She bit down on a cookie and felt a tooth wiggle. Then she tasted a little bit of blood from where her tooth had come loose. The cookies were awful! Stale and hard. They tasted like sawdust.

That Effie! *Grrrrr!*

Joseph waved a big arm in a circle so that Lily would hurry. She ran to catch up with him. He was eager to start on his summer plans, but Lily wanted to enjoy this walk for one last time. It would be three whole months before she would take this walk again.

Suddenly, she heard loud clopping boy-sounds behind her, then *splash!* Aaron Yoder jumped in a puddle as he dashed past her, his laughter ringing behind him. Cold, muddy water splattered her dress.

That Aaron! *Grrrrr!*

Another thing for her summer list:

3. I will not have to see Aaron Yoder for three whole months, except for church when I can pretend he is invisible.

When they got home, Mama wanted to see the handkerchiefs Teacher Rhoda had given them. Joseph had a big one like Papa used in church. Lily was glad she was a girl and had a nice flowery one instead of a boring men's handkerchief. As Lily went to get her handkerchief, she realized Effie had taken it! Lily hadn't been clear about the cookie trade. No wonder Effie had such a big smile on her face. Lily could have cried. She knew Effie would never give it back.

Oh, this was a terrible day. The worst.

"Let me see your report cards," Mama said, but Joseph was already halfway upstairs to change into his everyday clothes. He was in a hurry to go outside and start climbing trees.

Lily handed her report card to Mama. She watched her face when she read it. Mama looked pleased. "What does promoted mean?" Lily asked.

"It means you will advance," Mama said. "You will be in third grade when school starts this fall."

"Was Joseph promoted too?" Lily asked.

"Yes, he was," Mama said. "He will be in second grade." She sighed. "My little children are growing up so fast." She handed Lily's report card back to her.

Lily went upstairs to change out of her mud-splattered dress. What would she say when people asked her what grade she was in this summer? She couldn't say second grade

101

because she was already done with that, but she couldn't say third either because that wouldn't start until the fall. Finally, she decided she would have to say she was in grade two and a half.

On top of that thought rushed in a new worry: what if Aaron Yoder hadn't been promoted to grade four? He hardly ever paid attention in school. Maybe that's why Teacher Rhoda had been talking to him in such a serious voice. Maybe that was the "or else." Aaron Yoder would remain in third grade until he could learn to behave himself. He might be there for years and years.

Oh, that was a terrible worry for Lily.

Raindrops and Ice Cream

Not a leaf stirred during the first week of June. The sun beat down on Lily as she crawled beside a long row of strawberry plants. She paused at each plant to pinch off all the blossoms, leaving only one to ripen into a strawberry.

Mama and Joseph and Dannie were doing the same thing in the row next to her. Joseph was working on the other side of the row. Lily felt sorry that the strawberry plants were losing their pretty white flowers. Mostly, she felt sorry for herself. It was tiresome work to pinch off all the flowers. Worse still, it meant that each plant would give only one strawberry. This year there would not be many berries to eat. Lily loved to eat strawberries.

Next year, though, Papa and Mama said that they would have thousands of strawberries. There would be so many that they could sell them and still have plenty to eat fresh and can for winter. This year, the plants needed to put their energy into growing big and strong. That was why they could not allow them to produce a lot of strawberries this year. They were too small and young.

As Lily came to the end of the row, she stood and stretched her arms high above her head. "Do you want me to go bring some water out for everyone?"

"That would be nice," Mama said. "But hurry back out so we can get done before it gets late."

Lily ran to the house. Almost anything was better than working in that big strawberry patch.

She found the water jug and opened the faucet to let the water run until it was as cold as could be. As she waited, her mind drifted off to the beautiful books that Grandpa Miller had given to her for her last birthday, when they still lived in New York. Those books were extra special because they used to belong to Grandpa. Their covers were made with glossy leather-like material with little swirled patterns engraved all over them. On the inside were pretty, old-fashioned-type pictures and charming short stories. Lily thought they were the most beautiful books in the world. It had been awhile since she had had time to sit and read them.

She stuck her finger under the faucet to see how cold the water was. It was getting cold, but not too cold yet. She would have plenty of time to get those books upstairs.

Lily ran to her dresser and opened the top drawer. She looked through each book, trying to decide which one she wanted most to read. Finally, she grabbed both of them. She slammed the drawer shut and ran downstairs. She placed the water jug under the faucet, filled it to the top, and hurried outside with the books tucked beneath her arm.

Lily stopped at the big spruce tree beside the house and tucked both books next to the tree trunk. After the strawberry plants were done, she would sit here in the cool shade and read her books.

Mama, Joseph, and Dannie were happy to see Lily come back to the strawberry patch with the water. They each took a long drink. Then Mama closed the lid and set the jug at the end of a row. It was time to get back to work.

Lily started on another row of strawberries. Her back ached from bending over. She was hot. Her fingers were getting sore from pinching so many flowers off. She wished that Mama and Papa had never planted so many strawberries. An acre of strawberries was too much work! Thousands of plants that needed to be cared for. No matter how many blossoms she had pinched off already, she could hardly see a difference when she looked across the field and saw how many more were left to do.

Mama drew her watch out of her pocket and looked to see what time it was. "It's almost time to start making supper. We can work again tomorrow. You all helped me so much that I think we all deserve a treat for supper. Lily and Joseph, you can go to Wilson's Store and buy a box of ice cream."

Suddenly, Lily didn't feel as hot and tired as she had a moment ago. Joseph was excited too. They jumped to their feet and ran to the house to wash their hands.

After Mama was satisfied that they had scrubbed enough, she counted some money and handed it to Lily to buy the ice cream. She gave her a thick comforter. "Use this to wrap up the ice cream to keep it from melting," she said. "You can take the wagon so you don't have to carry it."

Lily put the comforter on the wagon. She and Joseph both held the handle of the wagon and started up the road to Mr. Wilson's store.

Mr. Wilson was always pleased to see some customers

come into his store—even little ones. He got up from his chair behind the counter. "What can I do for you today?" he asked.

"We need a box of ice cream," Joseph said before Lily had a chance to answer. As usual. Lily thought he should have let her talk to Mr. Wilson. After all, she was older than Joseph and she was the one who had the money to pay for the ice cream. Her little brothers were getting very bossy. It was a continual worry for Lily.

Mr. Wilson didn't seem to understand how wrong it was for Joseph to pipe up like that. Maybe, Lily thought, Mr. Wilson didn't have any older sisters. He walked over to his freezer and slid open the lid. "What kind do you want?"

Lily and Joseph both peered into the freezer to see what flavor of ice cream they wanted. Joseph wanted chocolate, but Lily didn't like chocolate. Lily wanted vanilla, but Joseph

said he didn't like vanilla. Finally, they compromised on an ice cream with cherries in it.

Lily handed Mr. Wilson the money and he counted out the change. After wrapping the ice cream in a paper bag, he went outside and helped them tuck it beneath the comforter. "Wait just a minute," Mr. Wilson said. He hurried into the store and came out with two green popsicles. He handed one to Lily and one to Joseph. "This will help you stay cool on the way home."

What a nice surprise! They thanked Mr. Wilson and started for home. Lily had planned to scold Joseph on the way home for speaking up in the store, but as she started to lick her popsicle, she decided it could wait. Then she forgot.

When they got home, Mama carried the big bulky comforter into the house. She covered it with another blanket before turning her attention to preparing supper.

Papa and Dannie came in from doing the chores, and everyone sat at the table to eat. Lily took tiny helpings of potatoes, meat, and vegetables. She wanted to save room for ice cream.

When everyone was finished, Mama dug the box of ice cream out of the comforter and placed it on a plate in front of Papa. He opened the box and spooned a big pile of ice cream onto everyone's plates. They would have to eat the whole box tonight before it melted away. How wonderful!

Lily savored every bite. Joseph gulped his down and asked for a second helping. Papa gave him another spoonful and then scooped the rest on his own plate.

When they were done, Lily helped clear the dishes away. Everyone sat in the living room while Mama read several stories out loud in her clear, sweet voice. When she closed the book, Papa said, "Bedtime for little lambs," just like he did every night. Lily wished Mama would read another story. They would have to wait until tomorrow evening to find out what was going to happen next in the story.

Lily snuggled under her thin summer cover on her bed. It had been a good day. They had worked hard, but the ice cream and green popsicle had been a happy treat. Maybe if she worked extra hard tomorrow, they could have more ice cream. And maybe Mr. Wilson would give them another green popsicle.

Just as Lily was drifting to sleep, she heard the distant sound of thunder as it rumbled across the sky. Then she heard raindrops patter against the window.

Rain. *Rain!* Grandpa's books! Her beautiful birthday books! She had left them under the spruce tree.

Lily wondered what she should do. Should she go wake Papa and tell him her books were out in the rain, or should she wait until tomorrow morning and hope that the branches had kept her books dry?

As Lily listened to the pitter-patter of the rain, she couldn't wait any longer. She slipped out of bed and tiptoed over to knock on Papa and Mama's bedroom door. She heard Papa stir. Then the door opened. "It's only a gentle thunderstorm, Lily," he said kindly. "You don't have to be afraid."

"I'm not afraid," Lily said. "I took my birthday books outside today and put them under the spruce tree. I forgot to bring them back inside."

"I'll run out and get them for you," Papa said. He picked up a flashlight and headed down the stairs. Lily followed him and stood inside the door to wait while Papa dashed out into the rain to find her books.

When he came in, he handed the books to Lily. They were soggy and the pages stuck together. Some of the pages tore as

Lily tried to turn them. The inscription Grandpa had written inside the front cover was blurred so that Lily couldn't read it any longer.

Lily's eyes filled with tears. Papa took the books and laid them on the kitchen counters and said, "We'll leave them here until they have dried."

"But they'll never be nice again," Lily sobbed.

"No, they will never be as nice as they used to be," Papa said. "But you should still be able to read them."

They went back upstairs. Papa tucked Lily into her bed before heading to his room. Lily lay in bed and listened to the rain. It didn't sound nice and soothing to her like it would have on any other spring night. All those little raindrops had ruined her beautiful books.

Lily's "Get Rich Quick" Plan

On a rainy afternoon in late June, Mama told Lily that she could go down the road to spend some time at Grandma Miller's. There was always something fun to do at Grandma's house. Lily and Aunt Susie would play dolls or color in books. Sometimes, they would help Grandma with her work.

Lily's favorite times of all were when she watched Grandma work on her scrapbooks. Grandma planned to make a nice scrapbook for each one of her grandchildren. She said she wanted all of them to have something pretty to remember her by. Lily was sure she would always remember Grandma. She loved Grandma Miller and didn't want to think about her passing away one day, but she was looking forward to receiving one of those scrapbooks.

Using old calendars, Grandma carefully glued a piece of plain paper over the numbers. She wrote poems and sayings on the plain paper and glued pretty pictures on the empty spaces of the pages. Grandma would let Lily and Aunt Susie cut pictures out of catalogs for her. Once in a while, she would let Lily look through her big supply of stickers and choose a few to take home with her. Collecting stickers was one of Lily's favorite things too, right behind playing dolls. Dolls first, then stickers.

Today, Grandma let Lily dig through her big box filled with stickers to choose one. Lily had a hard time deciding which one to choose. They were all so pretty. Should she choose flowers or butterflies or cute animals? She wished she could have one of each, but that would be greedy. Finally, she chose the butterflies.

At home, Lily took the sticker to her bedroom in the hallway. She had a special sticker box in her dresser drawer. She was saving pretty pictures and stickers to make a scrapbook for Grandpa and Grandma Lapp. She looked through everything she had collected already and decided she had enough to start making the scrapbook. Tonight, after all the supper dishes had been washed and put away, she would have time to start the scrapbook.

Mama and Lily took turns washing and drying the supper dishes. It was Lily's turn to wash. First, she had to rinse everything. Lily didn't like this part. The dirty dishes had to be swished in a big bowl of lukewarm water. Lily didn't like feeling the little bits of food that floated in the gray water. She was always glad when the last dish had been rinsed and she could wash the dishes in hot soapy water. Mama and Lily sang and talked while they worked. That part, she liked best.

That night, as Lily handed a clean dish to Mama to dry, she told her about the scrapbook that she wanted to make for Grandpa and Grandma Lapp.

"That sounds like a good idea," Mama said. "I'm sure Grandpa and Grandma would enjoy getting a scrapbook from you. I think I might have some nice paper that would work very well for your project. After we're done with the dishes, I'll look and see what I can find."

When the last dish had been dried and put back in the cupboard, Lily ran upstairs to get her special scrapbook box. She brought it back to the kitchen and spread everything out on the table, including scissors and glue. Mama had found paper and brought pens for Lily to use. They had purple and green ink. Lily got right to work.

Mama suggested she might like to trace some pictures and color them with colored pencils. She could glue them to the scrapbook sheets. Lily paged through some old *Family Life* magazines to see if she could find some little pictures. She chose several different pictures of birds and flowers and carefully traced and colored them. Just as she was spreading glue on the back of them to put into the scrapbook sheet, a horrible sound came from the hallway. *Bang. Bump. Thump.*

Silence.

Then, bloodcurdling screams.

Everyone jumped up and ran to see what had happened. Dannie had tripped on the stairs and fallen all the way to the bottom. He had bitten his lip and it was bleeding badly.

Papa carried Dannie to the kitchen as Mama hurried to find a clean washcloth. She soaked it with cold water and began to gently clean his lips. Lily and Joseph patted Dannie gently, trying to comfort him. His lip was swollen, but at least the bleeding had stopped. The crying too. Dannie could be loud.

Joseph brought Dannie's favorite book for Mama to read to him. He pulled a little chair up next to Mama's rocking chair to listen too. Usually, Lily liked to listen to Mama read, but tonight her mind was on her scrapbook project. When she went back to the kitchen table to sit down, she was dismayed to see that the glue she had spread on the back of the colored picture had dried.

She looked at it more closely. It almost seemed like a real sticker. She carried the picture over to the kitchen sink and wet her finger and rubbed it across the dried glue. It became sticky again and she pasted it to the sheet.

How fun! She had invented homemade stickers. She decided to make a whole pile of stickers. All evening, she traced and colored pictures. She spread glue on the backs and let them dry. She thought Grandma Miller would enjoy seeing Lily's invention.

The next time Lily went to Grandma's house, she tucked a sandwich baggie filled with her homemade stickers into her pocket.

Grandma admired her invention. "I think I'll have to buy these from you," she said. "How does a penny per sticker sound to you?"

Lily had only wanted to show the stickers to Grandma. She had never even thought of selling them. This was so much better! "Oh, it sounds just fine." She counted all the stickers she had made. "There are twenty-three stickers." She held out her hand as Grandma counted twenty-three pennies into it. "Thank you, Grandma. I think I'll go home right away." She couldn't wait to show all of those shiny copper pennies to Joseph and Dannie.

Grandma smiled. "Don't run too fast or you might lose your pennies." Lily dropped the pennies into her pocket and ran home. She held her hand over her pocket the whole way to make sure she didn't lose any of them. Not one.

After she had showed the pennies to Joseph and Dannie,

she dropped the pennies, one by one, into her penny bank. *Plink, plink, plink!* She liked the sound. A plan started forming in her mind. She would spend all her spare time making stickers for Grandma. Lily was going to be rich!

That evening, after supper, Lily traced and colored as many little pictures as she could. She didn't do it as slowly and as carefully as she had been doing. The faster she worked, the more stickers she could make. More stickers meant more money. She could already see her pile of pennies growing in her penny bank. *Plink, plink plink!* She would probably need a second penny bank soon. Maybe a third.

When the time came for the next visit to Grandma Miller's, Lily had made seventy-five stickers. Seventy-five! Lily could hardly wait until Grandma counted out all those pennies into her hands.

Lily knocked on Grandma's door. When Grandma opened the door, Lily held up the bag of stickers. "I made more stickers for you to buy," she said.

"Let me see what you have," Grandma said, pleased.

Lily spread out all the stickers on the scrapbooking desk. Grandma looked them all over carefully. Lily watched as Grandma sorted them into two different piles. What was she doing?

"It looks as if you rushed on some of these," Grandma said. "I can only buy the best ones."

Grandma counted eight stickers. Only eight. She gave Lily eight pennies. Lily was disappointed. She had been planning on bringing home seventy-five shiny pennies. Eight pennies was a big disappointment. She walked home slowly with the unsold stickers in her pocket.

Lily decided she would try again. She would slow down and take her time. She wouldn't rush. She would make sure each sticker was colored very neatly. She didn't want to bring home any more unsold stickers.

She looked at the stickers. She couldn't blame Grandma for not wanting them. She wasn't sure even she would want to use these sloppy stickers in the scrapbook she was making for Grandpa and Grandma Lapp. She decided to give all of the unsold stickers to Dannie to play with. Little brothers weren't fussy like grandmas.

The Fireworks Competition

Papa had just finished milking Pansy and handed the pail of milk to Mama, who was standing by the kitchen door. "I have to go over to the Beals' to make a phone call right after we get the chores done. I thought Joseph would like to go along."

Not fair! Lily thought. She wished she could be the one to go with Papa. It was always fun to listen to Papa talk on the phone, but it was even more fun to get a glimpse of the inside of an English house. The Beals were nice neighbors and always welcomed Lily inside. Joseph wouldn't notice anything different in the Beals' home. He wouldn't have anything new to report. But, of course, he was eager to go and hurried to get his shoes on by the door.

Papa tilted his head as he looked at Joseph. "You had better go wash your hands and face again before we go."

Lily started to set the table as Papa and a freshly scrubbed

Joseph walked across the field to the Beals' house to use their phone. When she finished setting the table with utensils, she sat down to fold the napkins to make them look like flowers. Most evenings there was not enough time to fold them in a special way. Tonight, they had to wait to eat until Papa and Joseph came home, so Lily had time to create beautiful napkin flowers.

When the last napkin was folded, Lily ran to the window to see if Papa and Joseph were coming. She couldn't see any sign of them, so she went to the kitchen. Mama was trying to keep the food warm. What was keeping them?

Dannie was hungry and impatient. And noisy. Mama spooned a pile of potatoes into a little dish for him to eat. It seemed to Lily that little boys were always hungry. Always hungry and never full.

Finally, Papa and Joseph came through the door. Joseph was practically bursting with excitement. Lily wondered what the news could be but knew she should wait until Papa was ready to tell them.

After they had prayed and started to eat, Papa looked at Mama, eyes twinkling. "Mr. Beal said that there is going to be a big fireworks show in Cloverdale on Friday. He said there will be singers to entertain the crowds of people and fun things for children to do. Lots of good food to eat. All to celebrate the Fourth of July. He invited us to go with them."

Mama looked hesitant. She didn't like to go into town when it was crowded.

Papa seemed to read her mind. "He said if we'd prefer, he wouldn't mind if we drove half a mile up the road, to the top of the hill in one of his fields. We should be able to at least watch the fireworks from there." He reached out for a basket of rolls. Lily knew Papa was taking his time, giving Mama plenty of room to think about this.

Papa buttered his roll, ever so carefully. "What do you think, Rachel? Does it sound like a nice family evening?"

Lily held her breath. It sounded wonderful! Even if they weren't going to town to hear the singers and eat the good food, at least they could see pretty fireworks. Mama had to say yes. She just had to!

Mama was in no hurry. She ate a few bites of the stew and helped Dannie with his last bite of potato. At long last, she gave her answer. "It does sound nice. I could pack some treats to snack on while we sit there."

Lily wanted to jump up and down and yell, "Yahoo!" Friday was only two days away, so that meant they wouldn't have to wait very long. Joseph was grinning like a cat in cream.

Friday was a beautiful day. Sunny, but not too warm. Not humid and sticky like so many days had been lately. It would be a perfect evening to sit outside after dark and watch the fireworks.

Papa hitched Jim to the buggy. Mama tucked a picnic basket filled with special treats under the front seat. Lily wasn't sure what she was more excited about: watching the fireworks or eating the yummy things in the basket. Papa had bought special things in town on his way home from work today. There were seedless grapes, potato chips, and little packs with crackers and cheese. Lily was sure that no one in town had better snacks than they did tonight.

When everyone was in the buggy, Papa lifted the reins and said, "Giddyup." Jim trotted down the driveway and up the road until he came to the field lane that led to the top of Mr. Beal's field. Jim slowed to a walk as the buggy bumped over the ruts in the lane. When they came to the top of the hill, Papa tied Jim to a tree. He spread a blanket on the ground.

He pulled out an empty five-gallon pail and turned it upside down for Mama to sit on. Everyone else sat on the blanket.

Mama blushed. "You make me feel like a queen, Daniel."

Papa winked at her. "You deserve to feel like one. I want you to be comfortable."

Lily thought it seemed strange that Mama wouldn't think the blanket on the ground was comfortable enough. She had often sat on blankets when they went on picnics.

Mama opened the picnic basket and started handing everyone snacks. Lily thought that there was nothing better than seedless grapes. She traded one of her packs of cheese and crackers with Joseph for a handful of his grapes. "When will the fireworks start?" Joseph asked. His mouth was full of half-chewed crackers. Lily nearly gagged at the sight.

"We don't speak with our mouth full of food, even when we're outside," Papa said. "It's getting dark quickly. The fireworks should start any minute."

Papa had hardly finished talking when a bright flash of lightning lit the sky. Then another and another. Thunder boomed and rolled across the hills. Everyone jumped up and ran to the buggy as the rain began. Papa quickly untied Jim from the tree and hopped into the buggy to guide him down the field lane. It was too bumpy to go fast, so Jim walked slowly and carefully. Lightning flashed across the sky and thunder continued to roll. One rumble barely stopped as another one began. Suddenly, little balls of hail started pinging against the buggy. As calm as Jim was with lightning, he did not like hail. He broke into a trot. The buggy bounced and jostled wildly the rest of the way down the field lane.

Joseph and Dannie started to wail. Lily felt like crying too, but she was older than they were. "Now, children, everything will be okay," Papa said in his reassuring way. "God will take care of us."

That made Lily feel a little better. God could take care of them in the middle of a big storm. But she wished He would make the storm stop.

When they reached home, Papa pulled up right beside the basement door so they could hop out and run inside. Papa drove Jim to the safety of the barn where he could unhitch him and put him in his stall for the night.

When Papa came inside, he was soaking wet, head to toe. "I've never seen anything like that," he said, toweling off his hair. "One minute the weather was beautiful. No raincloud in sight. The next minute, we're in the middle of one of the worst thunderstorms I've ever experienced."

Lily felt sad that they didn't get to see the fireworks. Not even one. At least no one in town did, either. That thought cheered her as she made her way up the stairs to her hallway bedroom to get ready for bed. Outside, the thunder and lightning continued to rage and roar. The lightning flashed so often that she didn't even need to use a lamp. The hallway was brighter with all those lightning flashes than it would be with her dim oil lamp.

The next evening, Mr. Beal stopped by. "Some storm we had last night, wasn't it?"

Papa nodded. "Do you have storms like that often in this area?"

"I've lived here all my life," Mr. Beal said, "but I've never seen anything like that. What a doozy. They were just about to start the fireworks last evening when it hit. Right before that, they had a comedian onstage keeping the crowd entertained. He said that they were going to give God a fireworks competition and that they were going to win. Just as he finished, the storm started and everyone had to hurry for home. They didn't have time to set off a single firework."

Papa looked sober. "It's never wise to challenge God like that. Now the storm makes sense."

Mr. Beal seemed uncomfortable. He shuffled his feet a little. "I'm sure it was just a coincidence." He put his hand on the door, then turned back. "Strange, though. There was no sign of rain or anything until he made that remark."

Lily could feel a shiver go up and down her spine. It seemed just like a miracle in the Bible.

Papa closed the door behind Mr. Beal. He lifted his eyebrows and his eyes twinkled. "Well, looks like God won that fireworks competition."

Sleeping in the Barn

*L*ily closed the book she had been reading. It was a wonderful story. She was sad she had come to the last page. The children in the story had slept in their barn on freshly mown hay.

Wouldn't it be fun to sleep in the barn for a night? Maybe for an entire week.

She slipped the book back onto the bookshelf and ran to find Joseph. She could talk him into sleeping in the barn. Joseph was always interested in adventures. She found him in the sandbox, playing with Dannie. Lily explained her idea.

Joseph's eyes lit up. "I'd like to sleep in the barn."

"Me too," Dannie piped up. "I like sleeping in the barn."

What? *Uh oh*. Lily hadn't thought this through. She wasn't thinking about Dannie when she came up with this idea. He was too little. Each night, he went through a ritual that made Lily crazy. First, he would call out to Mama and Papa.

Then he wanted to be re-tucked into bed. Then he needed a drink of water. What would happen in the barn if Papa and Mama weren't there to come for him when he called? "I don't think you would like sleeping in the barn, Dannie," Lily said. "You're too little."

Naturally, Dannie didn't pay her any mind. He jumped out of the sandbox and threw his little shovel on the ground. He ran to the house. "Mama, Mama, Mama! Can I sleep in the barn?"

Mama was at the kitchen table writing a letter. She looked up, confused, as Dannie, Joseph, and Lily burst into the kitchen. "Who is sleeping in a barn?"

"Lily and Joseph are sleeping in the barn for a whole week," Dannie said. "Lily says I'm too little to sleep there."

Mama turned to Lily. "Why would you want to sleep in the barn? You have a nice, warm, comfortable bed upstairs."

Upstairs in the hallway, she meant.

Lily told Mama about the story she had just finished. "Can we sleep in the barn?"

Mama hesitated. "Let's talk to Papa about it first."

That meant two things to Lily: First, Mama didn't think it was such a wonderful idea. Second, Mama didn't want to discuss it anymore.

Lily went upstairs to her hallway bedroom to play with her doll while she waited for Papa to come home. Papa, she hoped, would understand the excitement of sleeping in the barn. He remembered how it felt to be young. Sometimes, Mama forgot.

Lily made plans to build a blanket-nest hay pile in the barn. She created a make-believe hay pile of blankets for her doll. She didn't even hear Papa arrive until the hinge on the kitchen door squeaked opened and she heard his deep voice downstairs.

Lily jumped up and hurried down the stairs. Papa was telling Mama about his day, so Lily tried to wait patiently until he was done. She knew it wasn't polite to interrupt unless it was an emergency. This did feel like an emergency to Lily, but she doubted Mama would agree.

When there was a little pause in Papa and Mama's conversation, Lily wedged right in. "We want to sleep on the fresh hay in the barn tonight, Papa. Can we?"

Papa was washing his hands at the kitchen sink. He finished rinsing and grabbed a clean dishrag to dry his hands. He turned to Lily. "Why would you want to sleep in the barn when you have nice comfortable beds in the house?"

How strange. How could Mama and Papa have the same response? Lily explained about the story she had read. "It sounds like so much fun. Please, can we?"

Papa and Mama exchanged a look. "Not tonight," Papa said. "Mama and I will talk about it later. Right now it's time to do chores."

Lily went to the barn with Papa. Her job was to hold Pansy's tail to keep it from swatting Papa in the face while he milked her. But Lily's gaze was fixed on the stack of hay. She couldn't stop thinking about how much fun it would be to curl up in a blanket on the very top of that fresh, sweet-smelling hay. Oh, how she hoped Papa and Mama would give them permission to sleep out here. They just had to!

At breakfast the next morning, Papa had his answer. "Mama and I decided you can sleep in the barn on the next Saturday night before our in-between Sunday. That way you can sleep as late as you like in the morning."

That was good news and that was bad news. Lily was thrilled that Papa and Mama gave them permission, but it meant a long, long wait. Next Sunday was church Sunday.

She counted the days until the next in-between Sunday. Nine more days. That was a long time to wait. Joseph and Dannie were too little to realize how long a time nine days could be. They thanked Papa for saying yes and chattered together about what toys they would need to bring to the barn for the sleepover, as if it were happening tonight. Those little brothers had no sense of time whatsoever.

❧×❧

Finally, the in-between weekend had arrived. On Saturday morning, Lily worked extra fast as she helped Mama with all of the cleaning. Lily wished Mama would work faster. She wasn't hurrying any more than she did on normal Saturdays, and this was not a normal Saturday.

As soon as lunch was over, Lily asked Mama if she could start taking blankets and pillows out to the barn. She wanted to fix their hay-nests to sleep on. She had given these nests quite a bit of thought.

"You can get the blankets and pillows ready to go," Mama said, "but I want you to wait to take them out to the barn until after supper. Papa and I want to help you."

Lily ran upstairs and yanked the quilt and blanket and pillow from her bed. Then she hurried to get them from Joseph's and Dannie's beds too. She folded them and piled them next to the kitchen door. All ready! They were just waiting to be taken to the barn right after supper.

Lily never knew the hands of a clock to move around numbers as slowly as they did that Saturday afternoon. When it was finally time to eat supper, she thought she had never seen Joseph and Dannie eat so slowly. No one could leave the table until everyone was done with their meal. Didn't those little boys understand? *Hurry, hurry, hurry,* she wanted to tell them, but she knew she shouldn't. She sat and waited until everyone was done. Papa helped Dannie scrape the last bit of food from his plate. At last, supper was over. All that was left to do was to clear the dishes from the table and take them to the sink. Then, they could go to the barn and build their hay-nest beds.

Papa pushed his chair back from the table and stood. He smiled at Lily. "Tonight, I will help Mama wash the dishes. Let's all go out to the barn and get the three of you settled for the night."

Lily could hardly believe her ears. How wonderful! Not only was she going to sleep in the barn, but she didn't have to do dishes tonight! She hurried to the door to pick up the pile of blankets and pillows. Mama and Joseph came to help her while Papa went to get the thick winter buggy robes. He said the hay would feel better if the buggy robe went on top, then the rest of the blankets.

In the barn, Papa climbed up on the haystack and spread out the two buggy robes. Joseph and Dannie could sleep on one of them. Farther up the stack of hay, Lily would sleep on the other buggy robe. Once the blankets were spread out and the pillows puffed up, Mama gave each one of them a flashlight. "If you wake up in the middle of the night and change your mind, you can just come to the house."

Dannie, she meant. Certainly not Lily or Joseph.

Papa and Mama tucked them in and said good night before going back to the house to do the dishes.

Lily and Joseph and Dannie talked and giggled for a little bit. Soon, they ran out of things to talk about. Lily stared at the rafters in the barn ceiling. The sun was beginning to set. Streams of light shone through cracks in the barn wall. The cobwebs that dangled off the rafters looked thick and dusty.

She hoped the spiders would stay in their webs. She didn't want any of them crawling over her face while she slept. Just the thought of it gave her the shivers. A few wasps buzzed lazily near the pitch of the roof.

The goats munched the hay in their manger. Their sharp teeth made a loud crunching sound. The chickens made soft, sleepy clucking noises as they settled on their roosts to sleep.

There were so many strange night noises. During the day, the animal noises in the barn were familiar and peaceful. Tonight, she thought they sounded creepy and scary. Soon, she heard the whiffling sound of Joseph's snore. Then Dannie's deep, steady breathing. How could they sleep? She wasn't sure she could sleep at all. She started to think this idea wasn't so wonderful. Her bed in the hallway seemed very appealing.

A strange piercing squeal filled the air and then a *thump*! Lily bolted up in her hay-nest. She reached under her pillow to get her flashlight. She shined the spotlight on a big tomcat.

He had caught a mouse and was playing with it. The terrified little mouse squealed and tried to escape. The cat swatted it with its paws, let it run, then caught it again. The shine of the flashlight woke Joseph and Dannie. They sat up to see what was happening, but then they went right back to sleep.

Normally, Lily did not like mice, but she did feel sorry for this little mouse. It was horrible. She wished the mouse could make an escape.

At long last, the cat grew bored with the game and the horrible squeals stopped. But then new sounds started: the cat was eating the mouse. Lily pulled the covers over her head and held her hands over her ears to try to block the sound.

Sleeping in the barn wasn't nearly as much fun as Lily thought it would be.

Lily was glad when the first streaks of dawn tinted the eastern skies. She hadn't slept at all. Not one little wink. She clambered off the haystack and rolled up her blankets. Joseph and Dannie woke and hurried to pack their things. They ran back to the house, glad that the night of sleeping in the barn was over.

Inside the house, everything was quiet. Papa and Mama were still sleeping. Lily set the table for breakfast. The three of them sat at the kitchen table and waited patiently for Papa and Mama. They tried to be very quiet so they wouldn't wake them. The in-between Sunday meant that Papa could sleep late.

A little while later, Mama came into the kitchen. She looked surprised to see them sitting there. "Did you sleep well?" she asked.

"I slept well," Joseph said, rubbing his eyes.

"Me too," Dannie said. He had hay in his hair.

Lily scowled at them. "There were too many barn noises."

Papa came into the kitchen, yawning and stretching. He picked up the clean pail to go milk Pansy. Even on an in-between Sunday, the cow needed milking and the animals needed to be fed. "Do you want to sleep in the barn next Saturday night?"

"No!" Lily, Joseph, and Dannie said at the same time, as if it had been rehearsed. But it wasn't.

Papa and Mama grinned at each other. "Why not?" Papa said.

"My bed is more comfortable," Joseph said. "And I got cold."

"Too cold," Dannie echoed.

And cats, Lily thought, *don't catch mice and chew them in our bedrooms.*

Sunday Church at the Lapps'

Grandma Miller and Aunt Susie had come to help Mama clean the house to get ready for church on Sunday. It was the Lapp family's first time to host church in Cloverdale. Everything had to be extra sparkling clean. Grandma said that they couldn't let one speck of dirt or dust remain.

That seemed like an impossible task to Lily. How could anyone live on a farm, with two little brothers, and not have one speck of dirt or dust in the house? She hoped Grandma's eyesight wasn't too keen. It was hard work to get ready for church—all the furniture had to be cleaned. The insides of every drawer needed to be washed out. The silverware needed polishing. The pots and pans were scrubbed and scrubbed until they looked brand-new. All this work wore Lily out.

But there was a fun part. Whitewashing the basement. Lily loved dipping a paintbrush into the whitewash and painting the walls with it. It was fun to watch the gray cinderblocks transform into clean, shiny white walls.

After taking a break for lunch, Mama told Lily and Susie to go outside to wash the basement windows. "Grandma and I will finish whitewashing the basement."

That was a disappointment. Washing windows wasn't fun, not like whitewashing. Lily had to wash the kitchen and living room windows every Saturday. Basement windows would be a little different, but they were still windows. Windows were windows.

Aunt Susie helped Lily fill a pail with hot water and added a big splash of vinegar. Lily found two sponges and several old rags they could use to dry the windows.

They went outside to start to wash the windows. They were so close to the ground that they had to bend over to wash them. At least it didn't matter if their sponges dripped water everywhere. In the basement, they couldn't spill a drop of whitewash. Not a single drop.

As Lily and Aunt Susie finished up one side of the house, they went around the corner for the other windows and nearly bumped into the billy goat, munching grass. "Oh, that pesky goat!" Lily said. "I'll have to run and tell Mama that he got out again."

Aunt Susie started to work on washing windows as Lily ran to the basement. "Mama! The goat escaped from the pasture again!"

Mama sighed. She did not like those goats. She laid her paintbrush down and followed Lily outside. As they rounded the corner of the house, they saw Aunt Susie bent over, drying the window she had just washed. The billy lowered his head and started to run at Aunt Susie.

"Look out!" Mama shouted.

Too late! The billy charged right into Aunt Susie's backside. She fell down, knocking over the pail of water. The billy looked surprised too. He shook his head as if he wasn't sure what had gotten into him. Lily wondered the same thing. That billy was a nuisance, but he had never butted into anyone before.

Mama untied her apron and snapped it at the billy to chase him away from Aunt Susie. She seemed stunned for a moment, then frightened. Lily helped her scramble to her feet and move away from the billy. Mama went to get a rope to lead the billy goat to the barn. He would have to be tied up until Papa came home from work. That billy, Mama grumbled, had caused enough excitement for one day.

Before the sun had risen, Lily's family was up. Church would be at the Lapps' house in just a few hours, and Lily could hardly contain her excitement.

Yesterday, Jonas Raber, Beth's father, had brought the wagon filled with church benches to their house. He had stayed long enough to help Papa carry all the furniture that had been in the kitchen and living room upstairs and place it in the hall. Lily had to climb over chairs and a sofa to reach her bed.

After Jonas left, Papa and Mama carried the benches into the house and set them up to get ready for church. Lily and Joseph and Dannie tried to walk on top of the benches to cross the rooms without touching the floor.

Papa put three kitchen chairs in the doorway between the kitchen and the living room for the ministers to sit on. A little table stood next to the chairs. Mama put her best water pitcher on it and two glasses. Ministers often got thirsty after they preached for a long time and would need a drink.

"I have an idea," Lily said, trying to be helpful. "The ministers shouldn't talk so long."

Mama silenced Lily with a look.

Papa placed the big German family Bible on the table next to his little black prayer book. Everything was ready. All they needed to do now was to change into their Sunday clothes and wait.

When the first buggy rolled into the driveway, Papa, Joseph, and Dannie went outside to the barn to be with the rest of the men until it was time for church to start. The women came inside and removed their shawls and bonnets and placed them on Papa and Mama's bed. They visited quietly in the kitchen until the bishop's wife gave the signal that it was time to sit down.

Everyone found a seat. The men and boys on one side. The women and girls and babies on the other. The ministers filed in and shook hands with everyone. When the first song was announced, the ministers stood and walked to Mama and Papa's bedroom. Earlier this morning, Lily asked Mama what the ministers did when they went to a bedroom during the hymn.

"I think they probably pray and discuss what they are going to preach about," Mama said, not sounding at all certain.

No one really knew because ministers never talked about it to anyone. Even Effie didn't know and her father was one of the ministers. Lily thought they probably snooped through all the dresser drawers and closets. Why else did everything have to be so clean? She wanted to ask Mama if she agreed, but after her very helpful suggestion about asking the ministers not to talk so much didn't seem to be appreciated, she thought twice.

When the ministers came back out, everyone put their songbooks away. Lily tried to be still and listen to what the minister was saying, but what she really wanted to do was to play with her pretty flowered handkerchief that she kept in her pocket. Little girls in this Pennsylvania church weren't allowed to play with handkerchiefs once they were old enough to go to school. In New York, they could, but not here. She made a special effort to ignore Aaron Yoder, even when he looked at her from across the room and crossed his eyes. She tried not to giggle when she imagined his eyes stuck like that.

Lily watched the pendulum of the wall clock swing back and forth, back and forth. It made her feel sleepy and she started to nod off. Mama noticed and gave her a little nudge. Lily was too big to sleep in church. She had to sit up straight and listen to what the minister was saying.

When the first minister finally finished his sermon, everyone knelt to pray. After the prayer was over, everyone stood as the deacon read a chapter from the New Testament. While he read, Mama and Lily slipped down to the basement and lit the oil stove. It was time to start the peppermint tea and coffee. Lily worked as slowly as she could, trying to stretch this task out as long as she could, until Mama noticed and lifted an eyebrow. It was more fun to be able to do something—anything—than head back upstairs and sit ramrod straight on that hard backless bench. Lily was getting hungry too. Her stomach rumbled at the thought of the delicious lunch she and Mama had prepared for everyone to share: special church peanut butter, stacks of homemade bread, pickles, red beets.

At long last, church was dismissed. After the men ate, the women and children had a turn. Mama and Lily would be the last to eat today. Effie and her mother, Ida Kauffman, were first. As Effie filled up her plate, she leaned toward Lily and said, "It's too bad your parents couldn't afford sliced bologna and cheese."

Under normal conditions, Lily would have ignored Effie. But today wasn't a normal condition. Lily was hungry and cranky. She knew how hard Mama had worked to make this special lunch. Lily stepped on Effie's toe so hard that Effie howled. "Lily hurt me!" Effie wailed. Ida came sailing across the kitchen to comfort Effie.

In her puniest voice, Lily apologized to Effie for being clumsy, but Ida was not easily consoled. She took Mama aside and suggested that it was high time Lily work on becoming more ladylike. She lifted her nose and her spectacles gleamed. "And I understand that Lily has been sleeping in a barn this summer!" Ida Kauffman filled up every space, even in this large room.

Lily was furious. Mama was quiet. Effie was pleased.

Lily's Gray Jell-O

One evening before bedtime, Mama finished tidying up the kitchen as Lily swept the floor. "Next week is Grandma's birthday," she said. "Papa and I thought it would be nice to invite them over for a special dinner on Sunday."

Lily stopped sweeping. "Can I help plan the menu?"

Mama pointed to the broom. "We can sit down and figure it out as soon as we have finished up our evening work."

Lily carefully swept the dirt pile into the dustpan and dumped it into the trash can. She hurried to hang the broom and dustpan on a nail inside the basement door.

Mama was already at the table with a tablet and pen. She wrote down the type of potato, meat, and vegetable she wanted to make.

"Can I make Jell-O?" Lily asked. She loved Jell-O. She liked how it jiggled on the plate and how it felt as it slipped down her throat.

Mama thought for a moment. "I think Jell-O would work if we mixed it with some fruit. Then we could serve it with Grandma's birthday cake."

"Can I make it all by myself?" Lily asked. She wanted to show Grandma that she was growing up by making at least one thing all by herself.

"Jell-O is fairly easy to make," Mama said. "I think you can handle most of it, but I should measure the boiling water for you so you don't spill any on yourself."

On Saturday morning, Mama sent Joseph and Dannie down the road to Grandma's house with an invitation to come for a birthday dinner on Sunday. Lily stayed at home to help Mama with the cleaning. The house needed to be spotless for Grandma's special dinner.

Not much later, Joseph and Dannie returned home with a note for Mama. As she read it, the corners of her mouth slipped into a smile.

A good sign. "Are they coming?" Lily asked.

"Yes, they are," Mama said. "Which means we still have a lot of work to get done before then."

By midday, the house was clean. It was time to start cooking and baking Grandma's birthday meal. Time for Jell-O making.

Lily filled the big teakettle with water and set it on the front of the stove so that it would heat faster. "What kind of Jell-O shall I make?"

"You can choose whatever flavor you like," Mama said.

Lily climbed up on the counter and looked through the supply of Jell-O Mama had in the cupboard. Mama bought Jell-O in big bags at the bulk food store. Lily tried to think how much to make so that everyone could have as much as they wanted to. A cup full of Jell-O for everyone would be just about right. She counted up: Mama, Papa, Lily, Joseph, Dannie, Grandma Miller, Grandpa Miller, Aunt Susie. Uncle Jacob and Aunt Lizzie would stay with Great-Grandma, so that made eight people. Lily would need at least eight cups of Jell-O.

Next: which flavor should she choose? Sometimes Mama mixed a few flavors together. Lily decided she would choose several flavors and mix them together. She chose a bag of orange, blueberry, apricot, and strawberry. She hoped that mixing these flavors together would make the best Jell-O they had ever tasted.

Lily hopped off the counter. She found a big bowl and carefully measured eight cups of Jell-O powder into it. The teapot was whistling, but Mama was in the basement to select potatoes, onions, and apples. Lily didn't want to wait to stir the Jell-O until Mama came upstairs. She knew Mama was

worried she would burn herself, but she knew she could do it. She would work slowly and carefully, measuring out the teakettle of boiling water.

She put her hands in big potholders and lifted the handle of the teakettle. Grasping the heavy kettle with both hands, she carried it off the stove, holding it out in front of her. She shuffled her way slowly, cautiously, over to the sink. She was relieved when she safely set it into the sink. She found a measuring cup, set it in the sink, and carefully tipped the teakettle of boiling water into it. Then she poured the cup of hot water into the bowl filled with Jell-O powder. Cup after cup. She had just finished pouring the water over the Jell-O when Mama came back upstairs.

"Oh, Lily, I wanted you to wait until I came back." She hurried to the sink. "Let me measure the boiling water for you." When she reached the bowl, she stopped abruptly. Lily looked up at her. Something wasn't right. The Jell-O was gray.

"How much Jell-O did you measure into the bowl?" Mama asked.

"Eight cups full," Lily said. "One cup for everyone. I mixed flavors."

Mama's eyes went wide. Then she burst out laughing. "Eight cups full!" She laughed until tears rolled down her cheeks. "Well, it looks like we will be eating Jell-O for a long time."

Gray Jell-O.

Lily wished she had waited until Mama had come before she added the water. She had not thought how much Jell-O it would make if she measured eight cups full into her bowl. At least Mama wasn't upset with her. Lily had never seen Mama giggle so much before. It made Lily giggle too, even though she wasn't sure what the problem was.

Mama wiped away her tears and took a deep breath. "Okay. Right now what we need is a bigger bowl. A much, much bigger bowl." She looked in the sink at the Jell-O again. "I think we'll have to use a five-gallon pail." She hurried down to the basement to find one. She brought one upstairs and washed it out with soap and hot water to make sure it was clean. She set the pail on the floor and then dumped the bowl of Jell-O into it. Next she started measuring and pouring in the boiling water. She handed a wooden spoon to Lily and told her to stir it until all the Jell-O had dissolved.

After Mama was satisfied that the Jell-O was dissolved, she was ready to measure the cold water. After all the water had been measured, Lily discovered that they had at least forty cups of Jell-O. She had never seen that much Jell-O in her life. She had certainly never seen such a gray color of Jell-O before. No wonder Mama had laughed.

The rest of the day, Lily helped Mama prepare other food. They had to walk around the pail of Jell-O in the middle of the kitchen. It was too heavy for Mama to move by herself, so it would have to wait until Papa came home. He would be able to carry the heavy pail down to the basement where it would stay nice and cold until tomorrow's dinner.

When Papa finally came home, his eyebrows shot up when he saw the pail of gray Jell-O sitting in the middle of the kitchen. He looked questioningly at Mama. "Is there a reason you made enough Jell-O to feed the church?"

"It's all part of the adventure of having a young cook in the house," Mama said.

Lily told him the story of the Jell-O. Papa looked at Mama, and then they both burst out laughing. Why was it so funny?

Papa patted her head. "It looks like Lily is practicing to cook for lots of people." He bent down and lifted the pail with an extra grunt. He winked at Lily and she knew he had only pretended that it was very heavy for him as he carried it to the basement.

◦×◦

The next morning, Mama sent Lily to the basement with a big bowl and a dipper to scoop Jell-O out of the pail. She had some fruit ready to mix into it. Lily hoped it might not have quite such a gray tinge after the fruit was added.

Lily pushed the dipper into the Jell-O to scoop some out and put into the bowl. It made a funny slurping noise as she pulled the dipper out. Once the bowl was full, Lily looked at the pail. There was still so much Jell-O in it that she couldn't even see the bottom of the pail through the glassy gelatin. They would have to eat Jell-O for breakfast, lunch, and dinner, for weeks and weeks, months and months, if they were ever going to empty that pail.

When Grandpa and Grandma and Aunt Susie arrived, Lily ran to the door to meet them.

Aunt Susie had brought her doll along to play with. She and Lily loved to play dolls together. "First," Lily whispered to her, "I have something to show you in the basement."

Grandma went to the kitchen to help Mama finish getting dinner ready while Lily and Aunt Susie slipped quietly down to the basement. Lily walked over to the pail of Jell-O and pointed. "Look how much Jell-O I made yesterday."

Aunt Susie peered into the pail. "Gray Jell-O. Is this all we will have to eat today?"

"No, Mama made a good dinner," said Lily. "But we do have a lot of Jell-O." They both peered into the pail again. "Quite a lot."

They went back upstairs. Grandma filled the water glasses

141

as Mama dished out bowls of steaming food. Mama saw Lily and Aunt Susie come into the kitchen. "Go tell Papa that dinner is ready."

Lily went to the living room to tell Papa and Grandpa that it was time to eat. As everyone sat at the table, Papa bowed his head to ask a silent blessing. When it was over, Papa lifted his head and reached for the platter of fresh homemade bread to pass it around the table. When it came to Aunt Susie, she passed the bread on to Joseph without taking a slice.

"Are you sure you don't want any bread today?" Grandpa asked. Everyone knew that Aunt Susie liked bread.

Aunt Susie shook her head. "Not today," she said in her slow, thick way. "I'm saving room for Lily's gray Jell-O. She made a whole pail full and we need to help her eat it."

Mama explained about the Jell-O and everyone laughed, especially Joseph, which got Dannie giggling. Lily nudged them under the table with her toe.

"Send a bowlful home with us," Grandma said.

"You mean, a bucketful," Grandpa murmured.

Grandma ignored him. She turned to Lily. "It takes a lot of practice to become a good cook. I'm happy to hear that you're already starting to learn."

Grandpa leaned toward Lily and lowered his voice. "Someday, you might want to ask Grandma about your mother's adventures as a beginner cook." He winked at Lily. "I seem to remember something about gravy on the ceiling."

"Dad!" Mama said, pretending to be horrified, and everyone laughed.

While everyone helped themselves to second and third helpings of Jell-O, Lily made a point to remember to ask Grandma about Mama and the ceiling gravy story on her next visit.

Summer was deepening. It would soon be time for the start of another school year. Mama was working hard to make sure that Lily and Joseph had new clothes to wear. Lily stood at the edge of the sewing table. She liked to watch Mama sew new shirts and dresses.

Mama pumped the sewing machine's treadle up and down with her foot as fast as she could. The stack of finished shirts, pants, dresses, and aprons grew bigger and bigger every day. When the last piece of clothing had been sewn, Mama asked Lily to dig through the button box and find enough matching buttons for all the new clothes.

Lily liked digging through the button box. She carefully counted out little piles of buttons that matched the dresses and shirts. She needed seven buttons for each shirt, five buttons for each dress, and one for the apron. Nine buttons for each pair of pants. Pants didn't have nice buttons. They all looked the same. Big and black. Lily was glad she was a girl and all her buttons could be pretty.

After Lily had counted out the buttons into little piles, Mama told her to put them into an empty pill bottle. Mama folded the clothes and put them into two grocery bags. "Take these to Grandma Miller," she said. "Ask her if she has time to sew the buttons and buttonholes. I'm already way behind in the garden and everything that needs to be done around here."

"Can I stay for a while?" Lily asked.

"You can stay for an hour," Mama said. "But then I need you to hurry home and help me weed the garden."

Lily picked up the bags and hurried down the road to Grandma's house. She could hear the noisy hum of Grandpa's sawmill before she reached the driveway.

When she reached the house, Lily knocked on the door

and waited for Grandma to open the door. Lily explained how busy Mama was and asked if Grandma could sew the buttons and buttonholes for their new school clothes.

"Sure," Grandma said, "I'll get started on them right away."

"Mama said I can stay for an hour today," Lily said.

She followed Grandma into her craft room. Great-Grandma was sleeping in the bed against the wall. She slept most of the day, which was a relief to Lily. Grandma sat on her rocking chair in front of the window and pulled a shirt out of the bag. Lily counted out the matching buttons for her. Grandma carefully cut buttonholes down the front and on the cuffs of the sleeves. She threaded a needle and started to sew the first buttonhole with tiny, even stitches. So tiny! Lily's stitches were still crooked and clumsy.

Aunt Susie came into the room to see what they were doing. She pulled chairs in from the kitchen so she and Lily would have a place to sit. The only sound in the room was Great-Grandma's whiffling little snores. She slept through it all.

As Lily watched Grandma make the needle fly in and out of the fabric, she waited for the right moment to ask Grandma a question that had been buzzing around her brain. "Can you tell me some stories about teaching Mama to cook?"

Grandma smiled. "It was an adventure to teach my little Rachel how to cook." She cut another yard of thread from the spool and threaded the needle for another buttonhole. "Your mama used to think that there was nothing more special than an angel food cake. She would ask me over and over if she could bake one. I thought it was much too hard for a little girl to beat those egg whites. Making an angel food cake is hard work. My own arms always grew very tired."

Aunt Susie pulled her chair closer to listen to the story. Rachel, Lily's mama, was her older sister, and she didn't remember these stories. "One day," Grandma said, "when she asked me again, I told her she could make a regular cake and bake it in the angel food cake pan." Grandma paused and looked at Lily. "You know what an angel food cake pan looks like, don't you?"

Lily nodded. Mama still liked angel food cake best of all. Whenever they had too many eggs on hand, she would make the cake. The pan was deep and round, with a long tube up the middle. The whole bottom could be lifted out.

"Rachel was happy to use that cake pan," Grandma said. "She started mixing up our favorite chocolate cake. She got everything mixed up nicely and poured it into the cake pan and spread the batter around the tube until it was nice and even. She licked the empty bowl and spoon and put them into the sink to soak until we were ready to do the dishes.

"She wanted to put the cake into the oven by herself. She carried it over with two hands—one on the bottom, one on the side. Then, all of a sudden, before I realized what was happening, she reached out with one hand to open the oven door. The bottom part of the cake pan dropped out and cake batter ran everywhere. She was covered in chocolate batter! It ran down the front of her dress, her shoes, and the floor." Grandma chuckled. "We didn't get any cake that day, but your mama learned the proper way to carry a tube cake pan."

Lily tried to imagine Mama as a little girl. She couldn't believe Mama could make such a big mess. Nowadays, she was so tidy.

Aunt Susie giggled and giggled, so much that Great-Grandma stirred. "Tell another story about Rachel, Mom."

"Maybe . . . the gravy story," Lily reminded.

Grandma finished one shirt and picked up a dress. She took her time finding just the right thread color. When she was ready, she leaned back in her chair and started to sew another buttonhole. "We often had biscuits and chicken gravy for supper. Your Mama wanted to make the biscuits by herself. I thought she had helped me often enough that there shouldn't be a problem. If she needed help, I would be right there to help her. But she was feeling particularly grown-up that evening and said she wanted to make supper all by herself.

"I told her if she needed me, she could call for help. I went into the living room to do some sewing. After a while I could smell the biscuits baking. I thought they smelled a little different than usual, but I didn't say anything.

"Finally, she announced that supper was ready. I went to the kitchen to help her put everything on the table." Grandma started laughing now, so hard that tears rolled down her cheeks. "Those biscuits were the sorriest looking things I had ever seen. Instead of nice fluffy biscuits, they had run together into a flat mess. They even dripped right off the edge of the cookie sheet. I tasted a corner, and it was so sweet, I had to go get a drink of water right away. I asked her how much sugar she had added, and she said, 'Just what the recipe called for.' Turns out she had used one and one-half cups of sugar instead of one and one-half teaspoons. We ate those biscuits with fruit for dessert that night and spooned the gravy on bread instead." She wiped her eyes and took a deep breath.

Lily felt sorry for Mama! She was trying so hard to be grown-up. "Was that the ceiling gravy that Grandpa talked about?"

Grandma looked confused. Then a laugh burst out of her. "Oh, I'd forgotten about *that* cooking lesson. Another time, Rachel wanted to make flour paste to thicken the gravy, and things didn't work quite so well. We used to have a plastic can with a snap-on lid to shake the paste until it was nice

146

and smooth. Rachel thought it would be better to use hot water instead of cold to make the paste. The only trouble was when she tried to shake the can, the hot water created pressure and made the lid pop off. The entire kitchen was splattered with flour paste. There was paste on the ceiling, the walls, and the cupboards. It was an awful mess to try to clean up. It dries fast like glue."

"Did Rachel do other funny things?" Aunt Susie asked.

"Yes, she sure did," said Grandma. "But I think those stories will have to wait until some other day. Lily's hour is up and I'm sure her mama needs her little helper at home."

Lily said goodbye and started for home. It had been fun to hear that Mama had made funny mistakes when she had been learning how to cook. It made Lily's gray Jell-O not seem so bad. Not so bad at all.

But the thought of eating one more bite of Jell-O made her want to gag.

Summer's End

*I*t was a nice summer day in mid-August. The kitchen windows were steamed up from the boiling pot of water on the stove. Lily felt hot and sweaty as she sat at the kitchen table with Joseph and Dannie. In the middle of the table was a mountain of green beans, freshly picked from the garden. Each bean needed its ends pinched off and to be broken into pieces. Mama wanted to spend the day canning beans.

Lily pinched off the ends while Joseph and Dannie snapped the beans into little pieces and tossed them into a big stainless steel bowl. *Plink, plink, plink.* The boys thought it was fun, like playing ball, but Lily had grown tired of this tedious work. Beans, beans, beans. That's all she had been doing lately: picking them, snapping them, breaking them into pieces. Before beans, it was peas. Soon, it would be tomatoes and squash. She was as busy as a bird dog.

Taking care of a big garden was so much work. Canning

food for the winter was even more work. If they weren't canning, they were weeding and watering the garden so that the vegetables would grow and produce more . . . which meant more canning. Over and over and over, all summer long. Something had to be done every single day.

She looked out the window and saw Jim and Pansy grazing in the pasture. The sun shone brightly and a nice breeze made the tall pasture grass look like rippling waves. Sometimes, Lily wished she could be a horse or a cow. They could do whatever they wanted to all day long and never had to worry about canning food.

Mama noticed. "Is something bothering you, Lily?"

Lily sighed. "I'm tired of canning."

Mama nodded her head. "It's a lot of hard work. I will be very glad once all the shelves in the basement are full again and the garden is done for another year."

Lily was surprised to hear Mama admit that. She had no idea that Mama ever grew tired of this kind of work. Mama never complained.

Mama smiled at her. "As soon as we are done getting these beans ready to put in jars, you can have the rest of the day off to do whatever you want to do."

Instantly, Lily cheered up. She knew exactly what she wanted to do with the rest of the afternoon. A big patch of burdocks grew in the pasture behind the barn. She had wanted to gather the pretty pink and purple burrs and make little baskets with them.

Finally, the last of the green beans had been snapped and were ready for Mama to put into jars. Lily ran to find several little pails. She handed one to Joseph and one to Dannie and they raced each other to the pasture to gather burrs.

The patch of burdocks behind the barn looked even prettier

than it had when Lily had last noticed them. There weren't very many green burrs any longer. Most of them had turned pretty shades of pink and purple.

Lily started to pick the burrs and drop them in her little pail. Joseph and Dannie filled their pails too. When a pail was full, Lily found a place in the cool, shady barn to dump them. After picking several more pails, Lily thought they had enough to start making the baskets.

Inside the cool of the barn, Lily sat on the floor and showed Joseph and Dannie how to stick the burrs together. She tried to help Dannie make a basket, but he didn't seem to care what he was making. He ended up sticking one burr to the next and made a big ball. Then Joseph added his burrs to Dannie's to make an even bigger ball.

Lily finally gave up trying to show those boys how to make a pretty basket. The boys started to kick the big burr ball around the barn. That was the problem with boys. They didn't know how to play quiet games.

Lily started to make a basket for herself. She made a little one just big enough to hold an egg. It was beautiful, so she decided to make a big basket. She started by making the sides. She sorted through the pile of burrs to choose only the prettiest purple burrs. Purple was her favorite color. She wanted this basket to be the prettiest one she had ever made. Once the sides were completed, she was ready to start making the bottom, but first she had to lift it and admire it a little more.

As she looked at it more closely, it looked like a crown. Dannie came over to see what she had made. "Would you like to wear a crown, Dannie? You can pretend you are a king."

Dannie liked that idea. He bowed his head while Lily placed the burdock crown carefully on the top of his head. Dannie stood up straight and pretended he was a very important king.

Now Joseph was interested. Dannie pretended he was even more important. The two boys started to get silly again, so Lily decided it would be best to get the crown off Dannie's head and finish making her basket.

Uh oh.

The burrs were stuck to Dannie's hair. Stuck like glue. Lily pulled harder. Dannie started to yelp. The crown wouldn't come off.

Lily forgot about trying to make a pretty basket as she painstakingly started trying to pick one burr at a time from Dannie's hair.

Dannie was crying now. Howling. This was a big mess and Lily was only making it worse. She had no idea what to do next. She would have to take Dannie back to the house and see if Mama could help him.

Dannie wailed like a siren all the way to the house. Mama must have heard him because she met them at the door to see what was wrong. Her eyes went wide when she saw the tangled mess of Dannie's hair. But Mama was a quick thinker. She led Dannie into the kitchen and told him to climb on the stool. She started to try to comb the burrs out.

Even Mama had trouble. The burrs wouldn't let go of Dannie's hair. Mama worked and worked while Dannie pitched a fit the whole time. Finally, Mama had enough. She decided there was nothing else that could be done but to cut the burrs out.

Lily watched as Mama snipped the burrs out of Dannie's hair. By the time Mama was finished, Dannie didn't look like a little Amish boy. He looked like a plucked chicken.

Mama stood back and squinted her eyes. It didn't look as if she liked what she was seeing. "Well, thankfully, hair grows back."

Lily had been lingering at the door and started to slip outside. But Mama saw her with the eyes in the back of her head. "And now, little lady. Maybe you can explain to me what happened."

"I was trying to make a pretty basket," Lily said. "I thought the sides looked like a crown and I set it on top of Dannie's head. I didn't think it would get stuck like that. I'm sorry."

"Lily, I know you're sorry when things go wrong," Mama said. "But it would be a good idea to think about what could happen before you do things instead of waiting to think until after something goes wrong."

The thing was, Mama made thinking sound so easy. She thought Lily just had to think *more*. But Lily knew thinking was so much harder than it sounded.

⤞⤝

One good thing about having a hallway bedroom was that Lily could hear everything going on downstairs. On this warm morning in late August, Lily heard Mama in the kitchen. Usually, Lily would wait until Mama called for her, but today, she jumped out of bed. She wanted to help Mama get breakfast ready.

It was the first day of school and Lily could hardly wait. Her new lunch pail hung on the wall peg by the kitchen door. It had been there for weeks, waiting and waiting for this day to arrive. Her newly made school clothes hung on several hooks on her hallway bedroom wall. A little paper bag had been filled with crayons, glue, scissors, and a pencil. Best of all, she had a brand new ink pen! She was in third grade now. Old enough to have a pen in school. She took it out every day to show to Joseph. He would need to wait a year for a pen. She liked to point that out to him. Finally, finally, the day had come when she could use all of these wonderful new school supplies.

Lily skipped down the stairs, happy and lighthearted. She said good morning to Mama and asked if she could pack the lunches.

Mama smiled. "Yes, you can. Let me slice the bread for you and you can start making the sandwiches."

Lily spread butter and salad dressing on the bread while Mama sliced a nice big garden tomato. Today, Joseph and Lily would have a delicious tomato sandwich.

Lily tucked a homemade cookie into each lunch box and closed the lids. She took a moment to admire her new lunch box. It was sunny yellow and the lid had a border of pink and purple flowers. In the center of the lid, a little girl sat on a grassy hill with purple flowers around her feet. Beside the girl were printed these words: "Herself the elf. Elf fun is for everyone."

Joseph trudged into the kitchen, rubbing sleep from his eyes. He wasn't nearly as excited about going back to school as Lily was. He hadn't climbed as many trees as he had wanted to and had gone fishing only once. He was sorry that summer was over. Slowly, much too slowly, he worked on his breakfast. His slow eating drove Lily crazy.

Lily couldn't wait until it was time to leave for school. As soon as the breakfast dishes were washed and dried, she hurried upstairs to change into her new blue dress. A few minutes later, she stood by the downstairs clock, waiting until it was time to start for school.

The clock didn't move. Maybe it was broken? Lily couldn't hold still any longer. "Mama, can we go now?"

Joseph groaned.

Mama looked at the clock and smiled. "I guess it doesn't hurt to get to school a little early on the first day."

Lily bolted to the door. "Come on, Joseph!" She paused at the door just long enough to toss a goodbye over her shoulder to Mama and Dannie.

It was a beautiful morning. Fall would be coming, but for now, it was warm enough to stay barefooted. Small finches sang and twittered as they gathered seeds from big thistles along the road. Lily liked to watch them flit from plant to plant. She wanted to hold one in her hands. She wished they would know that she would never hurt them. It would be fun to hold a bird.

Lily noticed a cluster of black-eyed Susans along the road. She handed her little brown paper bag filled with new school supplies to Joseph. "Hold this for me while I pick flowers for Teacher Rhoda."

Joseph patiently held Lily's bag while she waded through the tall grass. She gathered as many black-eyed Susans as she could carry. She knew Teacher Rhoda would be pleased.

"You'll have to carry my bag the rest of the way to school," Lily said.

Joseph wasn't very pleased that he had to carry two bags plus his lunch box. So Lily told him she would carry the bags if he carried the flowers and then he didn't seem to mind the bags.

At the schoolhouse, Teacher Rhoda filled a quart jar with water and Lily's black-eyed Susans, then she put it on her desk in the front of the room. She told Lily that her favorite flower was black-eyed Susan, and Lily couldn't stop grinning.

Little name tags sat on each desk. Lily walked up and down the rows until she found the desk with her name on it. She carefully unpacked her little bag of supplies. She wondered who might be sitting across the aisle from her this year. Beth, she hoped. She peeped at the name on the desk.

No. *Oh no.* Lily's heart sank. The name tag said "Aaron Yoder." Two years in a row! It was too much to bear. She wondered why Aaron had to sit there, of all places. If Lily were the teacher, she would have Aaron sit in the very front of the row where she could keep an eye on him.

If Lily had to sit next to him, she would not look at him. Not for the entire year. He would be invisible to her.

The Invisible Plan worked all morning long. She completely ignored Aaron. She didn't glance at him, not once. When it was lunchtime, Lily went to wash her hands and get her new lunch box. She sat at her desk and looked at the beautiful little girl elf on the lid.

Suddenly, a loud guffaw came across the aisle—from the invisible part. "Hey, Sam!" Aaron called to his friend. "Lily's lunch box says 'herself the elf.'" Aaron let out a few more guffaws. "She must be an elf! That's why she's so skinny."

Lily quickly opened her lunch box so the picture would be hidden.

"Elf, elf, elf," Aaron chanted.

Sam and a few more of his friends joined him with the elf chant until Teacher Rhoda stopped them with a stern look. "That's enough, boys."

The lunch box didn't seem quite so pretty to Lily since Aaron had made fun of it. It was spoiled for her.

When the children finished lunch and went outside to play, Aaron ran up to Lily and started to chant, "Elf, elf, elf. Lily is an elf." More of Aaron's friends gathered around Lily and chanted "elf." She felt surrounded by a pack of wild hyenas. She darted away and ran off to join the girls.

She thought she might hate Aaron Yoder. She had never hated anyone before, not even Mandy Mast in New York, and it wasn't a good feeling. She knew Mama and Papa would be sad to think she hated anyone. But still, she couldn't deny how she felt about him.

That evening, Lily stood in front of her mirror. Maybe Aaron Yoder was right. Maybe she was too skinny. Maybe that was why her eyes looked too big and she didn't have dimples in her cheeks like Beth did. She made up her mind to eat more. Then, Aaron Yoder would stop teasing her.

Lily went downstairs to help Mama prepare supper. Mama chatted pleasantly as she worked at the stove. Usually, Lily enjoyed talking about her day to Mama, but tonight she had too much on her mind. Mama noticed. "Is something bothering you, Lily?"

Out spilled the story about the lunch box and how the boys had called her "elf." She might have emphasized that Aaron Yoder started the teasing and that he was a horrible boy.

Mama studied the lunch box. "That wasn't very nice," she said. "But look at how pretty the little elf girl is. I wouldn't feel too bad about it."

"But he—I mean—they said I'm too skinny."

Mama was quiet for a long moment. "You are perfectly healthy and have nothing to be ashamed of. I think you look just right for our Lily."

That evening, Mama took a scouring pad and scrubbed the picture right off the lid of the lunch box. It was still a nice sunny yellow but the picture was gone. All because of Aaron Yoder.

CHAPTER
21

The Funeral

As the clock ticked toward eight, Papa stood and stretched. "It's bedtime for little lambs," he said. Bedtime always came too early. Lily looked forward to being a grown-up. The first thing on her to-do list was to stay up as late as she wanted to, maybe all night long.

As she headed to the stairs, a knock came on the door. Papa opened the door to Grandpa Miller. Lily paused on the stairs to hear why he had dropped by at this time of day. "Grandma passed away," she heard him say.

No, no, no! It couldn't be. Not Grandma. She burst into tears and ran to Papa's side. "There, there, don't cry like that," he said, patting her back. "We'll miss Grandma but she was ready to go. She had been wanting to go to heaven for a long time."

"It's not fair," Lily sobbed. "Why couldn't God take Great-Grandma instead of Grandma? She was so old!"

Papa and Grandpa exchanged an odd look. Grandpa crouched down so he was face-to-face with Lily. "He did, Lily," he said. "Great-Grandma passed away this evening. Your Grandma is doing just fine."

Relief flooded through Lily. She brushed the tears from her eyes. Grandma was fine! Lily brushed her teeth, changed into her nightgown, hopped into bed, and pulled the covers up beneath her chin. Downstairs, Lily could hear Papa and Mama talking at the kitchen table. Lily knew Mama was crying softly. She felt sorry for Mama—she had loved Great-Grandma the way Lily loved Grandma.

But now Lily wouldn't have to worry about shaking Great-Grandma's bony claw whenever she went to visit Grandma and Grandpa. She felt a tiny pinprick of guilt for feeling so happy about it. Death was supposed to be sad. As hard as she tried, as much as she scolded herself, she couldn't stop smiling.

Papa didn't go to work the next morning. Instead, the family dressed up in their somber black Sunday clothes and walked slowly up the road to Grandpa and Grandma's house.

Benches filled the living room, just like a church Sunday, even though it wasn't Sunday. It was Great-Grandma's viewing day. In the corner of the living room, a big black casket rested on several chairs. Papa and Mama led the way over to the casket and they all got a good long look at Great-Grandma. Every hair on Lily's head stood up. She thought Great-Grandma looked scarier dead than alive, if that was possible. She smelled funny too. Lily wanted to pinch her nose. She tried not to shudder as the family sat down on the benches.

Before long, people from their church started to arrive. Slowly, each person shook hands with the family and had a good long look at Great-Grandma, then they sat on the bench to visit for an hour or two. Paying respects, they called it. All day long.

Time passed—lots of it. Lily had never known a day could last that long. All of her friends were at school, having fun, while she was stuck here on a hard bench. Her back and legs grew tired. Joseph and Dannie fell sound asleep. Longingly, she gazed at the door. She would love to slip out the door and run, run, run. She didn't care where she ran as long as it was far, far away from Great-Grandma's smelly casket.

In the kitchen, the women had gathered to prepare large amounts of food to be served after the funeral in two days. For a while, Lily entertained herself by listening to Ida Kauffman order the women around and tell them what to do. She sounded just like Effie did during recess.

When Papa stood and said it was time to go home for chores, Lily had never felt so relieved. But the happy feeling quickly vanished when Papa said they would return tomorrow for more sitting and visiting.

Those two viewing days were the most miserable days of Lily's life. She was so happy when the day of the funeral arrived. School was canceled for the day, and that meant Beth would be at the funeral too. Lily was amazed that Great-Grandma had so many friends. Vans and buses arrived in Cloverdale, filled with people from other communities. Buggies rolled in from four neighboring church districts. There wasn't enough room at Grandpa's house for everyone, so the men put benches in the basement and in the barn. Even in the new sawmill. A minister would preach a sermon in each spot.

Only the families who were related to Great-Grandma stayed in the house. It felt like a church day, except that Papa and Mama sat next to each other, with Lily, Joseph, and Dannie beside them. Lily wished they could sit like this every Sunday.

Unlike church, there was no singing at the funeral. Only preaching. Long, long preaching. Just like church. When the minister was finally done, he sat down and everyone rose to file past the casket for one last look at Great-Grandma. Lily cringed. Not *again*.

Finally, it was time to fasten the lid to the casket. Several men carried it outside to a waiting buggy. Then a long line of buggies started for the graveyard, ever so slowly. The buggy horses weren't even allowed to walk fast or trot. Lily felt so sorry for Jim.

Mama stayed at the house instead of going to the grave-yard and told Lily she could stay too. The kitchen was bus-tling with noise as women hurried to prepare the meal for everyone to eat as soon as they returned from the graveyard. Ida Kauffman came into the living room to start setting up the benches to make tables. Her bespectacled gaze grazed over Lily and Mama. "I would think a person would like to be at her grandmother's burial."

Mama smiled in her sweet way. "Daniel thought it would be a good idea if I stayed here and rested instead of standing at the gravesite too long in the hot sun."

Ida Kauffman lifted a disapproving eyebrow, giving off a look that suggested she did not agree with Papa. Then she bustled off to the kitchen, peppering other women with in-structions about how to set things out properly.

An hour later, everyone returned from the graveyard. People were laughing and joking and visiting, as if it were just an ordinary church day and not a boring funeral day. How strange. Lily hoped she would never have to go to another funeral as long as she lived.

A Surprise for Lily

Before the sun rose on a Saturday morning, Papa woke Lily from a sound sleep. Lily blinked a few times, sure she was dreaming. "Wake up, Lily. Wake up." She saw Papa standing by her bed. "I need you to take your brothers to Grandma Miller's right away. Give her this note and stay there until I come to get you."

Lily scrambled out of bed and hurried to dress. She could hear Papa talking to Joseph and Dannie in the next room, trying to wake them up. He helped them get dressed and ushered them down to the kitchen where Lily was waiting. Papa handed them their thin coats and told them to be good while they were at Grandma and Grandpa Miller's. He helped them out the door, waved goodbye, and closed the door behind him.

Lily, Joseph, and Dannie stood on the porch, wondering what in the world was going on. Why didn't Papa want them to stay at home on a Saturday morning?

A wisp of a memory floated through Lily's mind. There had been another time, back in New York, when Papa had woken her up in the night and taken her to stay at Grandpa and Grandma Miller's. When she returned home, she discovered that God had brought baby Dannie to Mama. Maybe . . . maybe that's what was going on! God was bringing them another baby today. How exciting! And this time, Lily was sure He would bring a baby girl. He knew she needed a sister much, much more than she needed another brother. After all, God knew everything.

Lily tucked the note Papa had given to her into her pocket. She took Dannie's hand as they made their way down the porch steps and started walking slowly up the road. Faint pink streaks tinted the eastern sky. The gray dawn was starting to look a little more cheerful. A baby girl was getting delivered to their house today!

She tugged at Dannie's hand. "Let's walk a little faster."

When they arrived at Grandpa and Grandma Miller's, everything was quiet. Only the soft glow of an oil lamp showed faintly through the kitchen window. Lily knocked on the door. Knocked and knocked, a little louder each time. Finally, Grandpa opened the door. Grandma was behind him and invited them inside. She read the note that Lily handed to her. Lily hoped Grandma would tell her what was written on the note. Was God on His way with a baby sister? Oh, she hoped so! But Grandma didn't say a word. She simply folded the note and put it into her pocket. Her eyes twinkled, though. Lily took that as a good sign.

She started to think up names for her baby sister. Priscilla would be her first choice. Or maybe Isabel. She had never heard of Amish girls with those names, but she thought they were pretty names. She wondered what her baby sister would look like. She hoped she would have ringlets of red hair. Or maybe blonde. Either one. Just not mousy brown, like Lily's own hair.

And maybe she would have snapping green eyes. Big pink cheeks. Oh, wasn't it going to be wonderful to meet her baby sister today? This was the best day of Lily's life. The best one ever.

Grandma was already bustling around in the kitchen. Joseph and Dannie were hungry now and eagerly watched her break eggs into a bowl. "Looks like I will have helpers to make breakfast this morning," Grandma said.

Lily took Grandma's hint and started to set the table. It seemed strange to be at Grandma's home so early in the morning. Strange, but nice.

Lily handed Joseph and Dannie the silverware to place next to the plates. She went into the living room to find some of their favorite toys to play with while they waited for breakfast to get ready.

Grandpa came in from feeding his horse in the barn. He washed up at the sink, then sat in his creaky rocking chair. He took a piece of paper from the little table next to his chair and folded it into an airplane. The paper airplane sailed in the air and landed at Joseph's feet. Dannie's eyes were glued on the airplane as Joseph picked it up and sailed it back. He had never seen such a thing. "Looks like we need more than one airplane," Grandpa said.

Soon, the living room was filled with paper airplanes, soaring through the sky. Aunt Susie came downstairs and wanted to play too, so Grandpa made one more. They laughed and laughed, until Dannie sent his airplane sailing again. This time, it got stuck in Grandpa's thick, wavy white hair. Grandpa pretended he had been hurt and he slid off the rocking chair and onto the floor, as if he were dead. As Dannie rushed to his side, Grandpa let out a roar and everyone squealed in laughter. They helped Grandpa get to his feet just as Grandma came into the room, shaking her head at the loud noises. She put her hands on her hips and said, "Breakfast is ready, if you think you can all act your age."

Grandpa reached for his little black prayer book on the table as everyone found a place to kneel. Lily loved to listen to Grandpa's deep, rumbling voice as he read the prayer out loud. She tried not to think about that airplane stuck in his hair—but it was so funny! Each time she thought of it, she felt a giggle start in her belly. Oh, and wouldn't it be awful if she burst out giggling in the middle of Grandpa's solemn prayer? She bit her lip to keep from laughing.

After breakfast, Uncle Jacob walked up the driveway and Grandpa went outside to join him. They had a lot of work to do in the sawmill, and Lily knew she wouldn't see Grandpa until the end of the day. He was firm about that rule: no grandchildren were allowed near the sawmill. Lily knew that rule was given because of Joseph and Dannie. They were curious boys. Knowing them, they would try to saw wood when Grandpa was busy and end up cutting off their little fingers. Too dangerous.

Lily helped Grandma and Aunt Susie with Saturday cleaning while Joseph and Dannie played with wooden blocks and toy animals. Lily thought the boys should help too. Grandma seemed to think they would be a bigger help by playing instead of getting in her way while she worked. That made no sense to Lily. No sense at all.

By noon, the cleaning was done. Grandma said that Lily and Aunt Susie could have the rest of the day to do whatever they wanted to do—as long as they stayed away from the sawmill. Aunt Susie ran to find coloring books and dolls. Lily glanced at the clock. Why hadn't Papa come back by now? Maybe God was running behind on His delivery schedule today. After all, heaven was far, far away.

It was late afternoon before Papa drove up the driveway. Lily rushed out the door to meet him as he climbed out of the buggy and hitched Jim's reins to the rack. She had to know! "Did God bring us another baby?"

Papa was grinning from ear to ear. "He sure did!"

"A girl baby?" Lily just had to know.

"No. Another little boy. We named him Paul."

Lily was shocked. Thoroughly shocked. She had been con-fident that God would bring them a baby girl. He brought baby girls to a lot of other people. Why not to them? Disap-pointment covered her like a heavy blanket.

Papa didn't notice. He was already up the porch stairs, talking to Grandma. Joseph and Dannie were getting their coats on. She knew she shouldn't be so sad about this new baby brother. Her friend Beth would love to have a baby in her family—even if it was a boy.

Maybe having a baby brother wouldn't be so bad. Still, Lily had prayed for a baby sister. But maybe God was out of baby girls and that's why He didn't bring them a girl. Maybe, if she prayed hard enough, God would save a baby girl for her. With that thought, Lily cheered up. She hurried to find her bonnet and coat. She might as well go home and see the new baby.

Papa asked Grandma if she would come back with them to stay with Mama for a little while. He was going to pick up a girl who would help Mama for several weeks.

Another worry. What if the helper turned out to be like the helper who came after Dannie had been delivered? Lily hadn't thought about cross Frieda Troyer in a long, long time. What if the helper *was* Frieda Troyer, all the way from New York? Oh, this was terrible news to Lily. Two disappointments in one day. It was too much to bear.

Grandma plucked her bonnet and shawl off the wall peg and soon they were on their way. When they reached home, Papa tied Jim to the hitching rack and went inside with them. Everyone went to the bedroom where Mama was lying in bed. She looked very tired and very happy. Right beside her was a little bundle, wrapped in a blanket. Lily could see some wispy black hair and wrinkled red skin.

No. *Oh no.* Not another ugly baby!

Papa picked the baby up and placed him in Lily's arms. He was the ugliest baby she had ever seen—even uglier than Dannie had been. Red and wrinkled and blotchy. And he was squalling. He was a squalling, ugly baby. She quickly handed the baby back to Papa and ran upstairs to her room. She flopped on her bed and started to cry. It wasn't fair!

She had wanted a beautiful little baby girl with long red ringlets—not a red, wrinkled baby boy with black wispy hair. And Papa and Mama gave the ugly baby a horrible name. What kind of name was that for a baby? And he was so especially ugly!

Lily heard Papa leave in the buggy. She sat up and peeped out the window. She saw that Joseph and Dannie were going with Papa to get the helper.

Joseph and Dannie were lucky to be boys. They didn't mind that the baby wasn't a girl. They didn't care what his name was or what he looked like. And on top of that, they got to go on an errand with Papa and meet the new helper before Lily did.

Lily buried her face in her pillow, weeping. The day had

started out so nicely, so filled with hope, and it had ended so badly. Every hope was dashed. She felt a gentle touch on her shoulder. She lifted her head and saw Grandma by her bed.

Gently, Grandma asked, "Lily, what's wrong?"

Lily wiped away her tears and sat up to face Grandma. "I never wanted a baby brother!" she blurted out. Soon, everything else poured out too. "And he's ugly! Paul is a terrible name for a baby. I wanted a baby sister . . . and instead, I have an ugly baby brother with a horrible name." Was it asking so much to have one of these little babies be a girl? That was the worst disappointment of all.

Grandma listened patiently. She didn't seem to be shocked or horrified by what Lily confessed. She even smiled. "All newborn babies look a little funny. He'll start looking better in a few days. And you'll learn to like the name Paul. It's a good name for a little boy. He's going to need you and love you in a special way, you know. You're the only sister he has." Grandma rose to her feet. "Why don't you go wash your face and then come downstairs and help me start supper?"

Lily went into the bathroom and washed her face. She hoped Grandma was right—that Paul would stop being so ugly soon. She was terribly disappointed that he wasn't a girl, but maybe having a baby in the house would be fun. It was nice to think that Paul might need her and love her in a special way. She hadn't thought about the fact that she was Paul's only sister. Dannie and Joseph's too, but they needed reminding of that. Like she often did, Grandma turned everything around. Lily dried off her face and hurried to the kitchen.

Slippery Eggs

*L*ily woke up early, confused. Why was she on the floor instead of in her nice warm bed? Then she remembered. Yesterday, Mama had a baby. Carrie Kauffman had moved in to be Mama's helper for several weeks. She was sharing Lily's hallway bedroom. In fact, she was sleeping in Lily's bed. That's why Lily was on the floor in a nest bed.

Lily felt worried about having Effie Kauffman's older cousin stay with them. She didn't know Carrie very well and she hoped she would be much nicer than Effie. She hoped she would be less nosy and tattletale-ish than her aunt Ida. Otherwise, it was going to be a very long six weeks.

A horrible alarm went off on the dresser next to Lily's bed. Carrie jumped up to shut off the alarm clock. That, Lily decided, was a bad sign. The first bad sign of Carrie Kauffman. Lily did not like having an alarm clock in her bedroom. It was hard enough to have two noisy brothers right through the door. She would prefer to have Papa or Mama wake her up in their gentle way instead of a shrieking alarm.

Lily pretended to be asleep while Carrie dressed and went downstairs. She thought about staying asleep as long as she could, but then she changed her mind. She quickly got up and slipped into her everyday dress. She was going to go see what Carrie was up to. After Dannie had been born, Frieda Troyer came, and she rearranged everything in Mama's kitchen. That was no help at all. After Frieda Troyer left, Mama and Lily put everything back in its place.

When Lily came into the kitchen, she saw Carrie try to poke at the last few red embers in the bottom of the stove to coax them to burn. Lily quickly ran to the basement and brought an armful of kindling for her. Maybe, Lily reasoned, if she helped with extra chores, then Carrie could go home sooner.

Carrie thanked Lily as she took the kindling from her and added it to the stove. She blew gently until a little flame started growing, then closed the stove lid. "Lily, what would you like for breakfast this morning?"

"Mama makes porridge every morning," Lily said. "And everyone has one egg except for Papa. He gets three eggs."

Lily got the eggs from the pantry and showed Carrie where to find the pot to make the porridge. She set the table as Carrie stirred the porridge. Lily kept one eye on her, just in case she was thinking about rearranging cupboards. So far, so good.

Soon, Lily heard the basement door creak open. Papa was coming in from doing chores in the barn. She ran down the basement stairs to meet him. "Good morning, early bird," Papa said in his cheerful way. He sat down to pull off his boots. "What made you get up so early?"

"I got up to make sure Carrie doesn't try to rearrange Mama's kitchen."

171

Papa pulled one boot off. He glanced at Lily. "While Carrie is here, I want you to be kind and polite to her. Even if she does things a little differently than the way we're used to." He pulled the other boot off. "Okay?"

Lily nodded. She didn't think that was the best plan, but she would try to be quiet even if Carrie did things wrong. For Papa's sake. Then she brightened. If she were extra nice, then maybe Carrie would go home and tell Effie what a wonderful girl Lily was. Then, maybe Effie would be nicer to Lily in school. It was worth a try.

Papa went up the stairs with the pail of Pansy's fresh sweet milk. Lily followed behind him. He set the pail on the rug inside the door. "Go get a jar and show Carrie how to strain the milk."

As Lily went back down the basement stairs, she pondered how confusing grown-ups could be. Papa had just told her not to worry about how Carrie did the chores. Next thing, he told Lily to teach Carrie how to strain the milk.

After the milk was strained and safely stored in the refrigerator, Carrie started to prepare eggs. Lily watched as she broke them directly into the frying pan. She had to blink a few times as she saw Carrie pour a glass of water into the pan and cover them up with a lid. This was another bad sign. Sign #2. Mama never made eggs like that.

When the eggs were ready, everybody sat at the table to eat. All but Mama. Meals were delivered to her in bed. Papa bowed his head to ask a silent blessing. Before Papa raised his head to signal the end of the prayer, Lily quietly added, "Dear God, please help me eat those eggs."

Papa reached for the platter of eggs and slid three onto his plate. He passed the platter to Lily. She felt her stomach do a flip-flop. The eggs didn't look like anything she wanted to eat. The slightest movement of the platter made them jiggle all over. They were slippery eggs. She chose the least jiggly egg and let it slip onto her plate. She dipped a piece of bread into the yolk and ate it. Then she cut bravely into the egg white. It was still runny. Lily tried to keep from gagging, right there at the table. She pushed the jiggly egg to the very side of her plate and hoped Papa wouldn't notice it. Even porridge sounded better than this slimy, yucky egg, and she hated porridge.

As soon as breakfast was over and Carrie's attention turned to filling the sink with soapy water, Lily quietly scraped her leftover egg into the slop pail. The cats could eat that awful thing.

Carrie was humming to herself as she washed dishes. Maybe Carrie would wash the dishes while she was here. As long as Carrie didn't ask Lily to help, it wouldn't be wrong not to offer. Besides, Carrie seemed to enjoy washing dishes. Aunt Susie loved to wash dishes. Maybe Lily was doing a nice thing for Carrie—letting her do all the dishes.

This was a good sign. The first good sign.

❧⚬❧

On Monday morning, Lily was in a hurry to rush through the breakfast of slimy eggs. She couldn't wait to get to school and tell everyone they had a new baby at their house. She decided she wouldn't tell her friends that baby Paul was so ugly. They didn't need to know. In time, Grandma Miller had said, his looks might improve. Lily hoped so. After two days, Paul was still the ugliest baby she had ever seen.

Lily changed into her school clothes and ran down the stairs to get her lunch box. Carrie had not packed their lunches. Bad sign #3. Quickly, Lily spread some butter and jam on several pieces of bread and filled a bowl with canned pears. She put everything in their lunch boxes and shut the lids. There was no time to waste. Not today.

By the time Lily and Joseph arrived at school, most of the other children were already there. Effie was in a corner of the schoolroom, surrounded by the other third grade girls. Lily quickly hung her bonnet on a hook and went to join them. She could hardly wait! It wasn't every day that she had exciting news. In fact, today was the first time ever.

Beth smiled as Lily joined the circle. "I'm so happy to hear about your new baby."

Lily stopped abruptly. Her excitement popped like a balloon. "But . . . how did you know?"

"Effie told us," Beth said.

Effie. Since her cousin Carrie was the Lapps' helper, Effie would have found out about the baby. And if Effie had news to tell, she would tell it. Another reason why having Carrie Kauffman as the helper was not a good idea. Bad sign #4.

"Can I stop in on the way home from school and see the baby?" Beth said.

"Oh yes!" Lily said. At least she could be the one to show the baby to Beth first. Effie couldn't do that.

After school that day, Beth and Lily walked home together. Lily quickly ran to Mama's bedroom. "Beth is here and would like to see the baby."

Mama smiled. She still looked tired. "Tell her she can come in."

Lily motioned to Beth. She quietly came into the bedroom. Mama handed baby Paul to her. Lily cringed. With all the excitement, she had forgotten to warn Beth that Paul was red and wrinkly and ugly. But Beth didn't seem to notice. Her eyes were circles of astonishment as she cradled him in her arms. "Look at his tiny nose and mouth," she said softly. "And his cute little hands and his soft hair."

Lily took a closer look. If you didn't pay any attention to how red and blotchy his face was, his nose and mouth were kind of sweet looking. And his tiny hands were cute, even though they were wrinkled and had creases. She had never even noticed how soft his hair was, only thin and wispy.

Carefully, Beth handed Paul back to Mama as if she were holding spun sugar. "Thank you for letting me hold him. I've never held a newborn baby before."

After Beth went home, Lily looked more closely at baby Paul. She thought his looks might have improved since this morning. She couldn't call him cute, but he wasn't quite as ugly.

Carrie Kauffman wasn't too bad a helper, even if Effie was her cousin. Carrie liked to sing. She taught Lily a new song and helped her sing it every evening. And she washed all the dishes. Every dish! After all the evening work was done, Carrie would often play a game with Joseph and Dannie and Lily.

All in all, there was only one thing Carrie did wrong, but it was a doozy. Every single morning she served those slimy eggs. Lily wondered how Papa could possibly eat three of them every morning. It made her gag just to think about it.

One morning, as Lily pushed the runny egg white to the side of her plate, Papa happened to see her do it. "Eat your egg, Lily."

Lily stared at the egg miserably. How could she eat this awful egg? She cut into it tiny pieces, but as thin, watery egg ran along her plate, she could feel the pinprick of tears in her eyes. She couldn't make herself take a bite of those awful things! From somewhere deep inside of her burst out, "They're slimy and gross!"

Oh no. Did she really say that?

Joseph and Dannie stopped eating and looked at her. Carrie's face went beet red. Papa cleared his throat. "That will be enough, Lily. If you don't want your egg you can go and get ready for school."

Lily went upstairs to change her clothes. She felt sorry that she hurt Carrie's feelings. What if Carrie went home and told Effie about Lily's outburst? She would be teased about it for weeks. She could hear Effie's squeaky voice, chanting: "Miss Slimy Eggs!" She could only imagine what Aaron Yoder would do with that particular bit of information.

The next morning, the eggs looked different. Carrie had fried them until they were hard. Practically burnt. Lily didn't mind. She ate all of her egg. Every bite.

That evening, after Carrie had fallen asleep, Lily was wide awake. She went downstairs to get a drink of water. As she passed Papa and Mama's bedroom door, she heard Papa mention Lily's name. She tried not to listen, she knew it was wrong, but she just couldn't help herself. "I wish Lily would have had her outburst on the very first morning," Papa was saying to Mama. "It would have saved us from eating a lot of awful eggs." She heard them gently chuckling with each other.

Lily tiptoed to the kitchen to get her drink of water. So, Papa and Mama hadn't liked those eggs either. Her feet felt light as she skipped up the stairs to go to bed.

The Quiz

Friday afternoons were the best part of the week. Teacher Rhoda often saved a surprise for the children—a game or an art project. On this rainy Friday, she stood in front of the classroom and smiled. "We will be doing something a little different today," she said. "I have a pile of paper here in front of me. Each one is filled with the same set of instructions. I will place one upside down on everyone's desk from third grade on up. I don't want you to peek at them until I say, 'Go.' The pupil who follows the instructions the best will get a little prize."

Lily glanced over at Joseph and the other first and second graders. They didn't read well enough to take part in an important quiz like this one. She was sorry for them. She remembered how it felt to be their age. Too little for anything fun.

Lily was glad she was in third grade. She liked to win prizes and wondered what today's prize might be. She hoped it would be several stickers or maybe even a pretty eraser. In her mind, she reviewed the hint Teacher Rhoda had given them—to follow the instructions carefully. This would be easy. She was a careful instruction follower.

Teacher Rhoda walked from desk to desk, laying a sheet of paper facedown on each child's desk. Lily stared at the piece of paper on her desk. She wished she could start right away. When the last piece of paper had been handed out, Teacher Rhoda returned to her desk. The children held their pencils up in the air, ready and waiting. Teacher Rhoda looked around the room, making sure everyone was ready. "Go!"

How exciting! The race was off and running. Lily quickly flipped her sheet over and skimmed the line at the top of the page: *Read all the instructions before you begin.*

#1 *Write your name in cursive at the top of the paper.*

Lily quickly wrote her name in cursive at the top of the paper. Then she looked at the next instruction.

#2 *Draw a picture of a barn on the back of this paper.*

She flipped her paper over and drew a barn. It didn't look very pretty, but the instructions didn't say anything about it looking pretty and she wanted to get it done fast. She was going to win that prize.

#3 *Tear the bottom right-hand corner off your paper.*

Lily quickly tore a little piece off. She could hear the sound of paper getting torn from all across the schoolroom. She wondered if Aaron Yoder would know enough to tear the right corner instead of the left one. She didn't think he was very bright. She glanced at him and was surprised to see that he wasn't working on the paper. He leaned back in his chair, hands behind his head, studying the raindrops that pelted the window, as if he had all the time in the world. He would never get the quiz done in time if he didn't start soon. Wasn't that just like Aaron Yoder not to care what Teacher Rhoda told him to do?

Lily turned her attention back to her sheet of paper.

#4 Fold your paper into an airplane.

She quickly folded it. Grandpa Miller had taught her how to make paper airplanes. This was fun. Then she unfolded it again to see what was next.

#5 Write your name backwards.

The next few instructions were for some addition and subtraction problems. They tripped Lily up and slowed her down. She had to erase and do them over a few times.

#8 Go get your hat or bonnet and place it on your head. Then sit at your desk.

A flurry began with a hiss of whispers as the children ran to get their hats and bonnets. Lily sat back down at her desk, wanting to burst out laughing. Everyone looked so funny with a hat or bonnet on, inside! That never happened.

Then she noticed Aaron Yoder. He was bareheaded, still at his desk, at his ease. On his face was a goofy grin.

There were only a few instructions left to be done. Aaron would never get the paper done in time. It would serve him right not to get a prize.

Lily came to the last instruction and her heart sank to her toes.

#10 Now that you have read all the instructions, do only #1.

Suddenly, she felt ridiculous, sitting there in her bonnet. Teacher Rhoda could see that she had not followed instructions. It gave her some small comfort that no one else had followed them, either. No one except for . . . Aaron Yoder.

Teacher Rhoda asked Aaron to come forward. She opened her desk and pulled out a little wooden puzzle game. "Congratulations, Aaron," she said as she handed it to him. "You are the only one who followed instructions."

Not fair! This was the best prize Teacher Rhoda had ever given out. It wasn't fair that Aaron Yoder won it. He walked back to his desk with a smug look on his face. He strutted, as proud as a peacock.

The problem, Lily thought, was that winning this prize would only make Aaron all the more insufferable. So not fair.

One Saturday afternoon, Papa bought a baby calf from a neighbor. He led it into an empty stall in the barn. Lily and Dannie watched the small calf through the slats of the stall. Lily had seen plenty of calves, but never one like this one. It was a lovely golden brown, covered with white speckles. Papa said the farmer needed to get rid of it because it wasn't a girl calf. Lily understood the importance of girls—hadn't she been wanting a sister for years and years?—but she felt sorry that the calf wasn't wanted just because it was a boy. Papa and Mama would never get rid of baby Paul, even if they secretly wanted a baby girl. She was pleased that Papa rescued the calf. Papa was kind like that.

"What will we name it?" Lily said.

"We'll have to discuss different ideas," Papa said.

Dannie put his hand through the wooden slat to pat the calf's little head. "Let's call it Pretzel."

"Pretzel?" Papa said. He was trying not to smile. "Why would you want to call him Pretzel?"

"Because he's the color of a pretzel and all the white specks look like salt," Dannie said.

Papa's face broke into a broad smile. "That sounds like a very good reason. Pretzel it is."

Lily could think of so many better suggestions: Speckles. Spots. Goldie. But now the calf would be stuck with Pretzel for a name. She sighed. This was the problem with letting little boys name things. They came up with ridiculous names.

Each evening, Papa milked Pansy and poured the milk into a pail. He added some of her milk to Pretzel's pail to feed him. He set Pansy's pail down and held the pail for Pretzel. Lily watched as Pretzel slurped his mixed milk noisily out of his pail. His tail was twitching happily the whole time. It looked like fun. "Can I hold the pail for Pretzel?"

Papa let Lily hold the pail. "Make sure you hold it tight. When the pail is almost empty, calves like to bump their heads against it hard. They think it will make more milk appear."

Lily held the pail firmly with both hands. The milk disappeared as Pretzel slurped. He had almost buried his entire nose in the milk. Lily wondered how he could breathe like that. Papa, satisfied that Lily was holding the pail tightly, went to spread straw in Jim's stall.

181

Finally, there was only a little bit of milk left. Lily tipped the pail to help the calf get to it. Pretzel bumped the pail with his head as hard as he could. Lily went flying backwards and landed with a splash right in the pail of Pansy's milk that was waiting to be taken into the house.

Papa heard the *kersplash!* and stopped to see what had happened. He helped Lily stand up and looked her over to make sure she wasn't hurt. Then, he started laughing. He laughed so hard that he had tears running down his cheeks. Lily didn't think it was very funny. Her dress was soaking wet. Warm, sticky milk was running down her legs, making a puddle by her feet.

Papa wiped his face with his hands. "I'll clean up here. Run into the house and get changed."

Lily ran into the house, her long wet skirt slapping at her legs. Lily wondered how one little calf could be so strong. Tomorrow she would let Papa hold the pail to feed Pretzel. She was done with boy calves.

Papa and the Lightning Rods

Saturday was a dry, sunny, chilly day. Papa came in from the barn and found Mama in the kitchen. "I think I'll try climbing up on the roof and take those lightning rods off the peak before we get a serious snowstorm."

Lily was disappointed. "Why can't they stay on the roof? They aren't in anybody's way." She had always thought those lightning rods were the only pretty thing on their ugly olive green house. The long rods stuck up high in the sky with funny green balls on the top. She imagined that they looked like a steeple on an English church house. Maybe God would think their home was an extra special place.

"They might not be in our way," Papa said. "But we trust in God to protect us during thunderstorms, not in lightning rods. So we need to take them down."

After lunch, Papa went to get his ladder. He propped it outside the kitchen wall and climbed up on the roof. Lily watched the ladder disappear as Papa pulled it up onto the roof. She listened to his footsteps as he walked across the roof and propped the ladder against the attic roof. The ladder made funny creaking noises as he climbed. Then there was silence.

Lily helped Mama wash and dry the lunch dishes. Mama fixed a bowl of lukewarm water and sprinkled some baking soda into it. She swished it around with her hand until all the baking soda was dissolved. She stuck her elbow into the water. Mama said if she couldn't feel the water with her elbow, then she knew it was just the right temperature for baby Paul's bath.

Mama spread out a blanket on the countertop and put a towel on top of that. She laid Paul on it while she undressed him for his bath. Lily pushed the sleeve on her dress up as far as she could and stuck her elbow into the water to test it. How strange! Her elbow was wet, but she couldn't feel the water.

Mama carefully placed baby Paul into the water. He kicked and wiggled and waved his little starfish fingers. He liked taking baths. It was one of the few times of the day that Paul didn't cry. He was a wailer, especially in the evening. His face would turn bright red and he would stiffen his little body and let out window-rattling yells. Lily and Joseph and Dannie would run upstairs whenever the baby pitched his fits.

But bath time was a nice time with baby Paul. Mama took time to make sure he was clean and sweet smelling.

Suddenly, there was a loud thump on the roof, then a strange sliding, scraping sound. Lily looked out the window to see Papa fall to the ground.

Then there was silence. Mama and Lily stood frozen for a moment that felt far longer.

184

Mama wrapped the baby in his blanket and handed him to Lily. "Sit in the rocking chair with him until I come back," she said. Her voice sounded strange to Lily: firm but frightened.

Lily wished she could run out to Papa and see if he was hurt. She hoped baby Paul wouldn't start his hollering. She could hear Mama's voice through the window, but she didn't hear Papa's voice answer back.

Not much later, the door opened and in walked Papa, holding onto Mama. Papa's face looked pale and tight. "I'll be fine, Lily," he said. "I think I'll just go lie down for a little while." Mama helped him to their bedroom and onto the bed. Papa never went to bed in the middle of the day.

When Mama came back to the kitchen, she took Paul from Lily and started to dress him. Her face looked worried, which made Lily feel worried too. What if Papa was hurt more than he had wanted her to know? Papa never complained. Never.

When it was time to do chores, Mama asked Lily to stay in the house and keep an eye on baby Paul while she milked Pansy and the goats. It worried Lily even more that Papa stayed in bed instead of doing the chores. Maybe tomorrow, he would be all better.

But the next day, Papa still stayed in bed. And the next, and the next. He didn't go to his carpentry job. The only time he got out of bed was when Grandpa Miller came by to take him to the doctor. They were gone a very long time, and when Papa came back, his face looked white and strained. The outing had exhausted him. Grandpa spoke quietly to Mama about what the doctor had said. Lily tried to eavesdrop, but she couldn't make out what Grandpa was saying. Each day, she could feel the worry in the house spike up a notch. What if Papa never got better?

Mama looked tired. She had to do Papa's chores on top of her daily chores. Grandpa Miller and Uncle Jacob stopped by as often as they could to help, but they couldn't come every day. Lily and Joseph did all they could, but much of the work was too difficult for them. Mama had to milk Pansy and the nanny goats. Twice a day, Mama came in from the barn and told Papa they should sell those goats.

Lily couldn't help but think that Papa wouldn't have gotten hurt if they had stayed in New York. Their house at Singing Tree Farm didn't have lightning rods.

But if Papa had ever gotten hurt at Singing Tree Farm, the church in New York would have helped them more than this church did. She was sure of it. Sometimes, Lily thought that everybody in this church was as snooty as Effie Kauffman. Everybody except for Beth. And Malinda. And Teacher Rhoda. And Marvin Yoder. Otherwise, everything and everybody was better in New York. They should never have left. She made the mistake of complaining to Grandma Miller and was silenced with a look. Grandma didn't tolerate any whining.

One afternoon, Lily and Joseph came home from school and there was Papa, in Mama's rocking chair, rocking baby Paul by the kitchen stove. He was out of bed, at last! Little by little, day by day, he was able to do more and more. He did some exercises that the doctor had given to him. Mama would warm towels in the oven and wrap them around Papa's back. He had a funny limp when he walked. Lily thought Papa walked like Great-Grandma used to walk, before she had her stroke.

But Lily could see that Papa was feeling much better. Once, she even heard him whistle. She loved Papa's whistle. To Lily it meant all was well.

One evening, just as the family sat down to the supper table, they were interrupted by a knock at the door. Slowly and carefully, Papa eased out of his chair to see who was at the door. She craned her neck to see and saw a stranger. The man's voice was so low and quiet that Lily couldn't hear what he was saying.

When he left, Papa came back to the table with a broad grin on his face. "I don't think you could ever guess what that was all about." He couldn't stop grinning.

"Well, tell us, Daniel," Mama said as she spooned some peas onto Dannie's plate.

Papa took his time answering. "I don't know the man, never even heard of him before. He had never heard of us either." He buttered some bread, still smiling.

Now Joseph, who never stopped eating, suspended his fork in the air. "What did he want, Papa?" He shoveled the forkful of food in his mouth.

They were all watching Papa now. Even baby Paul was cooing in his bassinet. Something good had just happened and they couldn't tell what.

"When I answered the door to the man, he told me that he had a hip replacement this summer and wasn't able to walk up and down his basement stairs to fire his coal furnace this winter. He said he installed an electric furnace so he has heat, but . . ." Papa stopped to take a bite of bread.

Everyone was on the edge of their seat, waiting for Papa to finish the story.

"He said he has four tons of coal in his basement that he can't use. He said he was driving down the road and something told him that the people in the green house could use that coal. So he stopped and offered it to us."

Mama's eyes went wide. "But, Daniel, we don't have any extra—"

Papa held up his hand. Another smile lit his face and his blue eyes sparkled. "I asked him how much he wants for it, and he said he didn't want a thing. If we would remove the coal and clean his basement, that's all the pay he wanted. He gave me his name and address and said to pick it up whenever I was ready."

Lily was surprised to see Mama start to cry. "Oh, Daniel," Mama said in a whisper. "We really can trust God to supply all our needs. Here I was worried that we couldn't afford to buy coal since you haven't been able to work these past few weeks. I should never have worried."

Lily hadn't even thought that there might be money worries because of Papa's back injury. She had never worried about money before. It was a new thought for her, but then she noticed Mama's happy tears. God did supply coal for them, just in time.

It wasn't long before Papa's back had improved enough to hitch Jim to the spring wagon. He hauled load after load of coal into the wagon, brought it home, and shoveled it into the coal bin.

When the last load of coal had been unloaded, Lily knew she had never seen a pile of coal quite that big. Even though the lightning rods were gone from the rooftop, Lily decided that this olive green house wasn't so ugly after all. Maybe God did think their house was extra special since He sent such a kind and generous stranger to their door. The proof was in the pile of coal.

The very next morning, big fluffy snowflakes started to swirl through the sky and drift gently to the ground as Lily and Joseph walked to school. Winter was coming, but Papa was well again, and they would all be warm until spring.

Lily's Verses

After each student had finished reciting the Bible verse they had memorized for the week, Teacher Rhoda would give them a new verse to memorize. The next week, they would recite and get a new one. It was part of the rhythm of each week and Lily loved it.

"Next week's verse will be Proverbs 24:17," Teacher Rhoda said.

Lily wrote the reference on a piece of paper and slipped it into her dress pocket. Tonight, after supper, Mama would help her find it in Papa's big German and English Bible.

But Teacher Rhoda had more to say. "And I decided to have everyone choose a poem to memorize too. It can be any kind of poem you'd like to choose: funny, sad, happy, thoughtful. It must have at least eight lines. You will have three weeks to get your poem memorized. At the end of those three weeks,

I will have a special prize for everyone who recites their poem without forgetting a single word."

This, Lily thought, would be easy. She loved to memorize. She was already imagining how pleased Teacher Rhoda would be as Lily went to her desk to claim her prize.

Later that evening, Mama helped Lily find the verse in Proverbs to copy: "*Rejoice not when thine enemy falleth, and let not thine heart be glad when he stumbleth.*"

"That's a very good verse," Mama said. "We should copy it off and hang it on the wall above the table so we can see it every day."

"May I do it?" Lily asked.

Mama smiled, nodding. "I'll get a piece of paper and a marker for you."

Lily spread the paper out on the table in front of her. She wrote out the verse in her best handwriting. When she was done, she felt she had done a very nice job with it. She found several tacks in the desk drawer, then stood on the table and tacked her paper on the wall.

She stood back and admired her verse. Mostly, her handwriting. It wouldn't take long for all of them to memorize that verse. She wondered if Mama might let her copy more verses. Each week, she could post a new verse.

Mama liked that idea, so Lily sat at the table and read more verses in the book of Proverbs. Each verse seemed to stand alone. She could pluck a verse out and write it down. In other books of the Bible, verses were all connected to each other. She found several more verses that she liked. She copied them down carefully and put them in a safe place where the paper wouldn't get wrinkled by little brothers before she was ready to tack one on the wall next Friday.

On Monday morning, the third grade girls met in a corner

at the back of the schoolhouse to talk before the bell rang. "What poem did you choose to memorize?" Beth asked.

Poem? The poem! Lily had completely forgotten! She had been so excited about choosing Bible verses to hang on the kitchen wall that she forgot all about the poem. She would have to tell Mama she needed a poem as soon as she got home from school today.

"I already have most of my poem memorized," Effie said.

"What is it about?" Beth asked.

"About Jesus, of course," Effie said, as if everybody should know that. "Those are the only kinds of poems that we should memorize."

Effie's father was one of the ministers for the church. She liked to remind everyone of that fact.

"My poem is about two little kittens," Beth said.

"Mine is about trees and wind," Malinda piped up. Her eyes darted to Effie, anxious, hoping for approval.

Effie frowned at the girls. "You have to find one about Jesus. You don't want Jesus to think that you like kittens or trees and wind more than Him."

Beth rolled her eyes, but Malinda, naturally, looked worried. She often looked worried. Beth didn't seem to care if Effie approved of the poems they had chosen to memorize. Lily hoped Mama would find her a poem that would have kittens or trees in it. A little part of her was secretly thrilled that Beth wasn't listening to or obeying Effie's instructions. For once! Effie thought she was the boss of everyone.

Before bedtime, Lily told Mama that she needed to find a poem to memorize. Mama was quiet for a moment, thinking hard. Then, right out of the blue, like she had learned it last week, she rattled off,

I know that cows have little cows
And dogs have little dogs,
That pussy cats have little cats
And frogs have little frogs
I know that birds have little birds
And fish have little fishes
So why can't sinks have little sinks
Instead of dirty dishes?

Lily clapped her hands. "Oh, I like that! Would you write it down on a piece of paper so that I can memorize it?" She was sure no one would have a poem like that. It was perfect, just perfect. Lily did not like washing dishes. It seemed as if that was all she ever did! She thought that little sinks would be so much better than stacks of dirty dishes.

Early the next morning, Lily showed her poem to Beth, Malinda, and Effie. Beth and Malinda read it and laughed and laughed. They thought a big sink filled with little sinks would be better than a big sink filled with big dirty dishes. Washing dishes wasn't their favorite chore either.

Effie's forehead scrunched together in a big, scolding frown.

❧

It was Friday evening. Lily looked through her stack of verses she had copied from Proverbs and chose a new one to tack to the wall. Usually, Lily showed Mama first, but it had been a long day with baby Paul. He had cried and cried all day. He seemed to cry all the time. Mama was in her room, trying to rock baby Paul to sleep, and Lily knew she shouldn't disturb them.

Lily read the verse a few more times before she tacked it up to the wall. It was a good one. And her handwriting, she noticed, was quite lovely. Clear and slanted cursive. It was too bad that Joseph was too little to read cursive. Maybe next year.

On Saturday afternoon, Effie's mother stopped by with pumpkin muffins. Ever since baby Paul was born, the Lapp family seemed to see rather a lot of Ida Kauffman, but there was a lot of her to see. To Lily, Ida Kauffman had a way about her that felt like the sun slid behind a cloud. Birds stopped chirping. Dogs stopped barking. Cows stopped mooing.

Ida said she wanted to see the new baby, but as soon as she walked into the kitchen, her sparse eyebrows shot up at the sound of baby Paul's unhappy wails. She planted her fists on her hips. "That baby has colic," she said. "You should feed him goat's milk." As if that explained everything.

Ridiculous! Lily had never heard of anything so ridiculous in all her life. Babies didn't drink goat's milk. Everybody knew that. Babies drank baby milk. She thought Mama was being very polite to Effie's mother, who sounded just like Effie did: she liked to act as if she knew everything. Since her husband was the minister, she liked to be involved in everybody's business.

Lily wished she could be as nice to Effie as Mama was to Effie's mother. "Sit down, Ida," Mama said, waving the teapot. "I've got some tea left over and some English muffins. Would you like one with raspberry jam?"

"Well . . ." Ida wavered, then sat down. "Don't mind if I do." From her chair, she gave instructions to make a cup of tea just so—two lumps of sugar and a dash of cream—when suddenly, Lily heard a loud, "Harrumph!" Ida jumped up from the kitchen table and said, "I suppose I should be going." And away she went, out the door and down the driveway.

Mama looked at Lily, astounded. "What just happened?"

Lily shrugged. She had been walking baby Paul in a big

circle around the kitchen and the living room, trying to settle him while Mama made the tea. "I don't know!" She looked out the window and saw the rather substantial backside of Ida Kauffman marching down the road. My, she was a big woman. "Effie gets like that too. Right as rain one moment, mad as a wet hen the next."

Mama shot Lily a warning glance. She was always encouraging Lily to see the good side of others. Lily handed baby Paul back to Mama. For some people, especially people like Effie and her mother, it was very hard to find the good side.

That evening, Mama gave baby Paul some fresh goat's milk. Baby Paul didn't yelp and holler at all that night.

One thing, Lily decided. She had found something good about Effie's mother. She might be right about Paul needing goat's milk. But it was just that one thing.

Sunday was an in-between Sunday. During the afternoon, Papa sat at the kitchen table playing a game of Sorry with Lily and Joseph while baby Paul napped. Dannie tried to play on Papa's side. That was exasperating. He wasn't old enough to play and only slowed the game down as Papa patiently helped him count and move around the board.

A knock on the door surprised all of them. They hadn't even heard a buggy drive up. In walked Uncle Jacob and his family. Lily was so pleased to have visitors on a Sunday afternoon. Uncle Jacob had interesting things to talk about and he always treated Lily as if she were a grown-up. She felt important. And the best thing of all was that no one worked on Sunday afternoon, and that included babysitters. Lily wouldn't be asked to watch Noah and Anna.

Mama popped some popcorn and made hot cider for

everyone to drink while they visited. Lily put away the game of Sorry so that everyone could sit at the table. Uncle Jacob had barely settled in when he bolted out of his chair. "Well, I think it's time we start for home."

Everyone was confused. The visiting had just begun. What had caused Uncle Jacob's sudden change of mind? It was just like yesterday, when Effie's mother had left in a huff.

Then Mama's eyes landed on the verse Lily had tacked above the table and she gasped. "We didn't choose that verse for you," she said, her cheeks turning pink. "Lily has been copying verses and placing a new one up each week. I didn't get a chance to see the verse."

What was so bad about Lily's verse?

Papa stood and read it aloud: "Withdraw thy foot from thy neighbor's house; lest he be weary of thee and so hate thee." He looked at Uncle Jacob, and the two men burst out laughing.

Lily was even more confused. First, her verse made people huffy, then it made Papa laugh. Mama hurried to take down the card from the wall. She told them about Effie's mother, and Papa and Uncle Jacob laughed even harder. Lily did not understand men at all.

After Uncle Jacob, Aunt Lizzie, Noah, and Anna went home, Mama asked to see the rest of the verses Lily had copied. "It would be a good idea to choose a different verse to hang on the wall," Mama said. "One that wouldn't accidentally hurt our visitors' feelings."

Mama found another saying for Lily to copy down: "The way to a friend's house is never long."

❧

The day had finally come! Today was the day when all of the children would recite the poems they had memorized. One by one, each student walked to the front of the schoolhouse to take a turn. The eighth graders went first. Lily enjoyed listening to all the different kinds of interesting poems. When it was the fourth graders' turn, Lily listened to Sam's poem about camping in the woods, but she refused to listen to Aaron's dumb poem about a little boy and a hornets' nest. To her, Aaron was invisible. Even when everyone laughed at Aaron's poem, Lily pretended he was invisible.

So far, Lily noticed that no one had a poem about Jesus. Effie was wrong. Lily hoped Jesus would understand if she felt a little glad that Effie was wrong, for once.

Then came the third graders. Malinda and Beth each recited their poems without a single mistake. Not one. Then came Effie's turn. She flounced to the front of the classroom and turned around, fixing her eyes on Lily. She opened her mouth and recited:

> *I know that cows have little cows*
> *And dogs have little dogs,*
> *That pussycats have little cats*
> *And frogs have little frogs*
> *I know that birds have little birds*
> *And fish have little fishes*
> *So why can't sinks have little sinks*
> *Instead of dirty dishes?*

Effie had stolen Lily's poem! Everyone in the class laughed and laughed about little sinks. Lily's face turned red and she felt tears stinging her eyes. What was she supposed to do for her poem? She wanted to run out the door and flee for home, but she didn't have time. Teacher Rhoda called out Lily's name. It was her turn. Slowly, she shuffled to the front of the schoolhouse and turned to face everyone. Effie sat in her chair with a cat-that-swallowed-the-canary smile on her face. There was nothing for Lily to do except recite her little poem.

She said it quickly and didn't make a mistake, but no one laughed. They had heard it already. She went back to her desk and sat down, refusing to look at Effie. Lily wouldn't give Effie the satisfaction of knowing how upset she was. But she was.

Thanksgiving Pudding

The goat milk cured baby Paul from pitching fits all evening long, and now Lily thought he had turned into the sweetest baby in the world. She had only one complaint about him: he was always asleep in his little bassinet in the kitchen. Other than sleeping too much, which Mama said wasn't possible, he was a very nice baby. Lily liked to hurry home from school every afternoon and warm her hands by the stove. Then Mama would let her sit on the rocking chair and hold baby Paul. Lily never got tired of watching him. She loved his chubby pink cheeks and his tiny fists that peeped out from under the blanket and waved in the air.

Lily would have liked to spend all afternoon holding Paul. But after a few minutes, Mama would take the baby and tuck him back into his bassinet. It was time for Lily to help make supper. Chores didn't stop even when a new baby arrived.

One evening after supper, Mama asked the family to come

to the kitchen table. She had spread a newspaper out on the middle of the table and dumped a bowl of hickory nuts on it. In front of Papa's seat was a wooden cutting board. Papa pounded nut by nut with a hammer until they cracked open. Then he would pass the cracked nuts to Lily or Joseph to scoop out the nutmeat. Lily hated this chore.

It had been fun to gather the hickory nuts in the woods. Papa had found several hickory nut trees, so Lily and Joseph and Dannie had searched in the grass and leaves until they had found enough nuts to fill a big bowl. Papa said they should leave the rest of the nuts for the squirrels because they would need those nuts to eat during the long, cold winter. "There's plenty of food in the basement for us," Papa explained. "We don't need to take a lot of nuts away from the squirrels."

Lily was glad there was a limit to nut collecting. Trying to get the nutmeat out of the shells was long, hard, boring work. Hickory nuts were the worst nuts of all, and her fingers would be stained brown. She wondered how the squirrels managed to get nutmeat out of those shells with only their big front teeth as tools.

Finally, the last nut was cracked and shelled. Papa scraped all the nutshells into the trash can while Mama covered the bowl of nutmeats and put them into the cupboard. They would stay there until Thanksgiving.

Lily loved Thanksgiving almost as much as Christmas. On Wednesday, school was dismissed an hour early. Lily and Joseph ran all the way home to help Mama get everything ready for tomorrow's big meal. When they burst into the kitchen, Mama was toasting the hickory nuts on the stove. They smelled good, all nice and sweet and cozy. Lily couldn't wait until tomorrow.

For the first time, Mama let Lily help her make the special

Thanksgiving pudding—layered with different flavors of orange and vanilla. It was as beautiful to gaze at as it was to eat. Mama told her to put the bowl in the refrigerator, and then she went upstairs to tend to baby Paul. Lily opened the refrigerator, but it was jam-packed with other dishes Mama had prepared. At first, Lily wasn't sure what to do, but then she had an idea. A brilliant idea. Just brilliant. It was cold outside, even colder than inside the refrigerator. So Lily simply set the big bowl of pudding on the porch and covered it with a kitchen towel. And then she saw a bright red cardinal at the bird feeder and she forgot all about the pudding.

Mama called Lily in to help with the turkey. Lily's favorite! Earlier today, Mama had roasted a big turkey. Now, it was time to pick all the meat off into bite-sized pieces. In the big roasting pan, Mama added diced bread to the turkey, plus seasonings. She poured turkey broth over everything and let Lily mix it all together. Lily's mouth watered at the thought of how delicious this turkey would be tomorrow. It was the best way to eat turkey. The very best.

The next morning, Lily jumped out of bed as soon as she heard Mama's light footsteps on the stairs. She didn't want to miss a single minute of the day. She hurried down the stairs to help. Mama gave Lily potatoes to peel. Mama cut each peeled potato into chunks and covered them with cold water so they wouldn't turn brown. The potatoes would have to wait to be cooked until after church.

Mama set the pies on the kitchen counter in a row: pumpkin, pecan, and cherry. Lily wasn't sure which one she wanted to eat, but she thought she might try a small slice of each one. Mama checked the oven temperature and slid the roasting pan filled with the prepared turkey into it.

After breakfast, Papa drove Jim up to the door, and they

climbed into the buggy to go to church. It seemed funny to be going to church on a Thursday, but Lily always enjoyed Thanksgiving church. Everyone seemed extra happy, thinking of the meal that was waiting at home. Even the slow church songs sounded a little faster and happier.

Lily tried to listen to the ministers but her thoughts kept drifting off to the good food in Mama's kitchen. Her stomach started to rumble and she tried to muffle it with her hands, but Effie and her mother heard. They sat right in front of Lily and Mama and turned to frown at Lily at the exact same moment. It seemed as if they had rehearsed it.

The very second church was over, people bolted off their benches and out the door. No one was interested in lingering to visit. Not today!

Lily and Joseph scrambled to the back of the buggy to peer out the little window. The buggies of Grandpa Miller and Uncle Jacob followed them home. The smell of turkey dressing filled the air as the buggies reached Lily's driveway. Mama hurried inside to start cooking the big pot of potatoes. Grandma and Aunt Lizzie helped Mama make the gravy and set the table. Lily was glad that Uncle Jacob didn't have to do anything except sit in the living room and visit with Grandpa and Papa. That meant he could watch Noah and Papa could watch baby Paul and Dannie. Lily could go play dolls with Aunt Susie.

It wasn't long before Mama called for Lily to come to the kitchen. Lily dropped the dolls on the floor and rushed downstairs. Thanksgiving dinner was ready! She looked at all the food on the table: mashed potatoes drizzled with melted browned butter, golden brown turkey gravy, sweet corn, seven-layer salad, freshly baked dinner rolls, and another bowl filled with Mama's secret cheesy peas. In the center was a large platter with turkey dressing, steaming hot and piled high. Three little bowls, one with honey, one with butter, and one with a special spread of jam and marshmallow cream, were tucked near the bread rolls.

Behind the table on the counter were the pies, a big bowl of fruit, and a chocolate layer cake with fluffy chocolate frosting.

Mama was looking at her list, frowning. "Lily, where is the pudding?"

The pudding? *Oh no!* The pudding!

Lily dashed out to the porch to get it and stopped in dismay. Two big barn cats were sitting in the bowl, licking the last of the beautiful Thanksgiving pudding. Lily snapped her apron at them. "Shoo! Scat! Get away from here!"

The cats didn't budge. They looked at her and started to clean their paws. Lily was so cross at them! She picked up the bowl and tipped it so they tumbled out. "Bad cats!" she said. They didn't look even a tiny bit sorry for what they had done.

Lily took the empty bowl and handed it to Mama. "I couldn't find a place for it in the refrigerator so I put it outside and covered it with a dish towel." Her eyes welled with tears. She was so disappointed. "The cats found it first."

Mama's mouth opened in a big *O*. She looked at the big empty bowl, then at Lily, then back at the bowl. "Well," she finally said with a reassuring smile, "I think we have enough food even without the pudding."

After dinner was over, Lily and Aunt Susie helped the women clean off the table and put the leftovers away. Then everyone sat in the living room to visit until it was chore time.

Lily waved and waved until Grandpa Miller's and Uncle Jacob's buggies turned the corner onto the road. Papa and Joseph and Dannie went to the barn to milk Pansy and the goats and to feed the rest of the stock. Mama asked Lily to stay inside and help her make their special Thanksgiving tea—the way they ended the day.

Mama spread all the bits and pieces of hickory nuts into the bottom of a saucepan and covered them with water. Lily watched as the water started to boil. As soon as the water turned a lovely shade of golden brown, Mama took the saucepan off the stove and added brown sugar and milk.

Papa and the boys came in from the barn just as Mama finished stirring the tea. She filled five little cups with it and everyone sat around the table to enjoy the last tradition of Thanksgiving. Lily loved the crunchy sugary nut bits that floated on top of the tea. She wondered why they called it tea when it really wasn't a tea at all. It was more like hot chocolate, only better. She sipped it slowly to make it last as long as she could, unlike Joseph and Dannie, who gobbled it down. They had this special tea only on Thanksgiving. They would have to wait an entire year before they could have some more. Joseph and Dannie had no concept of time. None at all.

It was a perfect day. Except for the pudding.

As Mama tucked Lily into bed that night, she whispered, "Don't feel too badly about the pudding, Lily. The cats work hard for us, keeping the mice away. They deserve a treat now and then."

Lily thought those silly cats had their best Thanksgiving meal ever.

The Christmas Program

It was Friday, the morning after Thanksgiving, and Christmas was in the air. "It's time to start thinking about Christmas," Teacher Rhoda said, right after devotions.

Lily sat up a little straighter in her chair. She didn't want to miss a word of this announcement. One seat in front of her and across the aisle—the invisible part—Effie waved her hand frantically.

"Yes, Effie?" Teacher Rhoda said.

"Will we be having a Christmas program this year?"

That was another thing about Effie that bothered Lily. She was so impatient. If Effie would just listen, Teacher Rhoda could explain everything.

Teacher Rhoda didn't seem to mind that Effie was so impatient. She smiled, as if she thought her enthusiasm was cute. "Yes, we will be having a Christmas program here at school. Today, I will give each student a part to memorize."

Teacher Rhoda walked from desk to desk and placed a piece of paper on each one. Lily quickly read her assignment. She had to memorize a Christmas poem, several verses from the Christmas story in Luke chapter 2, and sing "O Beautiful Star of Bethlehem."

Lily's heart sank. She didn't mind memorizing a poem and she didn't mind memorizing Bible verses, but the thought of singing in front of everyone made her stomach feel as if butterflies were fluttering around. She knew she had a month to prepare, but already her hands felt cold and clammy and sweaty.

At home, Lily showed the list to Mama the minute she returned from school. Mama skimmed the list. "I don't think you'll have any problem learning all of this in time for the program."

"I think I can memorize everything," Lily said. "But I don't think I can sing that song."

Mama looked surprised. "You already know it. Why do you think you can't sing this song?"

"My stomach feels funny when I think about it . . . I'm afraid I'll get sick. I might get sick and die, right there at the schoolhouse." That would be terrible. How embarrassing.

"I'll help you sing it often here at home," Mama said. "You will get so used to singing it that you won't even have time to get nervous at the program." She put the list away. "Did everyone exchange names for gifts like they did in New York?"

"No, we didn't," Lily said. "Teacher Rhoda didn't say anything about exchanging gifts."

"Maybe they don't exchange gifts in this school," Mama said. "I'll write a note to Teacher Rhoda and ask her what we're supposed to do. You can give it to her on Monday."

Lily forgot all about the Christmas program until Mama

handed her the note to give to Teacher Rhoda on Monday morning. She took the teacher's answer back to Mama that afternoon. As Mama read it, she said, "This sounds like a good idea." She put the note in her apron pocket. "They don't exchange names in this school. Instead, each child takes something small to school for each child. Maybe a balloon or a pencil or some candy. Any ideas of what you'd like to take the children?"

Gift ideas weren't hard for Lily. The hard part would be deciding on just one thing. Oh, so many choices! At first Lily thought of paper dolls, then stickers, then a few new crayons. But each time she thought of something, it was followed by the image of Aaron Yoder, sneering. He would find a way to mock anything she picked. Finally, she thought about what she would most like to receive: candy.

The best gift of all would be to fill a sandwich baggie with several different kinds of homemade candy, including a square or two of Mama's special fudge. She would ask Papa if she could buy Smarties to put in each baggie. Smarties were Lily's favorite candy of all. She was pleased with her decision. Everybody loved candy. Even Aaron Yoder couldn't make fun of candy.

Joseph decided to give each student a balloon. He was crazy about balloons. He was hatching a new plan to blow up a hundred balloons, tie them with strings, and hang on tight to the strings so that he could fly like a kite to his friend's house. So far, he had saved up only three balloons.

Mama thought they had made good choices for their gifts. "Don't tell any of the other children what you have planned," she said. "You want them to be surprised."

Effie, she meant.

Each afternoon in December, Teacher Rhoda asked the students to practice their poems and verses and sing their songs. Lily was relieved to learn that she wasn't singing alone—all the little girls were assigned the same song.

The days inched along. On the night before the Christmas program, as soon as Dannie and baby Paul were sound asleep, Mama set out different candies on the kitchen table. Smarties, of course. Little candy canes, tiny chocolate bells wrapped in different Christmas colors, red and green gumdrops, and small boxes filled with Mama's homemade candies: choco-late-covered pretzels, fudge, and raisin clusters. Lily started to reconsider her idea. Everything looked too good to give away. Maybe she should just give balloons too and save the candy for the family.

Mama would have none of that. She handed Lily a box of sandwich baggies. "Put one of each candy in the baggie. I'll help you fasten a twister on them."

Lily had fun filling the baggies, thinking how pleased her friends would be with her surprises. She thought of each child as she filled a baggie. The last person she thought of was Aaron Yoder. She wished she could fill his baggie with stinky brussel sprouts instead of delicious candy. That would serve him right.

The Christmas program was scheduled for the afternoon, so Papa and Mama would bring the special gifts when they arrived. The students, even the bigger ones, couldn't con-centrate on their lessons. Too excited. They could hardly sit still. Teacher Rhoda finally gave up trying to teach and told them to put their books away. "We'll spend the rest of the morning practicing the program to make sure everyone knows their parts."

Lily closed her math book with a snap. She was happier doing anything than long division. All she could think of was the program, anyway. And the candy.

At two o'clock, buggies started to roll into the schoolyard. The girls stood at the window to watch. Mothers carried little children in one arm and bags of gifts in the other as they hurried into the schoolhouse. Fathers tied the buggy horses to the long hitching rack. Each horse would be covered with a blanket so it wouldn't get cold while waiting. It was a chilly day. Big flakes of snow drifted lazily from the sky. *What a perfect day for a Christmas program*, Lily thought. She was so happy she could hardly keep it inside—her happiness kept spilling out.

Teacher Rhoda rang the bell. The students hurried to their seats while the parents found a seat on the benches at the back of the schoolhouse. It was time to begin. The children filed to the front of the schoolhouse and started to sing Christmas carols. Then they took turns telling the Christmas story, verse by verse. After a few more songs and poems, it was time for the best part: the gifts!

One by one, Teacher Rhoda called out a family's name. The children in that family would get the bags of gifts from their parents and hand them out. Lily was thrilled to see the pile of things on her desk grow and grow, as big as a mountain. She saw erasers and special pencils, pretty handkerchiefs and lots of candy. Every other desk had a small mountain of gifts too. Nobody was left out.

"The David Yoder family," Teacher Rhoda announced. Lily watched as Marvin, Ezra, and Aaron handed out gifts, even though Aaron was invisible to her. Marvin walked up one aisle and down the other, placing a shiny red apple on each desk. Ezra followed behind, giving everyone a banana. Last came Aaron. He gave everyone an orange. Even though Aaron was invisible to Lily, she did notice those oranges. Her mouth watered at the sight. She loved oranges, best of all the fruit. The only time she ate an orange was for Christmas breakfast. She couldn't wait to have one! Aaron started up her aisle, placing an orange on each desk. When he came to Lily, he hurried past her desk as if no one was there.

Lily was crushed. She was looking forward to that orange! She decided she would not give Aaron a pack of candy. He didn't deserve one.

"The Daniel Lapp family," Teacher Rhoda said.

Lily and Joseph got up and went back to Papa and Mama to get their bags of gifts. Mama handed Lily the bag and whispered, "Be sure not to miss any children."

Aaron, she meant.

Lily walked up and down the aisle, placing a baggie filled with candy on each desk. As she neared Aaron's desk, she wanted to skip past him. She wanted to so badly! But she knew Mama was watching and would be disappointed in her. She tossed the baggie on his desk and didn't feel at all sorry that it slid off and dropped on the floor. She hoped the Smarties broke into a thousand little pieces. She hoped all that would be left was Smartie dust.

When Lily sat at her desk, she set aside her invisible rule and glanced at Aaron. He had already eaten all of the candy that was on his desk. All of it! She hoped he would have a horrible stomachache all afternoon. Maybe even for all of Christmas. Just the thought of a green, sickly Aaron, languishing in bed during Christmas while she was having fun, satisfied her.

After the last gift was handed out, the program was over and it was time to go home. It had been a good day. A very good day. Lily gathered all her things into a big empty bag. She couldn't wait to get home to divide her candy with Dannie and Papa and Mama. Joseph, she knew, would do the same thing. Maybe, if she asked nicely, he might share his orange.

Sledding at School

Lily was excited. It had snowed and snowed and snowed last night! A real January blizzard. Snow made the world look so much prettier. She could hear Papa come into the basement from the outside. He stomped his boots to knock the snow off so he wouldn't track it into the house. When he came into the kitchen, he handed a pail of Pansy's milk to Mama. She would strain and cool the milk.

Papa smiled at Lily. "We got a little over a foot of snow last night." Lily couldn't wait to get started for school. It would be fun to walk through the snow. Joseph was already putting on his boots. He was in as much of a hurry to get ready for school as she was. Usually, Joseph dawdled over breakfast while Lily waited by the door. But not today. Joseph liked snow almost as much as she did. Maybe more.

Some of the children were already at school by the time Lily and Joseph arrived. Snowballs sailed through the air. Lily liked playing in the snow, but she didn't like snowball fights. She had two little brothers who liked to throw snowballs at her, two against one. Not fair. Always outnumbered. Snowball fights were just one of the many reasons she wanted a sister. She hurried inside the schoolhouse where there was no danger of being hit. She would rather stand at the window to watch the snowball fight until Teacher Rhoda rang the bell and the school day began.

During recess, the children piled back outside to play Fox and Geese. They lined up to trudge paths through the snow. One of the eighth grade boys was the leader and everyone followed behind him. They shuffled their feet to pack the snow down as much as they could. First, they made a wide circle on the playground, like an outline. They kept trudging through the snow, in smaller and smaller circles, until they had all reached the center and were ready to play. Lily thought the tracks looked like a giant snowy cinnamon roll.

Fox and Geese was a fun game: whoever was *it* had to run along the circle path to try to tag someone. Everyone else could jump from path to path, but when a person was tagged, then that person was also *it*. The more children who were tagged, the more were *it*.

Lily was glad she wasn't chosen to be *it* for a long time. She liked being able to jump from path to path to avoid whoever was *it*. By the time Teacher Rhoda rang the bell, nearly everyone had been tagged. All but Aaron Yoder. Lily could have tagged him once, but she didn't want to touch him. She shuddered. Too awful.

Lily went inside and straight to her desk, feeling happy, even if her pink cheeks stung from the cold. Recess on a snow-filled winter day was the best day of all. The very best.

During lunch, Lily tried to eavesdrop on the upper-grade

213

boys without being too obvious. They were debating what to play for the rest of lunch recess. Lily wanted them to play Fox and Geese again, but plans were brewing to sled down the long, steep hill behind the schoolhouse.

Lily wasn't sure that would be a good idea and not just because they didn't have sleds. The hill was long and steep and it wasn't even part of the school playground. It belonged to the farmer, Ben Fisher, right next to the schoolhouse. She was glad when Teacher Rhoda overheard the boys and said, "We don't go playing on other people's land without their permission."

Marvin Yoder raised his head. "May I go ask Ben if we can slide on his hill?"

Teacher Rhoda gave that some thought. "You can ask him on your way home from school today."

The boys were disappointed, but Lily was glad she didn't have to worry about sledding today. And maybe Ben Fisher would not want them to sled down his hill. She hoped so. Sledding was too risky. Somebody might get hurt. Somebody . . . like Lily.

Ben Fisher was waiting at the schoolhouse as the children arrived the next morning. He had brought a big stack of empty feed bags to use as makeshift sleds to slide down his hill.

Oh, this was not a good idea. Lily wasn't sure how feed bags would even work as sleds, but the big boys were thrilled. Even the little boys and some of the girls. Aaron Yoder wanted to try it out right away, but his brother Marvin said they would have to wait until recess. There wasn't enough time left before school to walk all the way up the hill and sled down before the bell rang.

When Teacher Rhoda dismissed the class for recess, everyone ran to get a bag. Lily was sure that Beth wouldn't want
to sled down that hill, but she grabbed a bag and ran after
the boys. They clambered over the fence and stood at the top
of the hill. Lily stayed by the fence and watched to see what
they would do next. She was the only one who didn't climb
up the hill to slide down.

Marvin Yoder placed a feed bag on the snowy ground
and sat on it. He held the front end up between his legs and
pushed off to start down the hill. He went faster and faster.
It almost looked as if he were flying! As soon as he reached
the bottom, he hurried back up the hill.

One by one, the children lined up to slide down. The snow
quickly packed down and became slippery as the children
went whizzing down the hill.

Beth was the first girl to slide down the hill. She squealed
and laughed all the way down. Joseph followed behind her.
He sounded like he was having the most fun he had ever had.

Lily was relieved when Teacher Rhoda rang the bell and
everyone trudged back to the schoolhouse. She hoped that
during lunch they would want to play something else.

Sadly, that didn't happen. Day after day, as soon as the
children were dismissed for recess, they bolted to get their
coats and mittens and a feed bag and hurried up the hill.
Day after day, Lily stood by the fence and watched them
slide down the hill.

One time, Teacher Rhoda came up beside her to watch
the children. "Wouldn't you like to try to sled down, Lily?"

Lily shook her head. She was absolutely positive that she
did not want to slide down the hill, and Teacher Rhoda didn't
say anything more about it.

Later in the week, Teacher Rhoda came outside and stood

next to Lily by the fence. "Everyone is having a lot of fun. I think you would too, if you ever tried."

Lily looked down at her boots. "The hill is long and steep."

"I could hold the bag for you until you get settled. If you try it and decide you don't like it, you won't ever have to again."

Lily faced a conundrum. She wanted to please Teacher Rhoda, but she was scared of that big hill. Teacher Rhoda held a hand out to her. Lily hesitated, then took hold of her hand and climbed through the fence. Teacher Rhoda helped her place the bag on the slippery path and held it until Lily sat down. "Hold it at the sides," Teacher Rhoda said.

It surprised Lily to think a teacher would know how to slide down a hill. She gripped the sides of the bag as firmly as she could. The hill looked so steep and long and she felt so small as she sat at the top.

Teacher Rhoda gave her an encouraging smile. "Are you ready?"

Ever so cautiously, Lily gave a brief nod. Teacher Rhoda let go of the bag and gently pushed her off. Lily started whizzing down the hill. Faster and faster. So fast it took her breath away! Her eyes started to water from the stinging wind. She could hardly see! The feed bag went faster and faster, then hit a bump, and Lily went sailing. Her hand got caught beneath her and scraped along the ice. Lily wanted to stop but couldn't. Everything was going too fast.

When Lily reached the bottom, she tipped over. Slowly, she rose to her feet, but her legs felt shaky. Her hand hurt. She looked at it and started to cry. Her mitten was torn and the back of her hand was bleeding. She looked up the hill and saw Teacher Rhoda waving to her. She looked so small up there. Other children whizzed past Lily, laughing and squealing. Lily knew she never wanted another ride. Not ever!

Teacher Rhoda came down the hill to see what was wrong. Lily held out her scraped-up hand. Teacher Rhoda took Lily inside the schoolhouse and gently washed the blood from her hand. She covered the scrapes with a bandage. "I'm sorry you got hurt, Lily. Did you enjoy any part of the ride?"

Tears filled Lily's eyes again. "No! It was too fast and lasted too long and I couldn't see anything."

Teacher Rhoda wiped Lily's tears from her cheeks with a handkerchief. "I'm sorry I encouraged you to try. I won't ask you to take another ride again."

The rest of the day, Lily tried to concentrate on her lessons. Her bandaged hand felt awkward. She couldn't hold her pencil very easily. When recess came, she went outside to watch the children slide down the hill. She felt lonely. The only thing the children wanted to do was slide down that dumb hill. She wished the snow would melt, at least for a while. She wished spring would come.

Even more so, she wished she weren't afraid of sledding. She wished she could join in the fun. But she would never ever slide down that hill again. Too dangerous.

The Dust Mop Battles

On Saturday afternoon, Mama sent Lily and Joseph upstairs to finish the cleaning. Lily was told to dust the furniture while Joseph cleaned under the beds with the dust mop.

They were in a hurry. They wanted to spend the afternoon building a snowman, but Mama kept finding more chores for them to do. Lily finished dusting the furniture in her hallway bedroom and hurried to dust Joseph and Dannie's room.

Their bunk beds looked rumpled and unmade. Several shirts were tossed on the floor. Lily sighed. Boys were so messy. She picked the shirts up and put them into the laundry basket. Then she made up the beds.

"I beat you!" Joseph yelled as he ran down the stairs. That wasn't fair. If Lily hadn't cleaned up his mess, she would have been done by now too.

As she walked through her hallway bedroom, she noticed

the handle of the dust mop sticking out from under the bed. She should go downstairs and make Joseph put the dust mop away. He hadn't beaten her after all.

Then she had a better idea. She decided to teach Joseph a lesson for being so messy. She took the dust mop and tucked it into Joseph's bed. She smiled with satisfaction. Joseph would have a surprise when he jumped into bed tonight.

Later that evening, Papa made his usual bedtime announcement: "It's bedtime for little lambs." Lily rushed upstairs to brush her teeth and jump into bed. She wanted to pretend she was already asleep by the time Joseph discovered the dust mop. She tried not to giggle when she thought how surprised he would be.

The boys got into their pajamas, brushed their teeth, and hopped into bed, just like every night. There were no sounds or squeals or screams. Lily was disappointed, but she said nothing.

The next night, as Lily climbed into bed, there was the dust mop, resting its head on her pillow. *Joseph!* Grrr. What a disgusting trick.

She set the mop in the corner of her room and turned her pillow over to sleep on the clean side. She would wait a few days, just to make Joseph think she had forgotten all about it, then slip it back into his bed.

Several days later, she put the dust mop back into Joseph's bed. The next evening, she checked her bed carefully before hopping in, but there was no dust mop. The next night, there it was, resting on her pillow again!

So much for teaching Joseph a lesson about being so messy. This was an entirely different kind of matter. She was going to pick a careful time to put that mop into Joseph's bed again, a time when he least expected it. She would win the battle of the dust mop.

At school that day, Effie had bragged that she had invited Teacher Rhoda home for supper and to stay for the night. When Lily heard, she couldn't wait to run home and ask Mama about inviting Teacher Rhoda to her house. How special! Usually, Mama liked to think things over for a while before she answered Lily. She liked to talk to Papa, think some more, talk to Papa again, and then . . . she would make her decision. But this time, Mama said yes, right away. She sat right down to write a note, asking if Teacher Rhoda would like to come for dinner next Wednesday.

Even better, Teacher Rhoda wrote a note right back to Mama, saying she was happy to accept their invitation.

Lily could hardly wait. She started making plans about what they would do. She thought Teacher Rhoda might like to visit with Mama and hold baby Paul. And maybe she would like to play a board game or read a story to them.

Of course, they would need a special meal. Mama had already told Lily she could help make Pineapple Fluff Pudding for dessert. It was Lily's favorite pudding and she was sure Teacher Rhoda would like it.

When Wednesday finally came, Lily could hardly pay attention at school. As soon as school was dismissed, Teacher Rhoda locked up the schoolhouse to walk home with Lily and Joseph. They chatted all the way home. Lily loved having Teacher Rhoda all to herself—well, almost all to herself. She had to share Teacher Rhoda with Joseph. But at least she didn't have to share Teacher Rhoda with twenty other children. Somehow, Lily thought, Teacher Rhoda didn't seem so teacher-ish tonight. She seemed younger and more fun.

When they got home, Teacher Rhoda helped Mama make supper. Lily stayed in the house to watch instead of going out to the barn to do chores with Papa and Joseph and Dannie. She didn't want to miss one single minute of the visit.

After the supper dishes were done, Teacher Rhoda held baby Paul on her lap while she helped Lily and Joseph play a game of Sorry. Lily thought Papa announced that it was time to get ready for bed much too soon.

As they headed up the stairs, Lily was so happy she was a girl. Teacher Rhoda would sleep in her room tonight, in her bed. Lily would sleep on a blanket nest on the floor. She hoped Teacher Rhoda didn't mind too much that Lily slept in a hallway.

As Lily slipped under her covers, she let out a contented sigh. It had been a perfect evening. Teacher Rhoda blew out the oil lamp on the dresser. As she climbed into bed, she said, "Good night, Lil—"

A scream came out of Teacher Rhoda that rocked the room. She jumped out of bed and reached for the flashlight she had placed on the dresser.

Lily jumped up to see what was wrong. Teacher Rhoda shined the flashlight on the pillow. The dust mop! *Oh, Joseph*, Lily thought for the hundredth time, *what have you done?* The sound of little giggles echoed through the boys' bedroom.

She apologized to Teacher Rhoda and explained all about the silly dust mop battle. Teacher Rhoda wasn't mad. She seemed to understand. She even laughed. A little. Lily swapped pillows with her. Teacher Rhoda climbed back into bed and it wasn't long before Lily could hear her even breathing and knew she was asleep.

Lily lay awake for a long time, upset. She was mad at Joseph for putting that mop in her bed, tonight of all nights. She wished she had never started the dust mop battle.

What must Teacher Rhoda think about Lily? What if she thought Lily were as mischievous as Aaron Yoder? Lily shuddered.

Even more distressing, Lily had lost the dust mop battle.

CHAPTER 31

Hannah's Visit

It was a cold evening in late winter. Lily sat by the window watching for a pair of headlights to come down the road and turn into her driveway. Uncle Elmer, Aunt Mary, Hannah, Levi, and Davy were coming for a visit all the way from New York and Lily couldn't wait. It had been such a long time since she had seen Hannah, her favorite cousin. The two girls exchanged weekly letters, but letters weren't the same thing as being together, talking and playing.

A pair of headlights appeared. Lily sat up straight but the car zoomed past the house. Mama was mending a pair of Dannie's trousers. Lily was sure Mama could hear her thirteenth sigh of disappointment as the car went past. "Lily, why don't you find something to play with while you wait? It will make the time go so much faster if you're busy."

Lily went up the stairs to her hallway bedroom. She opened the bottom drawer of her dresser and carefully lifted out a box filled with paper dolls. They were beautiful paper dolls, like new. Lily played with them only on special occasions. Tonight felt special.

Downstairs, she knelt in front of the sofa and took out the paper dolls. She set them up along the back of the sofa so they looked like they were standing tall. Next, she selected the clothes for each doll to wear. This was very hard work because all of the long dresses were so fancy and pretty. Mama said they were called hoop skirts. Lily thought there was nothing as pretty as those dresses. Even if she could never wear such a fancy dress, it was fun to pretend she was one of the dolls. She liked to make believe that she and her doll friends were invited to a party.

Lily became so involved with her paper dolls' party-going that she didn't even hear the knock on the door. Mama heard it first. She dropped her mending on the floor beside her rocking chair and hurried to answer the door. Papa had been reading a book to Joseph and Dannie. The boys scrambled off his lap to run to the door. The paper doll party would have to wait.

Uncle Elmer, Aunt Mary, Levi, Hannah, and Davy all stood patiently on the porch steps. "Come in, come in!" Papa and Mama said at the same time. There was a lot of laughter and talking as everyone came inside and removed their hats and bonnets. Mama offered them something to eat, but they said they weren't hungry for anything except catching up on news.

The grown-ups sat down to talk as the boys went to play with their toy farms. Lily was so happy to see Hannah that she felt suddenly shy. How strange! She couldn't think of a thing to say. Hannah noticed the paper dolls on the sofa and asked if they could play with them.

The two girls knelt in front of the sofa and soon they were talking and laughing like they had never been separated. Lily was so happy. This was much more fun than playing with dolls all alone.

Too soon, Papa came into the living room and said, "Bedtime for little lambs." Lily looked at the clock and was surprised to see how late it was. Later than she had ever been up! But tonight had been a special night and Papa understood that. Hannah helped Lily gather up the paper dolls and put them away so little brothers wouldn't find them. Then, they both went upstairs. Mama fixed a cozy blanket nest on the floor beside Lily's bed. Lily would sleep there while Hannah slept in her bed.

"No talking tonight, girls," Mama said. "It's late. There will be plenty of time for talking tomorrow."

Lily snuggled under her blanket and listened to the gentle

murmur of the grown-ups' voices in the kitchen. It didn't sound as if they were planning to go to bed yet. She fell asleep to the low sounds of Papa's and Uncle Elmer's laughter and Mama and Aunt Mary's soft buzz of conversation.

The next morning, Uncle Elmer decided to go to work with Papa while Aunt Mary helped Mama. Lily and Hannah were given some chores, but afterward they were free to play for the rest of the day. Having houseguests, Lily thought, was better than a holiday.

Hannah wanted to play with paper dolls, so Lily fetched the box and the girls lined the paper dolls up along the back of the sofa. They played with them all day, only stopping for meals. There was so much to pretend about: parties, visits to town, a day at school. Lily told Hannah about each of the girls in the third grade: Beth, Malinda, and Effie.

At supper, Uncle Elmer said that they were hoping to move to Pennsylvania. Tomorrow, they would go land shopping. Hannah and Levi hadn't attended school for two years, he explained, and it was time to make a change. Nearly all of the families in the New York church had moved away.

Lily couldn't imagine not playing with any friends for two years. How sad!

In the morning, the driver arrived early in the big van. Lily's family was invited to come along for the farm shopping. Joseph and Levi scrambled to claim the backseat. Dannie and Davy followed behind and squished in. Lily and Hannah sat in the bench behind Mama, Aunt Mary, and baby Paul. Papa sat in the front seat next to the driver to give him directions. Uncle Elmer was looking for a big farm, so they drove all around the area—up and down the hills and around the curves until Lily thought she could not sit in the van for another minute. It made her feel sick.

Mama noticed how pale and quiet Lily had become. "Maybe you should come up front, Lily," she said. Lily put her head in Mama's lap. She was sorry to miss time with Hannah, but it was better than getting sick all over the van. How awful that would be.

Uncle Elmer looked at several farms, but none suited him. Too hilly, too wooded, too expensive.

Finally, Mama said, "What about the farm right next to our house?"

Papa looked at Uncle Elmer, next to him on the front seat. "It's not in very good condition, but it wouldn't hurt to go see it." He directed the driver to take them back home. Lily was relieved to be heading home, but she was sure Uncle Elmer wouldn't like this farm. It had a little brown house even smaller than Lily's ugly olive green house. The barn looked old and weather-beaten. The yard was covered with overgrown grass and tangled weeds. It was hideous.

Naturally, Uncle Elmer thought it was perfect. He wanted to walk the property lines, so he and Papa hurried off to find the owner. Lily couldn't sit in that van for one more minute. She could see her house out the window. "Mama, can Hannah and I go home to play with my paper dolls again?"

Mama and Aunt Mary looked at each other and nodded their heads. Mama reached into her pocket and drew out a key. "Here you go," she said. "Enjoy yourselves, and we'll be coming home as soon as Papa and Uncle Elmer come back."

Lily and Hannah ran up the road and into the house. They spread the paper dolls out and started to play. At first, it felt funny to be in the house without grown-ups, but it wasn't long before they decided they liked it. Too soon, everyone else tumbled in the door, and Mama and Aunt Mary started to make lunch. Then came the worst, most dreaded moment of the entire week: Lily and Hannah had to have their hair braided to get ready for church tomorrow.

Lily tried to be brave and not cry while Mama combed out a week's worth of snarls, but she couldn't stop the tears from running. Hannah's lips quivered as Aunt Mary combed her long curly blonde hair. Mama and Aunt Mary took turns telling funny little stories to distract them. When they were done, Aunt Mary grinned. "I think we should work on their hair together each week. That was the least weepy braiding time I ever had."

Mama laughed. "Lily usually cries the entire time."

Lily and Hannah looked at each other, mortified. It wasn't very polite of their mothers to share such embarrassing moments, but at least they knew they weren't the only ones who cried.

On Sunday morning, Lily was so excited to have Hannah meet Beth. Oh, she hoped they might like each other! What if they didn't? That would be terrible. If Hannah moved to Cloverdale, Lily would have to divide up her time between Beth and Hannah at school. Recess with Hannah. Lunch with Beth. The next day, she would have to reverse it so everything would be fair. Lily wouldn't want them arguing over who got to spend time with her.

Today, Levi would be able to meet some fourth grade boys, but Lily thought that was unfortunate. Aaron Yoder had influenced all the other boys in that class to be troublemakers. She worried that Aaron might tease Levi about his stutter. It was better than it used to be, but Lily noticed that when Levi was nervous, it was more apparent. She hoped that Levi wouldn't be teased so badly today that Uncle Elmer would change his mind about moving here.

During church, Hannah leaned over to whisper to Lily, "Who is that cute boy?"

"Where?"

Hannah carefully pointed across the room, to the third boy from the left in the second row of benches.

Lily squinted hard, rubbed her eyes, then looked again. Hannah was pointing to Aaron Yoder!

Poor Hannah. For the last two years, she hadn't been around other children. She had lost all common sense about boys.

After church there was a light lunch and after that came the fun. The boys ran off to play softball. The girls had plans to gather under a tree and play a game. Lily looked for Hannah and was surprised to find that she and Beth were the first ones by the tree, whispering together. Lily felt a funny ping in her stomach. As the girls pretended to play school, the pinging feeling got worse. Effie said Lily had to be the teacher. Beth insisted that Hannah sit next to her.

Nobody liked to be the teacher when they pretended to play school. Everybody was having fun except for Lily. The pinging in her stomach got stronger.

Suddenly, a loud shout erupted from the yard. Levi was shoving Aaron Yoder against the fence. Lily knew Aaron Yoder would do something terrible to Levi. She just knew it!

Uncle Elmer and Lily's papa and David Yoder ran over to break up the scuffle between the boys. Lily hurried to Joseph. "What did Aaron do?"

"Nothing!" Joseph said. "It was Levi. Aaron told him about how he saw an old Indian in the woods, and Levi said that was nothing—there were old Indians everywhere in New York. Levi just kept bragging and bragging." He scrunched his face. "Were there Indians in New York?"

"None that I ever saw," Lily said. "Did Aaron hit him?" She wouldn't have put it past Aaron.

"No," Joseph said. "Aaron asked him why he was moving

here, then, if it was so much better in New York. That was when Levi went at him."

Lily was surprised at Levi. Bragging was no way to make friends, even if that new friend happened to be Aaron Yoder.

Papa waved a hand to Lily and Joseph. It was time to head home. Lily was quiet on the buggy ride home. She felt miffed with Hannah for becoming instant best friends with Beth. Hannah didn't seem to notice that Lily was left out. She chattered on and on about the plans Beth had made for her, just as soon as she moved here for good.

The minute they got into the house, Hannah suggested they play paper dolls again. As Hannah set the dolls up against the sofa, Mama motioned to Lily to come to the kitchen. "Lily, I think it would be nice if you would give half of your paper dolls to Hannah to take home with her when they leave tomorrow morning."

Lily looked at Mama, horrified. How could she give half of her paper dolls away? She loved each one of them. "I want to keep them all," she mumbled, sulky. Mama was serious, though.

Lily went back to the sofa and looked at her beautiful dolls. Which ones could she give away? They were all so pretty. Finally, she chose half of them and their clothes and handed them to Hannah.

Hannah was thrilled. Lily was miserable. The last day of this wonderful visit had been ruined.

Several weeks passed. One afternoon, a letter arrived from Aunt Mary. Mama opened it eagerly and started to read it silently. A smile spread across her face. She looked at Lily. "Uncle Elmer has bought the farm next to us!"

Lily felt a ping in her tummy. She was happy that her favorite cousin would live next door. But then she had a funny feeling too about being left out when Beth and Hannah played together. And what about Levi? He was a worry.

Mama turned the letter over. "Aunt Mary wants me to tell you thank you again for those paper dolls. Hannah plays with them every day."

Lily hadn't played with her paper dolls since Hannah had left. Not one time. She had packed them up and put them away. But maybe now she would be able to see her beautiful paper dolls again. Maybe Hannah would even give them back to her, since she would be living right next door in the ugly brown house. Lily brightened at that thought.

Papa's Building Project

*L*ily sat at the supper table. She peered into her bowl of chili soup. It was made with tomato juice, water, and beef broth, sweetened with brown sugar, with bits of meat and lots of kidney beans floating in it. It was thin and watery, and Lily thought it was the worst thing Mama cooked. Lately, she seemed to be making it so often. The most awful part of Mama's chili soup was those hideous kidney beans.

Lily wished Papa hadn't given her such a big helping. Everyone else was nearly done with supper. She had been working on this bowl of soup for the entire meal and had hardly made any difference in the amount that was left to eat.

She filled a spoon with several disgusting kidney beans. She put them in her mouth, then quickly gulped down water to swallow them like pills so she wouldn't have to taste them. She looked down into the bowl again. It was hopeless. Swallowing the kidney beans whole didn't seem to make much of a difference. Her bowl was still full. She knew she would have to stay at the table until she had eaten all of her soup.

Joseph helped Mama clear the table off and do the dishes while Lily tried to keep eating. She took one tiny awful bite after another. She definitely did not want to have any soup left in her bowl by the time Papa said it was bedtime. It had happened before: Mama would put her bowl into the refrigerator and Lily would have to eat it for breakfast. She couldn't think of anything worse than having to eat this awful, watery chili soup first thing in the morning.

It was growing dark outside. Papa came in from feeding the animals in the barn. He looked at Lily's bowl. "You're getting there. Try taking bigger bites and you will be done sooner." He spread several pieces of paper on the table and started sketching on them.

"What are you doing?" Whatever Papa was doing was much more interesting than Lily's soup.

Papa glanced up at her. "I'm drawing plans to build an addition to the house. I'm trying to figure out how much money I'll need to buy the materials to build it." He scribbled down a few notes on the paper. He glanced over at Lily. "That's part of the reason we have chili soup so often. It's nutritious and it doesn't cost very much for Mama to make it. That way, we can save a little more money for the house."

Lily looked down at her soup. If eating this lumpy broth would help Papa and Mama build an addition to the house, she would try to do her part. She would eat this awful soup. She took several huge spoonfuls, willing herself not to gag on those slimy kidney beans. Finally, the last bit of soup had been eaten and she could go wash her bowl. Hooray!

She sat next to Papa to watch him sketch the plans.

"I want to add a big kitchen," Papa said. "Over at the

other end, I'll build a big pantry with lots of shelves. Room for the refrigerator too. That way we won't have to have our refrigerator out on the porch any longer. Won't Mama be happy to have it indoors again?"

This was exciting! The ugly olive green house was going to turn into something pretty and cute and finally feel as if it belonged to them. Maybe Papa would even paint the outside wood a beautiful purple. Purple was Lily's favorite color. The best color of all.

Papa pointed to one corner of the sketch. "Over here at this end, I'll make a nice room that Mama can use for her sewing and quilting. And then I'll make a cement porch along this side of the house. Someday we'll enclose it for a laundry room and summer kitchen." He pulled out another sheet of paper with a floor plan sketched out. "We'll have a full basement underneath—not a little one like there is now—and then I can put some woodworking machinery in it and start making furniture." He rolled up that sheet of paper. "That way I can work at home with my family. Won't that be nice?"

Oh, that was the most wonderful news of all! Lily couldn't wait until Papa was finished with the addition and could stay at home each day. Then she had a horrible thought. She wrinkled her nose. It would mean she would need to eat lots and lots of thin chili soup. She made up her mind to eat it bravely no matter how awful it was.

The next week a man arrived at the house with a big crawler-type tractor to start digging earth away for the new basement. Before he could start digging, Papa had to cut down some small trees that were in the way. Lily felt sad as she watched Papa cut through the trees. They would start to creak and pop. Then, with a mighty roar, they would fall to the ground with a shudder and everything was quiet. Strangely quiet. Even the birds were silent. The man fastened the trunk of the tree to his crawler and pulled it into the pasture. Later, Papa would cut it up for firewood. But now, he had more trees to cut.

When the last tree had been pulled away, the man started to dig the earth. It was slow work, even with a big crawler. Every bucket load of earth had to be taken out to the pasture behind the barn and put on a pile.

While the man worked on digging the hole for the basement, Papa took Lily and Joseph out to the pasture to look at the tree stumps. They knelt beside one and Papa showed them tree rings. He told them that each ring stood for one year of a tree's life. Lily started to count the rings of a stump. There were sixty-eight. This tree had been sixty-eight years old. It made Lily feel sad, even more sad than when she saw the tree fall to the ground. The tree had spent a long time growing big and tall. In only a few minutes, it had been cut down. It would never make another ring.

Papa seemed to understand how she felt. "It had to be done, Lily. We need more room in our house and those trees were in the way." He rose to his feet. "But after we're finished building, we can plant new trees to replace the ones that had to be cut down. Those trees will grow up to be big and strong."

Such a thought made Lily feel much better. "Can we choose what kind of trees to plant?"

"That would be nice," Papa said. "We can each choose a special tree. But I want to plant a row of pines too."

Lily already knew what kind of tree she would pick. An enormous weeping willow. Its nice, long feathery branches would touch the ground, and she could sit underneath it and pretend it was a house. Aunt Susie or Beth could come to play and it would be a good spot to play dolls. Maybe even read a book.

❧❧

Lily, Joseph, and Dannie took turns swinging on the rope swing that Papa had made on the big chestnut tree in front of the house. A man with a big blue truck stopped beside the road. "Is your daddy at home?" he called out to them.

"Papa is at work," Lily said, "but Mama is at home."

Mama must have seen the truck from the kitchen window because she came flying out of the house, wiping her damp hands on her apron.

"I brought your load of cement blocks," the man hollered to her from the truck. "Where do you want 'em?"

Mama showed the man where Papa wanted the blocks. Lily watched as the man backed the truck up next to the house. He guided the crane on the back of his truck to unload big stacks of blocks and set them carefully on the ground. Lily wondered what kept them all from falling and crashing to the ground. One by one, the stacks swayed from the crane and were safely placed next to each other on the ground.

After the truck was empty, the man drove away. Lily and Joseph and Dannie ran over to see the blocks, but Mama told them to stay away from them. It would be too tempting to climb them and end up getting hurt.

That evening, Papa poured a bag of cement into the wheel-barrow and added water. He took a hoe and mixed up the cement and water until it looked like thick gray pudding. After he was satisfied, he scooped some wet cement on a board. He took a big cement block and placed it onto the footer he had built earlier. He spread wet cement on the top and edges of the block. Then he placed another one tightly against it. It was slow, tiresome work, and Lily, Joseph, and Dannie soon grew bored. They watched Papa as long as they could, then they ran to their swing. Swinging was so much more fun than watching Papa build a basement wall, block by block.

Each evening, Papa would hurry with the chores and work on laying more blocks until the sun set. Lily thought the walls grew so slowly. It was going to take a long time for Papa to finish them. She felt sorry for him. He worked so hard all day, and now he had to work so hard at night. And building a basement was such a slow, boring job!

On Friday evening, Papa came home from work and said that David Yoder had offered to come help him on Saturday. "We should be able to make nice headway laying blocks for a change."

Lily was glad to hear that Papa would have help, but she felt a small tug of worry. David Yoder was Aaron Yoder's father. What if Aaron came with him? That would spoil her whole day.

Aaron was known for telling whoppers. Lately, all he talked about was going to run off and live with an Indian. He said he had seen an Indian near an old railroad tunnel and was going to find out where the Indian lived. Even Sam, who hung the moon on everything Aaron said or did, said he might be sun-touched. What if Aaron talked Joseph into running off to find the old Indian? It wasn't hard to talk Joseph into crazy adventures. No one, especially Joseph, should listen to Aaron Yoder.

The next morning, Lily was relieved to see David Yoder drive his buggy into the driveway alone. She would not have to worry about Aaron today.

All morning long, Lily helped Mama clean the house, and then they started to cook an extra-special lunch as a way to thank David Yoder. Mama had hard-boiled some eggs and told Lily to cut them in half and remove the yolks. Lily followed her directions carefully and smashed the yolks with a fork until they were nothing but fine yellow crumbs. After mixing in salad dressing and spices, Lily spooned the yellow mixture back into the hollow egg whites. She dusted a sprinkling of red spice on top of the eggs, just like Mama did. The red spice looked so pretty against the yellow egg that she sprinkled some more. Lily felt very pleased. She had made stuffed eggs all by herself.

Mama told her to set the table with the blue willow dishes. They were prettier than their everyday dishes but not as pretty as Mama's special Sunday china. Lily carefully set the table. Papa would sit at his usual place at the head of the table. Mama would sit right next to him, on his right side, and Lily would sit next to her. Dannie and Joseph would sit in their usual places. Today, David Yoder would sit at the foot of the table.

Lily took special care to make sure everything was set very neatly. David Yoder was an important man. He was one of the ministers in their church.

When lunch was ready, Lily ran down through the basement and out the door where Papa and David Yoder worked on laying blocks. Lily was surprised to see how much they had done already. It was much faster with two people working on it.

"Time to eat," Lily said.

Papa looked up. "We need a few more minutes. We just have to finish using the rest of the cement so that it doesn't dry out."

Lily ran back inside and reported to Mama what Papa had said. Mama pushed the food to the back of the stove to keep it warm. Lily set the platter of stuffed eggs on the table near Papa's plate. She hoped he would ask who made them and then David Yoder would know that she was only eight years old and already a good cook. Almost as good as Mama.

It wasn't long before the men came in and washed up at the sink. Mama dished out the food into serving bowls while Lily filled the water glasses. She took care not to spill a single drop.

After a short silent prayer, Mama passed the food around the table. Papa picked up the eggs and slid several onto his plate before he passed them to Mama. David Yoder took a bite out of an egg, chewed, then stopped, as if he couldn't believe how delicious the egg was. Lily couldn't contain herself any longer. "I made these all by myself," she said. Somebody had to say it!

David Yoder's face had turned beet red. Mama took a bite of a stuffed egg and her eyes shot wide open in alarm. "Lily, what spice did you sprinkle on the eggs?"

"The red one on the counter."

Mama looked horrified. "Oh, Lily, that was cayenne pepper, not paprika." She jumped up and grabbed the platter of eggs, but David Yoder stopped her. His forehead began to look slick and it wasn't a hot day. "David, you don't have to eat those."

"I want to," David Yoder said, coughing through his words. "I don't know how you knew it, Lily, but I happen to enjoy spicy food." He helped himself to another egg as beads of sweat popped out on his brow.

No one else touched the eggs, not even Joseph, and he ate anything. David Yoder ate every single stuffed egg left on the platter, sweat running in rivers down his face and neck. He seemed very fond of her spicy stuffed eggs. Lily thought he might be one of the kindest men she had ever known. She didn't expect such kindness, considering Aaron was his son. Life was certainly a puzzle.

Spring Days

*B*aby goats, Lily thought, must be the cutest and funniest animals of all. They were never still, never asleep. They could find a way out of every pen, slip under every gate. Papa said they were called "kids," which explained the phrase "kidding around."

Tonight, when Papa and Lily and Joseph went out to the barn to feed the animals, they stopped short at what they saw. A kid was standing on one of the roof beams in the barn. It reminded Lily of a circus tightrope walker in one of Joseph's books.

Even Papa seemed stunned. "How did that little goat get up there? I'll have to get a ladder and help it down before it falls and breaks its legs."

Papa went to fetch a ladder while Lily and Joseph stood, necks craned, to watch the kid. Ever so daintily, it walked along the beam until it came close to the stack of hay, piled in the hayloft. It hopped nimbly into the hay. Joseph scampered up the hayloft ladder and caught the little goat. As he climbed back down the ladder, he handed the kid to Lily and she put it safely on the ground. The little goat went off to sniff around for more food.

When Papa came back with the ladder, he was surprised to see the kid back on the ground. He shook his head. "What a nuisance."

Papa sat on the little milking stool to milk the nannies. Lily liked to watch. It never took long to milk a goat, not like Pansy the cow. Tonight the kids jumped around the pen, like they were on pogo sticks. One kid plopped two front hooves on Papa's back and peered over his shoulder. He looked like he was supervising Papa while he milked the nanny. Lily and

Joseph laughed and laughed. Even Papa had to laugh. As he rose to his feet, the kid tumbled to the ground. It scampered off, bleating, annoyed.

"We'll miss these little goats when we sell them next week," he said. "They keep chore time interesting."

"Sell them?" Lily was horrified. "We can't let them go! We have plenty of room in the barn for them."

"We might have room," Papa said, "but we don't need more goats. We'll keep the nannies and the billy. It won't be long before we have plenty more kids."

Lily did not understand that logic at all. Why not just keep the ones they had? Then they wouldn't need new ones. Sometimes, grown-ups just didn't make sense.

❧×❧

It was a beautiful spring day. During recess, Marvin Yoder invented a new type of tag game that included everyone, oldest to youngest. Lily could tell this was going to be one of the children's favorite games to play.

Aaron Yoder was *it*. He stopped abruptly and pointed to the ground. "Hey, Sam. Look what I just found."

Sam Stoltzfus, who could never think for himself, ran over to see what Aaron had found. Both boys crouched down to look at the ground. It wasn't long before the rest of the boys ran over to see what Aaron and Sam were studying. Lily was curious, but she didn't trust anything Aaron Yoder said or did. He was full of whoppers. Just yesterday, he told everyone he was going to spend the entire summer in the woods, living off nuts and berries. That would last about two minutes, Lily predicted.

She turned her attention away from the boys and back to her friends. Not a minute later, Aaron came toward the girls with a squirming garter snake dangling in his hand.

Lily considered herself to be very brave about most things, but she took exception to snakes, with their slimy scales and fangs and evil eyes. They gave her the willies. She made a run for the schoolhouse. Too late! Aaron spied her and started running after her. Lily screamed a silent scream and burst up the stairs, sure that even Aaron had enough sense not to follow her inside.

He followed right on her heels.

Teacher Rhoda looked up from her desk in surprise as the doors to the schoolhouse opened up and Lily flew in with Aaron in hot pursuit. Lily ran behind Teacher Rhoda.

"Aaron!" Teacher Rhoda stood up so fast her chair fell over. "You take that snake outside and let it go. Then wash your hands!"

Even Aaron stopped short at the crisp tone of Teacher Rhoda's voice. He spun around and went outside. Teacher Rhoda picked up her chair. "Lily, you shouldn't let Aaron bother you. If it's not fun for him to tease you, he'll stop."

That, to Lily, would be like telling a rash not to spread. Aaron Yoder wasn't like most boys. He was far worse, far more troublesome. She thought he should be sent off to a school for bad boys, if there were such a thing.

A few days later, the children came in from noon recess and sat at their desks to listen to Teacher Rhoda read a story. The ten minutes of story time went too quickly and Teacher Rhoda always stopped at a good part. Lily had a hard time waiting until the next day to find out what was going to happen next. Someday, when she was a grown-up—age fifteen or sixteen—and if she were a teacher, she would read an entire book to her class in one sitting. No more waiting.

And she would definitely not schedule long division right after story time. It was difficult to go from happiness to sadness. She sighed as she opened her desk to get her tablet and math book. She screamed and slammed her desk shut! Inside were jumping grasshoppers and a wiggling earthworm.

Lily glared at Aaron Yoder. He sat at his desk with a cat-that-caught-the-mouse smile on his face. She wanted to smack him.

Teacher Rhoda hurried over to see what had caused Lily's shriek. Lily pointed to the desk, so Teacher Rhoda lifted it, peeked inside, and shut it tightly. She spun around to face Aaron Yoder. She knew, without being told. It was always Aaron. "Aaron, please come get these things out of Lily's desk. All of them. Then take them outside."

Aaron couldn't stop grinning as he fished out the grass-hoppers. He jammed the earthworm into the pocket of his trousers. Disgusting. He was just disgusting.

Lily recovered from everything but embarrassment. She kept imagining that grasshoppers were jumping around her feet. She could practically feel them climbing up her dress. And then she would feel angry with Aaron Yoder all over again. She wished he would just disappear.

With each passing week, Papa worked as much as he could on the new addition, but he also had Mama's garden to plow and corn to plant. Sometimes, Lily worried the new addition would never get finished. Now and then on a Saturday afternoon, Uncle Jacob or Grandpa Miller would drop by and help Papa for a few hours, but they had busy jobs and gardens to plow too.

Lily had a hard time making sense of the fact that the men in their church didn't come to help Papa. Even when Papa had fallen off the roof and hurt his back and couldn't work for a month, no one came to help with chores other than family. Catching Mama in a quiet moment, Lily shared her thoughts. "In New York," Lily said, "they would have come."

Mama stopped peeling carrots to look at Lily. "The church in New York was made up mostly of farmers. Our church in Pennsylvania has more people who work for other businesses."

"Like Papa," Lily said.

"Like Papa. Working away from home means that your schedule isn't your own. You can't just take a day off of work unless it's a funeral or a wedding or to help someone move in. That's one of the reasons Papa is going to try to start a carpentry business at home." Mama picked up the carrot peeler and started peeling another carrot. "Now do you understand?"

Lily gazed out the window at Papa. He was nailing floor joists. "It just seems as if friends should help each other."

Mama came over to the window and stood behind Lily. She watched Papa for a long while. "Lily," Mama added in a thoughtful voice, "it's good that you have happy memories of New York. But your imagination might be making New York seem like a perfect place, and it wasn't. No place is perfect. Papa and I made the move to Pennsylvania because it was the right decision for our family. It was the best decision for you children."

Maybe. But it made Lily sad to see Papa working away, all by himself.

Hannah Moves Next Door

ily was almost too excited to eat her breakfast. It was the last day of school. Normally, this would be a sad day for Lily, but not today. Not on this special day. Uncle Elmer and Aunt Mary and Hannah and Levi and Davy were moving into the farm right next to Lily's home. She suggested to Mama that it might be a good idea if she were to stay home today to be ready and waiting to welcome cousin Hannah the minute she arrived, but Mama said no, that the two girls would have plenty of time to play this summer. "Besides," Mama said, "school will only last an hour or so."

That was Lily's next point. The children would sing, they would get their report cards, they would be sent home. She wouldn't miss a single minute of learning today because they wouldn't be learning anything.

But Mama said no.

So Lily and Joseph walked to school. Today would be a

247

perfect moving day for Hannah. Spring was in full bloom with its bright green grass and delicate flowers. The sun was shining brightly and birdsong filled the trees.

When they arrived, all of the children were chattering about heading to Uncle Elmer's after school because their parents would be there to help with the move. As soon as school was dismissed, they would all walk there together.

Lily didn't like that idea. She had wanted time with Hannah all by herself. Instead, she would have to share Hannah with Beth and Malinda.

And Effie.

As Teacher Rhoda rang the bell for the last time this term, the children hurried inside to sit at their desks. They sang a few favorite songs, and then it was time to go up to Teacher Rhoda's desk, one by one, to get their report cards. She started with the big boys and girls and ended with the little ones. Just like last year, Lily had to wait until Aaron Yoder received his report card. Just like last year, Teacher Rhoda spoke to Aaron for a very long time. Lily was sure that Teacher Rhoda was telling him that he wasn't going to be promoted to the fifth grade because he was so horrible. He might be in fourth grade until he was thirty years old. Maybe eighty.

A smile crept across her face as she thought about Aaron, still in fourth grade, as a little old man with a cane. Toothless and bald as an egg.

Finally, Aaron was done getting his scolding. He turned around and strode to his desk, appearing pretty satisfied. He flashed his report card at Lily. It said, "Promoted to Fifth Grade." Astonishing. Just astonishing.

Teacher Rhoda didn't have much to say to Lily other than congratulating her for getting promoted to fourth grade. It sounded so much more mature than third grade. Lily went back to her desk and smiled. Why, she was nearly halfway to being all grown up!

Lily sat impatiently at her desk, tapping her toes on the ground, waiting until Teacher Rhoda had handed out the rest of the report cards and made her end-of-the-year speech. Lily was pleased to hear that she would be back to teach again in the fall. She had no doubt that Hannah and Levi would like Teacher Rhoda. No doubt at all.

A horse whinnied outside the schoolhouse. Lily leaned back in her desk and saw that Effie Kauffman's mother had arrived. As soon as Teacher Rhoda dismissed school, the children ran to get their bonnets and hats and started up the road. Effie climbed up on her mother's buggy and waved as the buggy hurried down the road, passing all the children.

How infuriating! Effie would get to Uncle Elmer's before the rest of the school children. Before *Lily* got there.

The boys ran ahead of the girls. Today, Joseph ran off with the boys instead of waiting for Lily. She wished she could be a boy and run ahead too. Beth and Malinda chattered pleasantly and compared the grades in their report cards. Lily's thoughts were too scattered to join in the conversation.

She felt a little mixed-up about having Hannah move to Cloverdale. Cousin Hannah had been her New York best friend. Beth had become her Pennsylvania best friend. What if Hannah and Beth liked each other better than Lily? What if they left her out? She hadn't even thought about Effie. What if Effie said mean things to Hannah and made her cry?

And then there was Levi. What if Levi and Aaron Yoder got into another fight? Lily sighed. There was so much to worry about.

As the girls walked past Lily's house, they could see a big truck in Uncle Elmer's driveway. Men from the church were busy carrying in furniture and boxes. The girls became quiet and shy as they made their way into the house. Lily felt relieved when she saw Mama in the kitchen with Aunt Mary and some other women.

"Where is Hannah?" Lily said.

"She's upstairs in her room with Effie," Aunt Mary said. "You girls can run on upstairs and help her get the room organized."

Lily had been in the house once before and knew the way to Hannah's room. Beth and Malinda bobbed along behind her. Hannah and Effie were unpacking a box that held a pretty pink oil lamp. Effie set it on top of her dresser. Lily felt a twinge of jealousy as she saw that Effie and Hannah seemed to enjoy each other. She hadn't expected *that*. Another worry.

Hannah saw them at the doorjamb and smiled. She waved the girls into the room. "Come help us unpack," she said.

Lily reached into the box and started to unwrap the newspaper that protected the candy dish. Beth handed the lid to her. They placed it next to the lamp. It was fun to help make Hannah's room look pretty.

Effie drew out a thin box and opened the lid. In it were the paper dolls that Lily had given to Hannah. Beth and Malinda stopped what they were doing to see the dolls. For months now, Lily hadn't stopped thinking about those dolls. She was hoping Hannah might offer them back to her, since she had moved to Cloverdale. She doubted it, but she hoped.

"They're so pretty," Beth said.

Effie narrowed her eyes. "You shouldn't have something so worldly. Those dresses aren't Amish at all. The dolls have their hair hanging loose." It sounded just like something Effie's mother would say.

They were only paper dolls. Secretly, Lily thought it would

be fun if she could dress up like that—with a ruffled hoop skirt and curly hair flowing down her back—but she would never dare tell Effie. Why, Effie would run and tell her mother. Then her mother would think it would be necessary to talk to Mama about it and then Mama would have a talk with Lily. No thank you! Some thoughts were better kept to yourself.

Beth and Malinda looked through all the paper dolls and admired all the dresses. "I wish we had time to play with them today," Beth said.

"Let's finish unpacking the boxes," Hannah said. "Then we can all play with them." The last box was quickly unpacked and put away. The girls sat on Hannah's bed and spread out the paper dolls. Lily was having so much fun playing with them that she didn't notice Effie wasn't joining in until Hannah scooted over on the bed to make room for her. "Here, Effie. You can come sit next to me. We still have two more dolls to play with."

Lily knew Effie. If Effie had wanted to play, she would have elbowed her way onto the bed. She wouldn't have waited for an invitation.

Suddenly, Effie gathered all the paper dolls and their clothes into a heap in front of her and then quickly crushed them all together in a big ball. She tossed them into the empty box of crumpled newspaper packing. "There!" she said. "Now you can't play with such fancy worldly things."

The girls stared at her in disbelief. The paper dolls were ruined. Tears prickled Lily's eyes. Those used to be *her* paper dolls. It had been hard enough when Mama made her give them to Hannah. Now Effie had destroyed them.

Lily peered into the box to see if she could try to make them nice again. She drew out a paper doll and almost had to squeeze her eyes shut when she saw it. Its head was twisted off and one arm was dangling. All the clothes were ruined. Lily knew without even asking Mama that they could never be made nice again. There was nothing left to do except throw them away.

Effie seemed smugly satisfied. No one was laughing or talking. There was nothing more to say. The girls didn't feel like playing anymore. They went downstairs to see if their mothers needed help.

Lily was glad when the truck was unloaded and everyone started going home. Grandpa and Grandma Miller and Papa and Mama stayed to help get everything in order before leaving.

Hannah and Lily went down to the basement to unpack jars with fruits and vegetables and place them on the shelves.

"I don't think Effie Kauffman was very nice today," Hannah said.

"She is never very nice," Lily said. "But most times she isn't quite as mean as today."

"Beth and Malinda seem nice. It will be fun having friends in school."

Lily felt better about sharing Hannah with Beth and Malinda. Apart from Effie's outburst of craziness, the time together had been fun. Working together, playing together, being with their families together . . . it *was* fun. She was finally feeling as if Pennsylvania were home.

Or maybe, Lily realized, you just couldn't escape people like Mandy Mast or Aaron Yoder. Or Effie Kauffman.

Lost!

One evening, the Lapps had just sat down to a supper of pot roast and fried potatoes when a rap on the door interrupted them. Lily and Joseph followed Papa when he went to answer it, opening it to David Yoder. Bending toward Papa, he spoke in low, urgent tones. Lily couldn't even hear him.

"Yes, of course I'll come," Papa said. "Just give me a minute and I'll be right out."

Papa came back to the kitchen. "Aaron Yoder has wandered off into the woods. David is worried he is lost, so a search party is gathering to go look for him. I'm going to have to miss your good dinner, Rachel."

Mama quickly grabbed two slices of bread and put a thick layer of fried potatoes between them. She wrapped it in a napkin and handed it to Papa. "Here, take this and eat it on your way," she said. "I hope you find Aaron soon."

Papa took the sandwich and hurried out the door. Lily ran to a window to see where he was going, her nose flat to the glass. She saw Papa climb into a big white van that looked as if it were filled with straw hats. Mama came up behind her. "With so many men looking for Aaron, they should be able to find him soon." Her voice sounded faint and far-off, as if she were talking to herself.

Lily shivered at the thought of being lost and alone in the woods. She hoped the men would find Aaron before it grew dark. Fear trickled down her spine. Aaron might be her least favorite person in the entire world, but she didn't want him to be eaten by wild animals. She wouldn't want that for anyone, not even Aaron Yoder.

Mama told everyone to go back to the table to eat. Lily wasn't hungry anymore. She was worried about Aaron. Joseph wasn't at all worried. He sat there eating his food as if nothing was wrong.

After the dishes were cleared away, Mama said, "Weeding the garden can wait until tomorrow. Why don't we sit in the living room and I'll read to you."

Lily was happy and sad to hear that. Listening to Mama read was much more fun than pulling weeds in the garden. But she was sad too, because she knew Mama was thinking about Aaron. Lily wondered what his mother was doing tonight. She thought Aaron's mother would like to trade places with Mama and have her boy home for a story.

Mama sat on her rocking chair and started to read in her clear, sweet, calm voice, with baby Paul in her arms. Lily curled up in the corner of the sofa to listen while Joseph and Dannie burrowed in right next to Mama so they could see all the pictures in the book. They weren't at all worried about Aaron Yoder in the wild woods. They were too little to worry.

Mama read one story, then another and another. Baby Paul fell sound asleep. The sun went down and darkness crept over the land like a big velvety blanket that was coming to tuck everything in for the night. Mama lit a lamp and then read some more. Lily should have been happy to hear so many stories, but she knew Mama was hoping Papa would be back by now.

The chimes on the grandfather clock struck nine. Mama closed the book. "It's getting quite late. Time for children to be in bed."

Before Lily went upstairs to brush her teeth, she stood by the kitchen window to look outside. Dark clouds scuttled across the sky. They blocked out the thumbnail moon and made eerie shadows on the ground below. Everything seemed scarier at night. She shivered as she thought of Papa walking through the woods in the dark, calling, calling for lost Aaron. She thought about all the times she wished Aaron would disappear, or pretended he was invisible, and a twinge of guilt pricked her.

Lily climbed into bed and drew the covers up beneath her chin. She prayed for Papa to come home soon. She prayed Aaron would be found.

Early the next morning, Lily found Papa seated at the kitchen table. He looked tired, like he hadn't slept all night.

"Did you find Aaron?" she asked.

Papa shook his head. "No, we didn't. We looked for him most of the night. We used lanterns and flashlights and kept calling his name, but we couldn't find any sign of him. We finally called off the search at three in the morning so that we could all get a little sleep. Right after breakfast, we're heading out again."

"You're not going to work today?" Lily asked. That shocked

her. Papa never missed a day of work. Only when his back had been hurt and he was stuck in bed.

"Work can wait until we find him." Papa took a long sip of hot coffee. "If you or Dannie or Joseph were lost, I would be very grateful if others dropped their work to search."

Lily was glad that Papa would keep looking for Aaron. She didn't know about Joseph or Dannie getting lost—they were much too curious—but she knew Papa would never have to worry about her getting lost in the woods. Lily was frightened by the deep, dark forests in Pennsylvania. It seemed there were forests for miles and miles everywhere she looked with little openings here and there for a house or farm. To get lost in the woods here would be very scary. Nope, not Lily. She was staying clear of woods.

Mama placed a bowl filled with scrambled eggs on the table. She put a piece of bread on top of the burner on the oil stove to toast it. Lily went to get a jar of jam. Toast with jam was always good and so much better than the porridge Mama made on most weekday mornings. At least there was one thing to be happy about on this summer morning. Toast with jam was always a happy thing. But then her smile faded. She wondered if Aaron was hungry.

Papa ate quickly and took his last bite of food as they heard the crunch of tires on the gravel driveway. He gulped down his glass full of water, rose to his feet, and plucked his straw hat off the hook next to the door. As he tugged it on his head, he said, "I'm hoping we can find Aaron before too long. It should be much easier to search since it's daylight." He gave Mama a sad smile, then hurried out the door to hop in the waiting van.

All day long, Lily helped Mama work in the garden. Each time they heard a car come up the road, they would stop and look up, hoping that Papa was coming home with good news. But the cars passed on by the house, and they went back to working in the garden. Waiting and working. And worrying.

Night had fallen by the time Papa came home. Joseph and Dannie had already fallen asleep, but Mama let Lily come downstairs to see Papa. "We still haven't found Aaron," he said, weary and troubled. "I feel awful thinking that he'll have to spend another long night out in the woods by himself."

The three of them sat at the kitchen table as Papa ate his warmed-up supper. He said many more people had joined the search for Aaron today. Police too. The police had brought some dogs that could follow Aaron's scent. They hoped the dogs could track Aaron.

Lily shuddered at the thought of those big scary dogs looking for Aaron. She was sure that if she was lost and some dogs started coming after her, she would try to run away from them. Then she would probably be even more lost. Lily didn't like strange dogs. She hoped that Aaron liked dogs. Maybe he did. After all, he was a boy and boys liked things that she didn't.

"I'm exhausted," Papa said. "Tomorrow, surely, we will find Aaron." He didn't sound at all certain.

That might have been the first time Lily noticed that it wasn't easy being a grown-up.

That night, Lily had a strange dream. She was in the schoolyard, playing tag, and Aaron Yoder was chasing her with a big snake. Suddenly, he dropped the snake and said he had to hurry. He was going off to live with—

Her eyes flew open.

She ran downstairs and into Papa's room. She shook him

gently until he finally woke. "Papa," she whispered. "Papa, I have an idea about where Aaron Yoder went."

Before dawn, Papa left to search again. This time, when he returned, he was smiling from ear to ear.

"You found Aaron!" Lily said.

"He's safely at home," Papa said. "We followed the trail to that abandoned railroad tunnel, Lily, just like you said. I went through it, came out the other end, and kept going until I saw a small trail of smoke. I followed it until I came to an old cabin. Would you believe who I found there?"

Lily knew. "Aaron Yoder!"

"Aaron Yoder keeping company with an old Indian."

Papa explained more about the old Indian. "He was ninety-eight years old and lived alone by foraging off the land. The Indian had hurt his foot, so Aaron was trying to help him. That's why he didn't come home for a few days. He had no idea that people were out searching for him. He felt badly about causing people worry."

It didn't surprise Lily that Aaron wouldn't have thought about causing others to worry, but it did surprise her that he would help someone.

"Aaron might have saved the Indian's life. David Yoder and his son Marvin are going to get back up there tomorrow to check on him, bring him some food. All in all, other than Aaron's mother getting a few gray hairs, it might have been a good thing. Our church came together in a crisis. We needed that, to know we can count on each other. And we're able to help a neighbor we didn't even know about."

The Indian, Papa meant.

"And you might have helped save Aaron too." Papa leaned over to whisper, "I'm not sure Aaron really knew how to get himself home. He might have been up there for quite some time."

Lily was truly glad that Aaron wasn't killed by wild wolves and that the old Indian wasn't going to starve to death. But as long as he was safe, a part of her wished Aaron could have stayed up there on the mountain a little longer. Just through the school year.

"It's a good thing you listened to Aaron when he talked about that old Indian, Lily," Papa said. "It's a good thing you listened to him."

She didn't *try* to listen to Aaron. But she did.

259

Home at Last

Early Saturday morning, Lily woke to hear sounds of Papa hammering boards on the new addition. She dressed and hurried downstairs to help Mama make breakfast and saw a buggy roll up into the driveway. She pressed closer to the window and saw another buggy turn into the drive, then another, and another. And another. Men jumped out of the buggies, grabbed tool bags, and walked over to the addition. Papa stopped working, surprised.

Mama came to the window and stood behind Lily. "Well, I'll be . . ." Her voice drifted off as a wave of wonderment swept through them. "Lily, go wake up Joseph and tell him he's needed outside to put the buggy horses in the pasture." She was grinning.

A few hours later, two more buggies arrived, filled with women bearing bowls and platters filled with food. David

Yoder had organized a work frolic for Papa. A small way to thank him, he said, for finding his lost boy.

As the day wore on, Lily was amazed to see the transformation occur: two rooms with shingles on the roof, windows, drywall, flooring. After lunch, a group of men worked inside to move old kitchen cupboards into the new kitchen. Lily was disappointed to see the bright orange countertops lifted up and moved into the new kitchen. She was hoping they would be replaced with another color countertop. Purple, maybe. How sad.

David Yoder and his three sons and Papa were up in the attic, hammering away. Mama told Lily to keep out of their way. She didn't have to tell Lily twice. Lily might be glad Aaron Yoder wasn't eaten alive by wild animals, but he was still invisible to her. She didn't even look at him. Maybe once.

By suppertime, the new kitchen was completed and the ladies had helped Mama put all the food back into the cupboards. Mama and Papa had a new bedroom too. It still needed some finishing touches and it would be awhile before they would move their bed into it, but the addition was nearly complete. Papa couldn't stop grinning. He would look at Mama and she would look back at him and then they would start smiling all over again.

When the clock struck eight and Papa said, "Bedtime for little lambs," Lily, Joseph, and Dannie didn't even mind. Today's excitement had worn them out. Lily climbed the stairs to her hallway bedroom and stopped short. Her bed was gone. Her dresser was gone. The hallway was empty. She spun around and saw Papa and Mama at the bottom of the stairs. Their hands were on Joseph's and Dannie's shoulders, holding them back with a firm grip. "Go through the red door, Lily," Papa said, eyes twinkling.

Lily went through her brothers' bedroom to the red door. She opened it and climbed the attic stairs, glad for the long summer light. When she reached the top stair, she couldn't believe her eyes. It didn't look like an attic anymore. A section of the attic had been walled off to create a bedroom, complete with a window under the eaves. It was a girl's bedroom. There was her bed, all made up. And her dresser with the little oil lamp, already lit. And a little purple rag rug on the floor. Lily had a bedroom of her own! A real bedroom.

❦❧

Later that night, Lily looked out the attic window before she slipped into bed. She could see a light in Hannah's kitchen from here. She looked at the sky and realized that she was closer to the stars in her attic bedroom. Closer than Joseph and Dannie were, and that pleased her.

She thought about the last few weeks, about the end of school, about Teacher Rhoda's news that she would stay for the next school term, about Hannah moving in. Hannah was the closest thing to a sister she would ever have. Maybe that was God's way of evening things out. He seemed to be perpetually out of baby sisters when the Lapps' turn came around for a delivery. She thought about Papa's back injury and how he was finally mended. She looked around her beautiful new attic bedroom—so much better than a hallway bedroom. Her mind drifted off to those frightening days when Aaron Yoder was thought to be lost and that she and Papa had helped get him home. Even though Aaron would always remain invisible to her, he had helped build this new bedroom for her. She thought about all of the people in their church who had come to help today.

Tonight, as she looked out over the quiet landscape, the darkness didn't look quite so scary. The future looked bright with hope.

Frequently Asked Questions about the Amish

Are there different kinds of Amish? Yes! There are over 1,900 Amish church districts. Each one has its own style of clothing, buggies, occupations, and rules about technology.

Do the church districts share anything in common? Most Amish groups share core values and common practices: use of horse and buggy for local transportation, rejection of electricity from public utility lines, prohibition against televisions and computers, some type of distinctive dress, beards for men, ending of formal education at the eighth grade, meeting in homes for worship every other Sunday, lay religious leaders, and living in rural areas.

Are all Amish farmers? No. In the past, they were all farmers. But today, like Lily's father who hired out as a carpenter, many Amish support their families by working in small shops, businesses, carpentry, construction, retail stores, or roadside stands. Others work for "English-owned" factories, restaurants, and shops. Farming is important to the Amish, though, and most every Amish family has plenty of space for a big garden.

Where do the Amish live? They live in twenty-eight states and the Canadian province of Ontario. About two-thirds live in three states: Ohio, Pennsylvania, and Indiana.

Lily reads a magazine called Family Life. *Is there really such a magazine?* Yes, and you can subscribe too. The Amish publishing house, Pathway Publishers, publishes three magazines: *Family Life*, *Young Companion*, and *Blackboard Bulletin*. The most popular of these three is *Family Life*, designed for adults and families. It contains articles on Christian living, parenting, and homemaking. It also contains editorials, letters from readers, medical advice, poems, recipes, and children's stories. *Young Companion* is targeted to teens and children. It contains stories with Christian messages—including lesson stories, adventure stories, and Amish romance. *Blackboard Bulletin* is designed for Amish schoolteachers but is also helpful for homeschooling parents. For more information, check out the website: www.pathway-publishers.com or write to:

Pathway Publishers
258ON – 250W
LaGrange, IN 46761

Mary Ann Kinsinger was raised Old Order Amish in Somerset County, Pennsylvania. She met and married her husband, whom she knew from school days, and started a family. After they chose to leave the Amish church, Mary Ann began a blog, *A Joyful Chaos*, as a way to capture her warm memories of her childhood for her own children. From the start, this blog found a ready audience and even captured the attention of key media players, such as the influential blog *Amish America* and the *New York Times*. She lives in Pennsylvania.

Suzanne Woods Fisher's grandfather was one of eleven children, raised Old Order German Baptist, in Franklin County, Pennsylvania. Suzanne has many, many, *many* wonderful Plain relatives. She has written bestselling fiction and nonfiction books about the Amish and couldn't be happier to share Mary Ann's stories with children. When Suzanne isn't writing, she is raising puppies for Guide Dogs for the Blind. She lives in California with her husband and children, and Tess and Toffee, her big white dogs.

Visit

www.AdventuresofLilyLapp.com

- Meet the authors
- Get to know Lily and her family
- Learn more about the Amish
- Find fun games and activities

Don't miss out on Lily's next *adventure* in
Book 3 of The Adventures of Lily Lapp series!

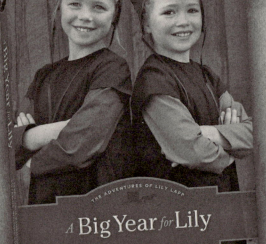

Mary Ann Kinsinger
Suzanne Woods Fisher

THE ADVENTURES OF LILY LAPP

A Big Year *for* Lily

· Book Three ·

AdventuresofLilyLapp.com

 Revell
a division of Baker Publishing Group
www.RevellBooks.com

Available Wherever Books Are Sold and in Ebook Format

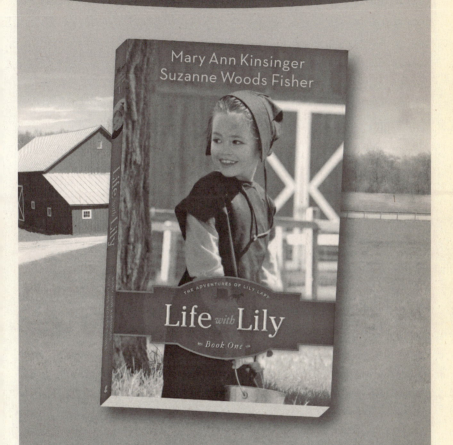